CW00666049

# CRUELTY'S
# DAUGHTER

### A riveting psychological suspense thriller

# ANNA WILLETT

THE
BOOK
FOLKS

Paperback edition published by

The Book Folks

London, 2018

© Anna Willett

This book is a work of fiction. Names, characters, businesses, organizations, places and events are either the product of the author's imagination or are used fictitiously. Any resemblance to actual persons, living or dead, events or locales is entirely coincidental. The spelling is British English.

All rights reserved. No part of this publication may be reproduced, stored in retrieval system, copied in any form or by any means, electronic, mechanical, photocopying, recording or otherwise transmitted without written permission from the publisher.

ISBN 978-1-7208-7988-6

www.thebookfolks.com

For my dear friend, Xee. I miss you.

# Chapter One

Mina stepped out of the shower and wrapped a fluffy white towel around her body. She pulled the band from her bun and let her long black hair fall around her shoulders. A glimpse in the mirror caught her attention. Stepping closer, she examined pale grey eyes. Her father's eyes—like cold skies, they hid a storm. Was it there for the world to see? If someone looked, really looked, could *they* see past the pleasing features? *Am I a monster?* A question she'd asked herself so many times, the words had almost lost meaning. Leaning closer, she searched her reflection for an outward clue. Finding nothing but her expressionless face, she turned away and headed out of the room.

The college was a good twenty-minute drive, even after the peak hour rush subsided. Mina glanced at the time on the dashboard: 7:02 p.m.

"Great. I'm late on my first night." She let out a long sigh and pulled into the parking lot.

After two laps, she found a vacant bay at the far end. Gathering up her handbag and notebook, she resisted the urge to check her reflection in the rear-view mirror. *What the hell am I doing?* Filling out the application online for a creative writing course seemed like a great idea after half a bottle of vodka. But what did she know about writing? *That's not why I'm here.*

She climbed out of the car and slammed the door. Almost without thinking, Mina turned and let her gaze settle on the darkened area to the left of her car. A few other vehicles were parked near the corner of the lot; around them, thick shrubs and trees crowded the bitumen. Far from the glow of the nearest light pole, the area sat in partial darkness.

As her eyes moved over the cars and unkempt shrubbery, she felt a familiar tightening in her gut as her skin prickled. It had been many years since she'd experienced the sensation, but she recognised it nevertheless. A tensing of the muscles as though her body were preparing for attack. The last time she'd felt this way... Mina stopped herself. A shiver worked up her back. *I won't let the memories keep ripping away at me.* She pulled the strap of her bag over her shoulder and hurried towards the squat concrete building where she could see people filing towards the entrance in dribs and drabs.

By the time Mina pushed open the thick, lime-green door and entered the classroom, she'd convinced herself the experience in the parking lot had been nothing more than first night jitters. She wasn't used to being around people she didn't know. It made sense that she'd feel jumpy.

A tired looking woman in her forties shuffled papers and checked her watch while waiting for everyone to take their seats. The unmistakable smell of whiteboard markers hung in the air over the disappointingly small, box-like room. Two rows of cream coloured rectangular tables, each furnished with four blue plastic chairs, faced the front of the room.

With only eight other students in the class, there was no shortage of seats. Mina made her way to the rear of the room, keeping her eyes on the concrete floor to avoid making contact with the few students still milling around the tables. She dumped her notebook and bag on a table, ignoring the flutter in her stomach that threatened to blossom into panic. She felt out of place, conspicuous in the cramped room. The desire to turn and leave arose, but she swallowed and forced her slightly hunched shoulders to relax. Once seated, she looked around and took stock.

It had been years since she had last set foot in a classroom and was struck by the odd assortment of people taking this particular class. They varied from a plump man with longish grey hair, who looked to be in his fifties, to a girl at Mina's table who couldn't have been more than nineteen. Two blue clips decorated with penguins held back limp brown hair next to a rather chubby, almost babyish face. The girl noticed Mina and smiled, revealing a mouth full of crooked teeth. Mina returned a tense smile and turned her gaze back to the front of the room—an automatic reaction designed to keep people away. *I'm supposed to be* connecting *with the human race*. Even so, she couldn't bring herself to turn back and make eye contact with the girl. The eagerness in her smile unnerved Mina. *I wish I'd sat somewhere else.*

The instructor glanced at the large metal clock over the top of the computer screen and coughed. There was a collective scraping of chairs and flapping of paper as everyone readied themselves for the class to begin.

* * *

At eight-thirty, the instructor, who'd asked everyone to call her Lyn, suggested they stop for a fifteen-minute break. Mina grabbed her bag and headed for the door, hoping to make it out of the room before the girl at her table could introduce herself. She wasn't looking to make friends nor did she want to spend her fifteen minute break hearing the girl's life story. Or worse, sharing hers. *Then what am I doing here?* Maybe sitting in a room filled with

3

strangers was enough for now. A small step, but still progress.

On her way in earlier, she'd noticed a vending machine by a large paved courtyard. Eager for a few quiet minutes before class resumed, she made her way out of the building.

The evening air felt crisp and fresh on her face, a welcome break from the stuffiness of the classroom. The courtyard, lit by four large, florescent lights on tall metal posts shed a pool of yellow over the faces of the few students beginning to gather. The lights reminded Mina of something she'd seen in an old science fiction movie; mechanical eyes staring out of space ships.

She fished some change out of her purse and walked over to the vending machine. Sliding a coin into the slot, she pressed the buttons and waited while the can was dispensed. She could hear voices and doors opening and closing as the courtyard filled up with an odd assortment of people from various classes. Mina grabbed her drink and made a break for one of the concrete benches that lined the courtyard.

She sat alone, bathed in that pool of unnatural yellow light, and opened the can. Sipping the drink, she made a big show of checking her phone in a move she hoped gave everyone the impression that she was far too busy to talk. Keeping people at arm's length was instinctual. A legacy left over from years of living with the enemy.

Maybe it was being back in a classroom, the smell of collective body odour, or the sounds of group chatter that prompted the memories but suddenly she found herself thinking of her school days. Lunchtimes pretending to read, listening to laughter and whispered plans, but always from the outside. What should have been a carefree time was spent avoiding friendship and isolating herself for fear of revealing how she and her mother were forced to live.

Mina stared at the phone in her hands and recognised the ridiculousness of what she was doing. Falling back into a stupid self-defence mechanism, still trying to keep the world at a safe distance. If the stack of self-help books under her bed were to be believed, she had to stop blaming her father for everything she did, or she'd remain his prisoner. She'd promised herself tonight would be the first small step, a chance to chat with someone new and see what happened. Yet here she was staring at her phone doing her best to block everyone out.

She didn't hear as much as *feel* someone sit down next to her, and assuming it was the girl from class, Mina decided to make an effort and be friendly. She stuffed her phone back in her bag and was about to turn and introduce herself when a male voice took her by surprise.

"Don't tell me, Conversational French?"

"What?" An edge accented her voice, sharp and annoyed.

Without fail, there was always some guy who was convinced he had all the right moves. The thought of another idiot with a pick-up line made her feel irrationally angry. She turned, mouth set in a hard line, intending to spell her feelings out with two words: *not interested.*

He smiled, they always smiled, but there was something different about the look on his face. Maybe the absence of the ever present excitement guys had in their eyes. The open, friendly expression caught her off guard.

Men's faces were always the same: excited, eager, calculating. She could almost see their minds working: *if I say just the right thing, if I strike just the right pose, she'll fall for it.* But not this guy. The deep sea-green of his eyes, flecked with brown sparks around the pupils threw her off balance. He couldn't have been more than a few years older than her, early thirties maybe. For a moment, she found herself unable to speak.

"Sorry, I was just trying to guess which course you were taking. You look like you belong in Conversational French," he said, shaking his head. "It's just something I do to pass the time during the breaks." He placed both his hands on his thighs, palms down and moved to stand.

"Creative Writing," Mina spluttered out the words, surprised by how pleased she was when he sat back down.

"Oh, Lyn's class." Then he pointed at the grey-haired man from Mina's class. He was standing near the vending machine smoking and chatting to a woman wearing a pair of orange and blue floral pants. "Now him, I pegged for the writing course right away, but not you. Huh." He frowned and a deep line appeared between his brows.

"Why not me?" Mina asked, anxious to know what he'd seen in her that made him so sure she didn't belong in the writing course.

"Your jacket," he said, indicating the navy leather.

Mina almost laughed with relief, but managed to keep her expression and voice even. "My jacket makes you think I'm in the wrong course?"

"It's Italian leather, definitely not something sold in Perth. I'm guessing you bought it overseas—probably Europe. You're drinking Pasito, the Kirks brand of Passiona. An Australian drink. I'd say you've been to Europe, but you *are* Australian. You like to travel and so that brings me to conversational French." He shrugged.

"I'm impressed." Mina found herself almost smiling. "There's just one problem with your reasoning."

"What's that," he asked, cocking his head slightly to the side.

"I could have bought the jacket online." She covered her smile by sipping from the can of soft drink.

He shook his head. "The fit's too good. *That* jacket..." He jerked his chin in her direction, "was made for you. And not in Perth." He held Mina's gaze with his strange green eyes and waited for her to respond.

"You're right. I bought it in Italy. And you are also right about the drink, but conversational French—you're way off."

He shrugged. "Okay, well I guess I need to work on my observational skills a bit more." His eyes shifted to his cell phone. "Time to get back to class." He stood and, to Mina's astonishment, turned to leave.

She'd been expecting him to ask for her phone number or at least her name. "Which class are *you* taking?" She tried to sound casual, not overly interested.

He stopped and looked back over his shoulder, but didn't turn around. "I'm not. I teach a course. Photography. See you," he called as he walked towards the adjacent building.

Mina watched him open the door and hold it for an elderly woman carrying a green enviro bag that was so full it looked like it might burst. She bustled her plump body under his arm and paused to say something. Mina couldn't hear the woman's words, but saw her gesturing towards the bag and nodding. He nodded back and said something that made the older woman chuckle loud enough for Mina to hear across the courtyard.

She watched the woman enter the building leaving him holding the door. As if sensing her gaze, he paused and looked back. She flushed and turned away, but not before he gave her one last smile. Feeling like she'd just been caught staring through her neighbour's window, Mina scrambled to her feet, dropping the can in the process. A small puddle of fizzy yellowy-orange liquid splashed across the cracked pavers.

Mina cursed silently and stepped forward to retrieve the can, but her shoe made contact with it before her hand, sending it rattling across the courtyard. Rosy-faced and flustered, she grabbed her bag and headed towards her class determined not to turn around for fear the guy had witnessed the clumsy scene.

# Chapter Two

The inside of her mouth tasted sour, as if she'd swallowed something bitter. Mina sat up and ran her hands through her hair. Milky bands of light streaked across the mess of clothes cluttering the bedroom floor. She couldn't remember what time she'd fallen into bed, only that she'd been sitting in her mother's study—she still thought of it that way, even after eighteen months—drinking vodka and staring at the ceiling. Her head ached with the memory and her eyes felt puffy. She'd probably ended the night with a crying jag before passing out on the bed.

She threw back the covers and rolled off the mattress. The room pitched, bile rose. With her hand clamped to her mouth, she stumbled down the hall. Gagging over the toilet-bowl, Mina reached out a trembling hand and tore off a wad of toilet paper. *I can't keep doing this.*

She stood and turned on the tap. Waking up hungover and confused had become normal—too normal. It had become so that Mina couldn't remember the last time she'd actually fallen asleep *unaided*. When she had finished rinsing her mouth, she brushed her teeth trying not to gag.

The chiming of the doorbell added to the pounding in her head. For a moment, she wavered, confused by the sound—then realising the ringing came from the front door and not the inside of her brain. She cursed under her breath and stumbled for the stairs. The bell sounded again, urgent and demanding. Mina winced. She paused at the foot of the stairs frowning. *How long has it been since someone's visited the house?*

In the months after her mother's death, there'd been a string of visitors—mostly from the office and her mother's small circle of friends. Over time, the visits dried up until Mina barely saw anyone for weeks on end. Now, at ten-fifteen on a Saturday morning, someone was at the door. The sudden intrusion unnerved her.

She considered ignoring the bell, running upstairs and hiding under the covers. She even went as far as turning and placing her hand on the banister when the bell rang for a third time. The high-pitched peel sent a dart through her aching head. If she didn't answer, they might keep ringing. Mina didn't think she could stand it.

Cracking the door open, a shaft of light fell on her face. She squinted and drew back slightly trying to adjust to the brightness. Two men stood on the door step, both dressed in jackets and ties. *Oh no, the God Squad*, she thought with a spark of irritation. Just what she didn't need, two freaks trying to convince her Jesus wanted to save her soul.

"Miss Constantine?" The younger of the two men broke the silence.

"Yes." She kept her voice even and met the man's gaze. He had cold eyes buried in a narrow face. *How does he know my name?*

"I'm Detective Worsten and this is Detective Drevelli. We'd like to ask you a few questions." He reached inside his jacket and produced his ID. "Can we come in?"

The doorway grew smaller. Her heart dropped like a rock smacking the bottom of a muddy pond. She'd been waiting for this day for twelve years. The time had come; she was almost relieved. A million questions filled her head: *how did they find out? What do they know? Will they handcuff me?* Relief turned to fear then panic. Beads of sweat broke out on the back of her neck and her knees wobbled.

She promised herself she wouldn't break down. Whatever they thought they knew about her, they'd have to prove.

"It's about Andrea Fields."

Mina looked at the man's mouth, not sure she'd heard him correctly. "What?"

"We'd like to ask you a few questions about Andrea Fields." He paused recognising the confusion on Mina's face he added, "She's a classmate of yours. We were told you sat with her on Thursday night."

"Classmate?" Mina was still trying to process what was happening. They weren't here to arrest her or accuse her of anything—not yet. It wasn't even about *her*, it was about some Andrea girl. She wanted to laugh out loud, but instead let out a long breath. She nearly smiled, but caught herself just in time.

"I'm sorry, Detective um…"

"Detective Worsten."

"I don't know anyone named Andrea." Mina folded her arms across her stomach and leaned against the doorframe. Now that the danger had passed she felt the need to sit.

"Can we come in? It will only take a few minutes." Worsten took a step forward and placed his hand on the half open door. Mina had the impression he was used to people doing as he asked.

"Okay." Mina nodded. The thought of letting the two police officers into the house made her already queasy stomach flip, but she couldn't think of a way to refuse that wouldn't make her look guilty of something.

The two men followed her as she led them through the house; their footsteps heavy, menacing.

They reached the kitchen, a spacious rectangular room overlooking the garden, modernised with marbled benchtops but still retaining the original 1940s feel. Mina grabbed a glass from the draining board and filled it under the tap. She took a long swallow before turning around. "You can sit if you like." She gestured towards the table and took another sip of water. Her mouth felt coated in dust.

Worsten glanced at the table and chairs but made no move. "Andrea was in a class you attended on Thursday night at the Alice College." He paused and reached inside his jacket, for a second she caught sight of the gun holstered beneath its folds. He pulled out a small photo and handed it to Mina. She hesitated and then took it from his outstretched hand.

The girl in the photo was leaning back, seemingly resting her head against an arm that had been cropped out of the frame. She had shoulder-length brown hair. Her wide smile revealed crooked teeth. Mina closed her eyes as a sinking feeling washed over her, draining the relief she'd felt only moments before.

"Yes. I remember her. We sat at the same table. Is she all right?" Mina asked, knowing full-well that if the girl *was* all right the police wouldn't be in her kitchen asking questions.

"We don't know. She hasn't been seen since Thursday night." Detective Worsten kept his gaze locked on Mina's.

"Oh." The sound escaped from her mouth like a limp puff of air. She handed the photograph back to Worsten, eager to be rid of it.

"When was the last time you saw Andrea?" The older detective spoke for the first time.

Mina turned her attention to Detective Drevelli. He was taller than Worsten, maybe early fifties, heavy-set and almost completely bald.

"I…" Mina hesitated. She thought of the girl. *No*, she stopped herself. *She has a name.* Andrea's eager smile and the way Mina had dismissed her flashed through her mind. "I saw her when I was walking to my car."

Worsten pulled a small notebook from inside his jacket and began writing. Absurdly, Mina wondered how many pockets his jacket concealed.

"What time?" Drevelli asked.

Mina thought for a second, "It must have been close to ten o'clock. Class had finished and everyone was leaving."

Worsten wrote something in his notebook while Drevelli continued to ask questions.

"Was Andrea with you when you walked to your car?"

Mina put the almost empty glass on the draining board and folded her arms around her body, concealing her hands as they clenched into fists. "Yes. She asked me where I'd parked. I told her that I was heading to the front lot. The one on Lyon Street. She asked if she could walk out with me."

"What did you talk about?"

"Talk about?" Mina felt confused by the question. In spite of the cool morning, she could feel sweat forming on her lower back. She wanted the questions to end and the two detectives to leave. Having the men in the kitchen made her feel dizzy. Drevelli stood near the fridge, his feet in almost the exact spot where her father had fallen. She wanted to look at his shoes, but forced herself to hold his gaze.

"When you walked out to the car park, what did you and Andrea talk about?" His expression softened, he spoke slowly. Mina realised that he thought she was about to cry.

"I don't remember," Mina said and turned her head to stare out the kitchen window. Thin streaks of sunlight splayed out across the back lawn as a light breeze ruffled the branches on the two jacaranda trees standing like crooked fingers on either side of the yard. The world outside looked so uncomplicated.

"Did she say where she was going or if she was meeting anyone?" Drevelli asked.

"No, not that I remember." Mina kept her gaze on the window.

Drevelli let out a long breath. "Okay, Ms Constantine, I know this is upsetting but we really need your help." He hesitated, "You might have been the last person to see Andrea before she disappeared, so anything you can tell us is important."

Mina looked back at the two faces, she wanted to tell them what happened in the parking lot and bring the inquisition to an end, but the truth wouldn't help Andrea.

"I'm sorry. I said goodbye and headed for my car. I didn't see her leave. That's all I know."

The two officers exchanged a glance. She realised how she must look to the two men: bleary eyed, hair uncombed, and wearing torn track pants and a rumpled T-shirt. *I probably smell like booze and vomit.* A wave of disgust and shame flowed through her. She could only imagine how they would look at her if she told them what had really happened. Mina expected Drevelli to continue pushing for answers, but instead he nodded.

"All right. If you remember anything else let us know." He nodded to Worsten who pulled a business card out of his pocket and handed it to Mina.

"Do you think it's the same man that took the other three girls? The one they're calling…" She stopped, not wanting to finish the question.

Drevelli sighed. He seemed about to say something, but then changed his mind. Mina wondered if he was about to give her a standard throwaway line.

"We can't be certain, but it looks that way." He shook his head. "I hope not, Ms Constantine."

After showing the detectives out, Mina walked back to the kitchen on stiff legs. A heavy marri dining table and chairs sat against the kitchen wall. When her mother was alive, she kept the table set with cheerful lime placemats and a bowl of fresh green apples.

Mina pulled out a chair from under the now-cluttered surface and sat down. She lowered her head and let her clenched fists relax on the cool wood.

She'd been so dismissive of Andrea, so self-involved. And now the girl was missing. *Missing*. Three girls had disappeared in Perth over the last eight months—Andrea was the fourth. The media were calling the man responsible the Magician. It started when one reporter wrote that each girl vanished without a trace; no one saw or heard anything, disappearing as if by magic. The name caught on and every news show and paper began using the creepy tag.

The sound of birds twittering in the garden, usually a cheerful noise, seemed harsh and grating. She wondered if Andrea was alive or dead, and shuddered. *Could I have changed what happened?*

* * *

Pulling off her clothes, she moved to the window. Ignoring the clear blue sky, Mina snapped the heavy wooden blinds shut. With the sunlight blocked out, the white walls of her bedroom turned grey. Mina shivered and climbed onto her unmade bed. For a while she lay uncovered, wearing only her bra and underpants, staring up at the ceiling, letting the sweat on her skin turn cold then dry. She replayed the moment Andrea asked if she could walk with her to the car park. The way the girl's voice shook with nerves and the eager, almost pleading look in her eyes. Her own impatient noncommittal nod. *Would it have killed me to be kind?*

Mina pulled the covers up and closed her eyes. She focused her mind on an image; a white stretch of beach. Using a visualisation technique she'd practiced and perfected during some of the darkest days of her life, she was able to almost hear the waves breaking against powder-soft sand. A shoreline laced with dry, black seaweed. The water looked light green and icy; the air clean, holding the tangy taste of salt. The image calmed her as it always did, and in minutes she was asleep.

*Her feet pounded the ground as her breath came in short bursts. Long wet grass brushed her hips, pulling at her clothes. She pushed her way towards a large, black shape. Her eyes darting from ground to sky catching snapshots of pale bare feet and black clouded firmament. Urgency and fear pushed her towards the darkened building. An explosion filled the air; the sound so intense it seemed to pull her backwards and suck the air from her lungs. The sky erupted in blue light and for an instant the structure came into view. Red brick, impossibly tall. The building rose out of the field like a ghost ship.*

*Mina stopped running, but the structure shifted, getting closer, cutting through the grass and moving towards her. She didn't want to see what was inside, knowing its horrors would destroy her. She tried to scream but her throat felt soft, empty of sound. Then a wailing filled her ears. Not hers; the building seemed to be screaming.*

# Chapter Three

Mina woke with a laboured grunt. Her mind, still draped in the horror of the dream, took a few seconds to reconcile with her surroundings. She was in her bedroom. The digital clock on her bedside stand read 7:12 a.m. Weak light filtered under her door, but otherwise the room lay in darkness.

She reached out a hand and fumbled with the lamp; flicking the switch, the room was bathed in light. Forcing herself to take deep breaths, Mina swung her legs over the side of her bed. *I'm in my room. I had a nightmare, nothing more.* Whatever fear lingered was just the result of the dream, yet the image of the tall red building still played in her mind as she crossed the room and opened the walk-in wardrobe door. She grabbed her thick wool dressing-gown and put it on; clutching it closed, she padded downstairs.

The open living room blinds revealed black glass as cold as slabs of frozen oil. Without thinking, she walked to the window and flipped the blinds closed. She plopped down on the sofa and clicked on the TV. Not really seeing the images as they flickered across the screen, her mind kept jumping between flashes of Andrea and the dream.

She closed her lids and rubbed her eyes, trying to push away the memories. When she opened her eyes, Andrea's picture filled the screen. Mina drew in a short breath and leaned forward.

The female reporter's voice oozed practiced concern as she described Andrea's last known movements and what she was wearing the night she disappeared. Then, Andrea's picture was replaced with photos of the three girls already missing. Re-enactments of the other three girls' last known movements were played before cutting back to the studio where the presenter asked for anyone with information on their whereabouts to call Crime Stoppers.

The whole story lasted about nine minutes. When the segment ended, Mina muted the TV. Seeing Andrea on the news somehow made her disappearance more real than the police visit. Mina ran her fingers across her lips trying to focus her mind on what the reporter had said: Andrea's mother arrived at the college at a little after ten expecting to find her daughter waiting. But Andrea never appeared and no one had seen or heard from her since.

Mina replayed her last moments with the missing girl, trying to ignore the way her gut shrivelled with guilt and focused instead on the details. Had whoever abducted Andrea been watching the two of them? She remembered feeling something earlier that evening when she first got out of her car. It was as if her whole body had reacted to a sensation of imminent danger. Mina shivered as goose bumps rose on her arms. Then another thought occurred. *If my instincts were right and he was at the college when I arrived, I might have seen him at some point. Maybe he'd even been in my class* ...

The police had already visited her. Surely they'd check out everyone in her class? Mina stood and wandered through the house. She felt jumpy—restless. In the kitchen, she spotted the card the detective had given her. She'd tossed it on the counter after she'd shown the two men out. Picking it up and flapping it near her face, she considered calling Detective Worsten. Would it do any good if she did?

She imagined telling them what had really happened between her and Andrea. The girl's voice had been stuttering and nervous. It was as if every syllable was etched into Mina's brain, never to be erased.

* * *

"My mum's supposed to be picking me up." Andrea hurried to keep pace with Mina. "Is it ... I mean can I ... um."

"What?" Mina headed away from the class and turned left on the paved walkway, the clacking of her boots echoing off the empty buildings. Away from the lights of the few open classrooms, the campus seemed vast and shadowy.

Andrea shuffled along next to her, an uninvited presence. Mina found the girl's awkwardness irritating. She'd only sat next to her because there was a vacant seat, but now she thought they were friends. As much as Mina had joined the class to reconnect with people, she found the idea of becoming friendly with a shy kid like Andrea off-putting to say the least. Maybe it was her nervousness or Mina's own anxiety about being around people, but whatever the reason she wanted to be rid of the girl.

"I'm heading the same way ... I mean ... um." Andrea stumbled.

Mina stopped walking. The girl's voice grated on her nerves. She could feel herself losing patience, almost ready to snap at her.

"What did you want to ask me? Because I'm really in a hurry." She glanced down at her watch to emphasise the point.

"Can I walk with you?" Andrea's words came out in a rush as if she'd stored them up and had been waiting for the courage to get them out.

Mina noticed the girl shift from one foot to the other. She wore jeans, too tight for her thick frame, and a light-coloured jumper with a bull dog knitted into the front. "Okay. I'm parked down there." Mina pointed across the lawn in the direction of the front lot.

The look of relief that lit up the girl's features took Mina by surprise. *God, she really is desperate,* she thought with a pang of guilt. She wished she could be kinder, but couldn't risk getting involved with someone so needy. *She's the sort that wants to talk and talk.* There'd be all sorts of probing questions. The more Mina thought about it, the more she regretted letting Andrea walk with her.

"Wow, there's not much light down here." Andrea sounded breathless, as if matching her stride to Mina's exhausted her.

Mina didn't bother to answer. She kept her eyes trained on the ground and focused on crossing the darkened lawn, hoping to get to her car as quickly as possible. When they reached the edge of the lot, Mina stopped. Andrea, trotting along a step behind, almost ran into her.

"Sorry," she said and shuffled back a step.

The lights around the parking lot didn't reach far enough, leaving the outer edges of the bitumen rectangle draped in darkness. Thick bushes and trees flanked two of the four sides of the parking area. During the day, the expanse of foliage probably looked lush and picturesque. At night, the trees appeared dense and spooky.

"Okay," Mina turned and faced the girl. "I'm parked over there." She jerked her head left. "See you." She reached into her handbag and felt around for her keys.

"Could…" Andrea coughed. "Could you wait with me?" Her voice was soft, almost a whisper. "My mum's picking me up at ten." She pressed her notebook to her chest and looked around. "I'm a bit early and… you know." A slight breeze blew through the trees, rustling the leaves and lifting Andrea's limp hair.

Mina knew quite well what the girl was talking about. The Magician. After the second woman disappeared and the media gave the creep responsible the catchy nickname, a subtle feeling of paranoia spread throughout the female population of Perth. While it didn't surprise her that Andrea was afraid to be out alone at night, Mina found the girl's fear irrational. Whoever the guy was, she felt certain he wasn't hiding behind every bush waiting to pounce.

"You'll be fine," Mina said, avoiding eye contact. "Just go stand under the light." She heard her own voice echoing in the almost empty parking lot and resisted the urge to look over her own shoulder. *I'm not getting sucked into the panic.* "Like I said, I'm in a bit of a hurry." Mina tried to force the corners of her mouth into a smile, but the effort felt stiff and insincere.

Andrea opened her mouth then closed it again, making her lips smack together. She looked over at the area about ten metres away where a yellowy light shone down on the bitumen in a shadowy arc. Mina could see the girl shiver. *Is she that scared?* She pushed the thought away. *It's night time in July, of course she's cold.*

"Okay. Yeah. Sorry." There was a tremor in the girl's voice. "See you next Thursday." Andrea turned and trotted over to the light pole.

Mina felt a stab of guilt. She *was* only a kid really, and the parking lot felt a bit creepy. She watched the girl step into the circle of light and glance over her shoulder at the gloomy bushes. Mina took a step towards the girl when another thought occurred to her. *If I wait with her, she'll think we're friends and be all over me for the next five weeks.* Mina only decided to take the course to push herself to meet people. With Andrea on her heels, she wouldn't get the chance to do anything but listen to endless teenage chatter.

Mina turned away and hurried in the other direction. The breeze whipped up a pile of leaves and sent them swirling around her feet. She side-stepped the flying debris and pulled her jacket closed against the chill. When she reached her car, Mina turned back for one last look. Andrea stood hunched over as if trying to block the wind with her shoulders. Still clutching her spiral notebook to her chest and glancing towards the heavily overgrown garden beds, she appeared forlorn and pitiful.

"Not my problem," Mina said aloud. Her voice, carried by the breeze, came out louder than she intended.

\* \* \*

Mina pulled out the top drawer and tossed the detective's card in with the cutlery. Telling the police she was a selfish, heartless, bitch wouldn't help Andrea. Besides, the last thing she needed was police hanging around questioning her. *But I could have helped.* There was no escaping the truth, Andrea had asked for her help and Mina had refused. She'd left the girl alone and frightened and now she was dead or going through God only knew what horrors.

Mina closed her eyes and clamped her hand to her mouth. *How many deaths can one person be responsible for before they go mad?* She turned away from the counter and opened the fridge. There was no vodka left, only half a bottle of wine. She grabbed the bottle and a glass from the cupboard before returning to the living room.

She left the TV on, the meaningless white-noise filled the silence. Mina tossed the wine back in sour mouthfuls, ignoring the acidic burning in the pit of her stomach. She continued to drink until the accusing whispers in her head went silent.

# Chapter Four

Andrea pushed her feet against the floor of the van trying to press herself farther back, away from the sound of the doors groaning open. She couldn't see. Rough fabric clung to her head, held in place by something thick at the back of her neck. The inside of the hood smelt earthy and damp like potatoes. Each time she sucked in a breath, the fabric clung to her mouth and nose, pushing the smell deeper into her throat. Her kidneys ached from the blows he'd delivered. Her hands were tied in front of her and her feet bound together. She felt the vehicle dip as he climbed in.

"Please, don't hurt me." The words caught in her throat, coming out in breathless gasps.

His hands wrapped around her ankles. Andrea screamed. He'd warned her not to, but the sound burst from her throat before she could stop herself.

She felt herself being dragged forward. She tried to reach over her head and grasp something, anything to stop herself from being pulled out of the vehicle. She thought she felt something metallic, but before she had the chance to grasp it, the floor dropped away. The back of her head hit something and then she collided with the ground.

Cold air rushed into her lungs. A spike of pain jabbed at the back of her head. She felt a floating sensation as if her head were being bounced on rough waves. Her feet were jerked upwards and rough hands tore at the tape freeing her ankles.

"Get up." His voice, muffled and deep, snapped her back to the moment. It was the only time he'd spoken since those first moments in the back of his van.

He'd come up behind her while she waited for her mother to pick her up after class. She'd been worried about the guy on the news, the one abducting women in Perth. As the minutes ticked by, she felt more and more certain that someone was watching her. *I'm being an idiot, he's not the Bogey Man, he can't be everywhere at once.*

Andrea had drummed her hand on the back of her notebook. She'd tried to focus on her writing. She had been working on a story for nearly six months, a novel about a young woman who meets and falls in love with a guy who is only human one week each year, the rest of the time spent transformed into a wolf. *Maybe I'll call the book Moon Dance.*

Andrea looked up, the moon remained hidden by heavy clouds. Outside the circle of light surrounding her, the parking lot looked spooky and filled with shadows. She thought she heard movement behind her but before she could turn, the world went dark. Something coarse and rough was flung over her head and she'd been lifted. Fingers like thick spikes pulled her into the bushes. The terror of the moment overrode every sense. It was as if the whole world had been pulled out from under her and she found herself in a nightmare.

She'd struggled, trying to lift her arms and pull free from the stranger's grasp. A scream burst from her lips only to be muffled by the man's hand. A blow landed on her lower back and the air burst from Andrea's lungs. Before she could draw breath, he'd punched her again in the same spot. Her legs had sagged and her bladder let go.

In seconds, she was in the back of a van and he was above her. She couldn't see because of the hood, but she heard him breathing and felt his fingers around her upper arms.

"If you scream again, I'll slit your throat." His voice was cold and clipped—each word snapped off like chips of ice. "Nod your head if you understand."

Before she had time to respond, he let go of her arms and punched her thigh. It was a sharp, heavy thump that sent spirals of agony up her leg and through her groin. Andrea nodded her head with as much vigour as she could muster, hoping he could see her acknowledging his demand. He grunted. She held her breath, not knowing when or where another blow would land.

The next time he touched her, she jolted and bit short a gasp before it could escape her lips. He shoved her onto her stomach and bound her feet together before securing her hands behind her back with thick tape. As he pulled the binds around her wrists with a series of jagged rips, Andrea shook—a deep, bone-jarring shudder that began in her belly. She tried to stop herself, but a cry built inside her like gaseous pressure inside a sealed bottle.

"Mum!" She'd opened her mouth and wailed until the cords on her neck felt as if they'd snap. A punch landed on her upper arm then another on her already throbbing leg. Andrea let her head drop back with a dull *thunk* as it hit the floor of the van. She'd turned on her side and pressed her cheek against its cold metal. Her mind raced with terrifying images. *How can this be happening?* Her thoughts stumbled to keep up with the reality of her predicament even as the van rumbled to life and she felt the vehicle move.

The tyres bounced over what felt like a speed bump and Andrea's head thumped the bed of the van with a cold *whack*. It was as if the blow had cleared her faltering thoughts and jerked her back to reality. She'd rolled onto her back. Her shoulders straining with the weight of her body. She gave a hoarse grunt and rocked herself into a sitting position. With the sack over her head, it had been impossible to see her surroundings. She could smell petrol and something metallic. Coupled with the stench of the sack and her own urine, she felt as if she'd choke on the mingling odours. *I have to get out,* was the first coherent thought she'd mustered since he'd grabbed her. Her terrified mind latched on to it.

By bending her knees and pushing off with her heels, she managed to shuffle towards what she guessed were the back doors. The slippery tray helped speed her progress and within a minute, her feet were pressed against something solid. Andrea had leaned back and raised her legs, pressing the soles of her shoes against the surface hoping to find glass or something she could kick through.

After an exhausting exploration of the rear of the van, she found nothing but a solid mass padded with something spongy. Wrists aching and shoulders burning from being compressed beneath her, Andrea rolled back onto her side and gave in to despair.

Time passed slowly. The rocking of the vehicle and the stuffiness of the hood felt like a weight crushing her lungs until it was difficult to draw breath. Her stomach churned as the constant vibrations jostled her body. Andrea pictured her mother arriving at the college parking lot and waiting for her. How long would she sit in the car wondering why her daughter was late? She could see her mother's face creased with worry, eyes straining to over the screen of her phone because she wouldn't have thought to bring her glasses. Why would she? The college was only a fifteen-minute drive from home.

The vehicle had turned, sliding her to the left and then coming to a slow stop. The engine continued to rumble then died. *He'll kill me now.* She clamped her eyes shut. *I don't want to die. I don't want him to hurt me.*

"I want to go home." The whispered plea drowned out the thumping of her heart and comforted her. She repeated the words over and over as if they'd shield her from what was to come.

The engine grumbled to life and the van rolled forward. Andrea let out a hiccupping breath. For the time being, she was safe. *He can't hurt me while he's driving.* She allowed herself no other thoughts. What would happen when they reached their final destination? Each time the question pushed its way to the front of her mind, she buried it under a blanket of prayers and images of her mum and dad. Outside, sounds of traffic and snatches of conversation had petered into silence as the van left the city and headed into the night.

Now, he pushed her forward. She remembered falling and hitting her chin on something sharp. Her jaw ached. His hands, large and rough, grabbed her by the shoulders and pulled her to her feet.

# Chapter Five

It had been close to a year since Mina had awoken before ten in the morning. But even with the assistance of alcohol, sleep was fleeting and occupied by dreams. *Not dreams, nightmares.* Dressed in jeans and a loose blue jumper, she pulled a plate out of the sink and rinsed it under the tap. Up early with nothing to do, she'd decided to clean the kitchen—which meant tackling the overflowing sink and loading the dishwasher. She used the side of a fork to scrape dried sauce off the plate then dumped it in the over-full rack.

Her thoughts returned to the nightmare. Sometimes her mother would feature, often morphing into Andrea. The one constant was the red building sailing towards her in a field of long grass. It began the day the two detectives visited with the news that Andrea had been abducted, and had continued to assault her over the next four days. Her rational mind told her the nightmares sprang from a guilty conscience. She'd abandoned the girl in a dark, deserted parking lot and now she was most likely dead. *God knows, I've got a lot to feel guilty about.*

Protecting guilty secrets was the reason she'd pushed Andrea's attempts at friendship away in the first place.

Mina slammed the dishwasher shut, pressed the start button, and the machine hummed into life. She'd made the decision to return to college tonight. It was important to show her face and act as if nothing had happened. At least that's what she kept telling herself. In truth, she felt the need to return to the last place she'd seen the girl. Maybe doing so would exorcise Andrea's hold over her. *It's like she's bored her way into my brain.*

With the kitchen looking relatively clean, Mina searched for something to occupy the hours until it was time to leave for her writing class. The income from her late father's business interests left her with no pressing need to work, a blessing and in some ways a curse that led to an almost reclusive life. She noticed the pile of unopened mail on the table. Paying bills and answering letters had always been her mother's domain. Since her death, Mina often let the mail pile up for weeks before forcing herself to tackle the mind-numbing task of wading through the river of bank statements, bills, and general crap that landed in her box.

She glanced out of the window over the sink. The stark blue sky, clear of clouds, looked austere and chilly rather than inviting. She dismissed any thoughts of venturing outside and dragged a chair back from the table. At first glance, the stack of envelopes contained nothing more personal than a gas bill. Mina contemplated leaving the chore for another day until she noticed a bulky looking packet free of writing.

She pulled it from the stack and held it in both hands. The paper felt rich and expensive like something used for invitations. She frowned, the only invitations she ever received were from the bank asking her to make an appointment with a financial advisor. When you had plenty of money, your bank was keen to tell you what to do with it. But this envelope hadn't come from a bank. Something about the dense, slightly dimpled feel of it unsettled her.

Mina dropped the envelope on the table and ran a hand through her hair. It couldn't be from the office. They'd never hand deliver something for her to sign. Constantine Accounting, founded by her late father and then taken over by her mother, now belonged to Mina. She had no interest in the accounting business, stopping by the office for only a few hours a fortnight. Not long enough to be involved in any real work, but enough to let the three accountants and two secretaries who worked for her know that she was still alive.

Herbert Longfellow, the senior accountant and an old friend of her father, believed in doing business the old-fashioned way. If there was something that needed her attention, he'd have his secretary contact her and arrange a time for Mina to come into the office. An unmarked envelope shoved in her mail box wasn't Herbert's style.

Mina tapped her index finger on the table and stared at it. "Oh, for fuck's sake." The words came out with more bravado than she felt. She snatched the thing up and tore it open.

Inside revealed a single sheet of paper, thick and dimpled, off-white like the envelope. Mina unfolded the paper and read the one-word message.

*Thanks*

The large, hand-written letters sloped to the right. She felt a line of sweat break out on the back of her neck. The single word, black and stark, was sinister, like a strange species of alien spider crouched on the page. She tried to make sense of the message but could think of nothing that explained the note.

She dropped the paper on the table and picked up the envelope, turning it over in her hands, hoping for some clue as to its meaning. Only then did she realise there was something else inside the folds. A hairclip landed on the note, slipping out of the envelope with a whisper. After a heartbeat of confusion, understanding dawned.

She gasped as if stung by the object and pushed away from the table with enough force to rake the chair legs across the polished jarrah floor. She staggered to her feet and moved around the chair, putting distance between herself and the offending item. A blue hairclip with two little penguins lay on the sheet of paper.

Her eyes darted around the room as if searching for the source of the letter. She could hear her heartbeat pulsing in her ears. *Andrea's hairclip.* She remembered thinking how cheap and infantile the thing looked in the girl's stringy hair. How was it possible that the clip now sat on her kitchen table? She ran her hand over her mouth, trying to bring her thoughts under control.

There could be only one explanation. *He sent it to me.* Mina took a step backwards and her butt hit the sink. *No,* she corrected herself. *He delivered it to me.* She felt the blood drain from her face and the sweat on her neck tinge like icy fingers against her skin. *He was here.* If he'd put the envelope in her mail box, he could have looked through the other letters, maybe even stolen some. If that was true, then he'd know her name and God only knew what else. Personal details, phone number? With each new thought came rising panic.

Since her mother's death, she'd been alone. Alone in the house. Alone in the world. She'd become used to relying on herself. Now she longed for someone to turn to. A reassuring voice. An offer of help. Her thoughts raced through the people in her life: business associates, friends of her mother's—no one close enough to call for help. The constant hum of the dishwasher remained the only sound in the empty house.

Another thought occurred to her, *he might be here now.* "Oh God." Mina scampered for the back door and slid the old-fashioned bolt into place. Then, turning, she jogged through the house and checked the front door. It was locked, but that left the windows on the ground floor. Her heart fluttered. In such an old house the window locks were only metal clamps. There was no real security.

She stopped moving and tried to force her mind to slow down. Even after everything that had happened, she'd never felt afraid to be alone in the house—until now.

She paced through the living room and back into the kitchen, her trainers squeaking to an abrupt stop. The light spilling in from the window threw a rectangle of gold on the floor just in front of the fridge. Mina stared at the spot where her father had died. It was as if she were back in the moment. She recalled the way her clothes had clung to her body, tight and restricting as if the energy flowing through her were more than her body could contain. Recalling that inner flood of strength, she felt the panic recede. *If I could get through that without fear, I can handle anything.*

The drumming of blood pounding in her ears lessened until her heartbeat returned to normal. The memory of her father's death, usually distressing, now calmed her. She'd been through more than most people could imagine. Done more than most would ever dare. Whatever the freak sending the letter had in mind, Mina wouldn't allow herself to run like a scared infant.

She pulled the chair back from the centre of the room and sat down at the table, staring at the note, but not yet touching it. *He's trying to tell me something, but what?* One word, *thanks*. Not a threat. But why thank her? What had she done?

Mina picked up the clip. It felt rigid and slippery. She rubbed her fingers over the little blue penguins feeling slightly repulsed.

He'd taken this from Andrea, of that she had no doubt. Had he killed the girl? Her repulsion turned to anger. Andrea was little more than a kid, annoying but harmless, and the crazy freak had abducted and done God knows what to her. She dropped the clip onto the note, the smiling penguins looked knowing and sinister as if they held secrets.

"Pity you can't tell me why he sent a thank you note."
As the words echoed in the empty house, realisation
dawned. *He's thanking me for giving him Andrea.*

Mina leaned back in the chair and let her shoulders
slump. It was the only explanation. He'd been watching
them last Thursday night. Waiting. He *knew* what Mina had
done. She'd refused Andrea's plea to stay and wait with her
and in doing so, offered the girl up to the killer who was
lying in wait.

"And now he's thanking me." The words tasted dry
and sour on her lips.

She slapped her hand over her mouth and rushed to
the kitchen sink. Her stomach spasmed, but nothing came
up. Staring at the drain, breathing in the damp, slightly
mouldy smell, she waited for her stomach to settle. All the
bravado she'd felt only moments before vanished, leaving
her with a sense of hopelessness. *I keep causing sorrow. Even
that crazy bastard, the Magician, can see it.*

She felt a dull ache in her kidneys as she straightened
her back. Not sure if the pain were real or just a phantom
memory of her father's kick, she ran the back of her hand
over her lips. They felt dry and numb. She considered
opening a new bottle of vodka. She'd put one in the fridge
two days ago, by now it would be icy. She could almost see
the beads of moisture running down the bottle as she
poured the clear liquid into a glass.

Grabbing the beacon and heading for bed was a
tempting option, but she had to think. She'd caused what
happened to Andrea. Not completely, but she couldn't
escape her culpability. Instead of just adding fresh guilt to
the pile that continued to fester in her mind, maybe she
could do something to undo the damage. But what? *I could
phone the police.* Mina reached up and grabbed a cup from
the shelf near the sink. She turned on the tap and filled the
glass. The water tasted fresh and clean, it helped quench
the queasy feeling in her stomach.

*What would getting the police involved achieve?* Her mind raced through the possibilities: they could do tests on the note and envelope. Maybe get a DNA match. If the Magician was in their database, they'd be able to trace him.

She moved across the kitchen and stood over the note. It wasn't written on a sheet of cheap copy paper. No, he'd taken great care with the way he'd contacted her. Would he be stupid enough to leave his DNA all over the envelope? She didn't think so. Still, he *had* risked coming to the house and putting the note in her mailbox. If the police staked out the place, he might show up again.

She took another sip of water and licked her lips. If she showed the note to the police, they'd start asking questions. She could hear Detective Worsten's voice, "Why is this guy thanking you? Does he think you're involved in some way?"

Mina had been the last person to see Andrea before she disappeared. If it looked like she might have been involved in the girl's disappearance, the police would at the very least take her in for questioning. Even if they couldn't prove anything, they might start digging into her life. Her past. She couldn't let that happen.

Mina picked up the note, grimacing at the feel of the thick paper between her fingers. *I should burn it.* Getting rid of the note and the clip would be the safest course of action, yet destroying it seemed like turning her back on Andrea a second time. Realising she was taking a risk, Mina shoved the note and the clip back inside the envelope.

She opened the pantry and grabbed the toasted sandwich press off the bottom shelf. The thing hadn't been used since her mother was alive. Deciding no one would ever think to look inside the old metal appliance, Mina opened the press and slid the envelope inside. She clipped the sandwich maker closed and returned it to its place on the shelf.

It was a relief to have the envelope and its contents out of sight. Mina let out a long breath. She felt calmer, more in control of her thoughts. Maybe the Magician would leave her alone now he'd had his fun with her. The note and clip might have been his sick way of frightening her. *I bet he gets off on seeing women shake with fear.* Her hands curled into fists, the thought of him standing over Andrea enjoying her terror sickened Mina.

Nodding her head, she crossed over to the sink area and opened the cutlery drawer. Ignoring Worsten's business card, Mina picked up a knife. The blade was about fifteen centimetres, the base wooden and sturdy in her hand. She turned the handle over, liking the size and weight of it. Her handbag sat open on the counter. Mina dropped the knife in and closed the zip.

She would return to the college tonight. If he did show up, she'd kill the fucker. She owed it to Andrea.

# Chapter Six

Following Mina home had been a huge risk. Grabbing the girl and getting her in the back of his van had been, well... like magic. He clamped his lips together cutting off the chuckle that bubbled up his throat. Thinking about the moment he emerged from the bushes and threw the sack over her head sent a shock of excitement through his body. He grinned and pressed his eye to the hole. Now wasn't the time to think of Mina. Watching the Dolly—he always thought of his girls as the Dolly—take off her dirty clothes and wash herself was the beginning of something special. His thoughts of Mina had to be kept separate from what he did with his Dollies.

He clenched a stained nylon blouse in his fist and let his gaze travel over the Dolly's body. She wasn't much to look at, but there was a soft vulnerable quality that made watching her even more exciting. The last girl had been too audacious and his anger got the better of him. This Dolly would last much longer, he'd see to it that the games didn't get out of hand.

The Dolly shivered and hunched over, trying to cover as much of her body as she could. Crouching with her knees together, she picked up the white fleecy pants and stepped into them. With her back to the door, she bent and scooped up the matching top. Her skin was so white it almost glowed in the dimness of her cell—the perfect canvas for the angry purple bruises on her back. She slipped the top down and the white flesh disappeared.

He sucked in a breath and felt his heart skip a beat. The moment had come. He'd had the Dolly for almost a week. Each step had been carefully planned—the tension building so that this moment would be perfect. He pulled his face away from the hole and the heavy fabric, pushed aside by his cheek, fell back in place. He slid back the bolt and took a deep breath before grabbing the long metal handle and rolling the door back.

She turned. Her hair was splayed in damp strings, her eyes wide and mouth drawn open in terror. He'd been right to wait, let the fear grow. He crossed the space, still clutching the old nylon blouse. The Dolly tried to scream and dart past him. He took hold of her, easily blocking her attempt at escape. Spinning her around, he slipped the blouse over her head and around her throat. The perfection of the moment was so pure, he almost lost control. Slowing his breathing, he managed to keep from squeezing the blouse too tight. The games were always better when he took his time.

# Chapter Seven

Mina grabbed her handbag off the seat and got out of the car. Even though she'd parked in the same spot as last week, the lot at Alice College seemed like a different world. A police van was set up along the curb where she'd last seen Andrea. Boards with pictures of the missing girls sat on both sides of the vehicle. Small clusters of students stood talking to uniformed officers while stragglers milled around the photo boards.

Had she been stupid enough to think he'd risk showing up? She recalled reading somewhere that serial killers often inserted themselves into investigations of the very crimes they've committed. He could be one of the people talking to the police officers. Maybe even putting himself forward as a witness. Mina walked past the crowd catching snatches of conversations:

"Can't believe it could happen here."

"Has a body been found?"

The voices, excited and breathless rang in her ears as she left the parking lot and crossed the lawn.

The atmosphere was no better inside the classroom. Lyn stood at the front with a group of people gathered around her. When Mina entered, the conversation stopped.

"Hi." Lyn moved past the plump man with the long grey hair. "How ya doing?" Puffy crescents hung beneath the woman's small eyes making her look sleepy.

"Fine." Mina responded automatically. She stood still, uncertain what Lyn expected her to say.

Lyn nodded and touched Mina's shoulder. "I'm glad you came." The woman gave her an encouraging smile. Mina looked around the group noting the sympathetic smiles and nods. She realised that they viewed her as a victim in all this. She'd been the last person to see Andrea so she *had* to be suffering. *If only they knew what I did.* She could feel the heat creeping up her neck, filling her face. Coming back had been a mistake, but it was too late to turn and leave.

"Thanks." The word came out as little more than a croak.

Before Lyn could say more, Mina scurried to the back of the room and sat down. She busied herself opening her notebook and uncapping her pen. She could feel the weight of everyone's stare, but kept her head down.

"I'd like to start by taking a moment to stop and think about Andrea." Lyn's voice trembled slightly. "I know none of us know each other very well, but I'm sure I speak for everyone when I say we're all thinking of her and her family."

Mina forced herself to look up and focus on the woman. "Let's just hope the police catch whoever's responsible." She seemed to be looking in Mina's direction.

A spattering of voices all muttered in agreement. Mina pressed her lips together and nodded along with her classmates. The room seemed smaller than last week; the collective body heat of the other people filled the air, making it stuffy and difficult to breath. Lyn began discussing *point of view* or at least that's what Mina thought she was talking about. It was difficult to keep track, her mind kept coming back to the police vehicle and the way everyone had stared at her when she entered the room.

She tried to listen to Lyn but guilt kept gnawing at her until her stomach felt like a ball of wire and her jaw ached from clenching. When Lyn finally suggested they take a break, Mina stood too quickly and her chair almost over balanced. For the second time that evening, all eyes were on her.

By the time she'd made her way to the courtyard, Mina wanted to keep on going and not stopping until she made it to her car. The thought of setting foot back in the classroom made her throat dry. Maybe leaving and putting everything that had happened since last Thursday behind her was the right idea. But could she do that? Would *he* let her?

"I was hoping you'd come back."

The sudden presence startled her. Mina's hand reached instinctively for her handbag and the knife hidden inside.

"Sorry. Did I make you jump?" He frowned and tiny wrinkles appeared at the corners of his sea green eyes. Mina puffed out a breath, relieved and a little flustered.

"No. I mean yes, a bit." Realising she was clutching her handbag like an old lady expecting to be mugged, she relaxed her grip and tried to smile. Her face felt stiff and unnatural.

People moved around the courtyard chatting in groups. A few sat on the grass just beyond the range of the lights. The glowing ends of their cigarettes moved up and down in the shadows. With so many people around, it was stupid of her to be jumpy.

"I thought you might need this." He held a can of soft drink out.

Confused, Mina stared at the can. He seemed to be waiting for her to speak. "Oh. Um, thanks." The moment felt awkward, as if she were missing something. She reached for the can and then it dawned on her. "Oh yeah. Pasito." She managed a forced laugh.

He shook his head. "I guess our last meeting was more memorable for me."

"No. It's not that." She didn't know why she felt the need to explain herself, the can of soft drink was a really lame way to make a move on her. It was the sort of thing she usually detested, but there was something in his expression, a guilelessness that appealed to her. "I'm just a bit—distracted."

His expression changed, became almost pained. "Yeah. Everyone's feeling it tonight. Did you know her?"

*Did I know her?* The question hung in the air while Mina grappled with an answer. "Not really." As soon as the words were out, she felt a rush of shame. In truth, she hadn't known the girl very well, but she'd delivered her into the hands of a psycho. Could there be anything more intimate between two people?

He let out a sigh. It was a desolate sound. "I'm sorry that happened to one of your classmates. You're brave to even come back here." He held up his own unopened can of soft drink and gestured around the courtyard.

"Thanks, but I'm not brave. It's really nothing to do with me." She fiddled with the tab on the top of the can, pulling it open with a hissing pop.

"Yes, of course not, but still …" He let the words trail off. "How's the course going?"

"Good. Very interesting." She took a sip from the can enjoying the way the sweet, fruity liquid cooled her throat. "But it's not for me." She took another sip stalling. "I don't think I'll continue with it." She kept her tone casual. She had no intention of returning next week. She'd made an appearance. Shown everyone that she had nothing to hide. There was no need to keep coming back. Whatever she thought might happen when she put the knife in her bag, clearly hadn't.

"Well, if I won't see you next week…" He hesitated as if searching for the right words. "We could… Why don't we, you know, have a drink together?" He scratched the skin just above his left eyebrow. Mina noticed he had a small scar that ran half the length of his brow. It looked white against his tanned skin.

"We *are* having a drink together." She felt mean, but liked the surprised twinkle in his strange green eyes.

"Just for that," he said. "I'm buying you a drink and then boring you with long stories about my childhood."

Mina tried to keep a straight face, but couldn't. She'd come back to Alice College expecting to encounter a crazed killer and instead she was about to agree to go on a date for the first time in years.

Behind her the doors clanged with the sound of people making their way back to class. "All right, but I've got some pretty boring stories as well."

"I bet you do," he said with a straight face. "See you back here at nine thirty." He turned to go, then stopped as if remembering something. "I'm Lee. Lee Danvers." He put his hand on his chest and took a step backwards almost colliding with a man carrying a take-away coffee cup.

* * *

The pub smelled like beer: piney and rich. They found a table in the corner by walls covered in black and white framed photos. Most were shots of Perth in the 1940s. Mina took a sip of her vodka and lemon.

"Mina." He said her name as if trying out a strange new word.

She liked the sound of his voice, deep and soft.

"That's an unusual name," he said. Then, after a pause, he added, "The children of the night. What sweet music they make."

"Well done." Mina couldn't help laughing. "You must be one of the only people I've ever met who worked that out."

"Dracula's one of my favourite books *and* movies." Lee lifted the pint glass and tilted it to his mouth. "So, I'm right? You're named after Mina Harker?"

"My mother was a fan of the book, not the movie." She ran her finger over a deep gouge in the dark wood table. "She liked the classics."

"Was?"

The classic Australian rock piped through the speakers seemed louder. "Yes. She passed away." The last thing she wanted to do was talk about her mother's death. Only a moment ago, she'd felt the weight of the last week lifting. It seemed important to hold onto that feeling.

"I'm sorry. I–"

"It's fine." Mina downed the rest of her drink. "I think I'll have another, do you want one?"

"No, I'm good. Let me get it." He put down his drink, but Mina was already on her feet and heading for the bar.

She didn't want to think of her mother or Andrea. Being with Lee, doing something as normal as sitting in a pub, made all the guilt and fear of the last week seem like an echo belonging to another life. Mina wanted the sensation to last. She ordered a double vodka and lemon and returned to Lee.

"You teach photography?"

He hesitated as if wondering how to answer. "Yes. But I mostly work freelance for online magazines." She watched his face as he spoke. The subtle nuances often mirrored the complexity within—or so she'd heard. He had clear skin, unlined except for a few creases around his eyes. His hair, the colour of sand, was tousled in messy half curls. Mina wondered what it would be like to slide her fingers through the blond tangle. Would his hair feel silky or coarse?

"Where do you work?"

She blinked, realising he'd asked her a question. "I sort of work at an accounting firm. Not very interesting," she added before he could ask for details.

"Is that why you're taking a writing course? Looking for something more interesting?"

She had the urge to say something clever, but the intense look in his eyes made her hesitate. There was kindness swimming in the strange sea of green and brown. Mina suddenly felt off balance, giddy as if the vodka had hit her all at once. Whatever she'd meant to say went out of her head and she found herself telling him the plain, honest truth.

"I need to … I don't know, make contact with the human race." She gave a nervous laugh and tucked her hair behind her ear. She wasn't usually given to bouts of nervousness. At least not making an outward show of being nervous. "I know that sounds strange."

"No. No, it doesn't." He put his glass down and let his hand rest on the table, his fingers only centimetres from hers. "Sometimes, it's easy to cut yourself off. Pull away from the world." He shrugged. "Not everyone needs to be constantly surrounded by people. It's not strange, a bit lonely maybe."

*Lonely*. He'd said the word she'd been avoiding. She'd told herself enrolling in the writing class was a form of self-help, a way of reconnecting with the world, but in truth, she *was* lonely. The sad pathetic fact was, at twenty-nine, she wasn't just lonely, she was completely alone. The realisation had a sobering effect.

Mina looked down at her hands, lying flat on the table. "Yes, it is lonely." The last word almost caught in her throat. *Jesus, what's happening to me? One kind word and I'm ready to start bawling.*

As if sensing her misery, Lee reached out and put his hand over hers. His skin felt warm. "So, did you do it?"

The question took her by surprise. "Do what?"

"Make contact with the human race?" A smile lurked around the corners of his mouth.

Mina let out a breath that was in equal parts relief and amusement. "I'm starting to think so."

* * *

Lee insisted on driving her home. He held his car door open and invited her in. Mina hesitated. She felt drawn to him in a way she'd never experienced before, but what did she really know about him? Only his name and where he worked. He'd told her he grew up in a small town about two and a half hours south of Perth. But apart from the basics, he was a stranger. This *was* only the second time they'd met and here she was thinking about getting into his car.

"I think I'm okay to drive." Mina pulled her jacket closed and crossed her arms around her body. The pub had emptied out while they'd been talking and the midnight streets were shiny with rain. "I only had a few drinks."

Lee rested his arm on the open car door and shook his head. "I can't let you drive. I'm the one who plied you with alcohol, the least I can do is drive you home."

"But my car is—"

"You can get an Uber back in the morning. Come on." He cocked his head towards the open door. "Jump in."

Mina looked back at the pub. Some of the lights were already out. The air smelled heavy with the promise of more rain and her head buzzed from the vodka. "All right. Thanks."

Lee waited until she was seated in the car and then slammed the door closed and walked around to the driver's side. *What am I doing?* She felt unsure about where things were headed. A flicker of excitement sat in the pit of her belly and the memory of the vodka warmed her chest. How far would she allow things to go with this man? It had been a long time since she had let anyone get close to her, even physically. Her mind threatened to turn towards darker thoughts, she tried to push them away.

*It can't last,* she told herself. *Whatever happens won't change anything. I'm dangerous. If I let this go too far, he'll get hurt.* A procession of images flashed through her mind: Andrea, her mother, and finally her father. Mina closed her eyes and pushed her head back against the car seat. When she opened them again, Lee was sitting next to her.

"You okay?" His voice was soft with concern.

"Yep. Fine." Mina managed a smile. "I think you were right about me not being fit to drive."

He nodded but made no further comment. Once they were on the road, Mina felt more relaxed. The car smelled piny with a hint of something sharp. It was a pleasant combination; masculine and clean.

Lee pulled up at the traffic lights next to a black ute. "Where to?" He turned to look at her waiting for directions.

"Civil Park." Mina thought her voice sounded loud over the soft music coming from the radio.

"Hmm. Nice." He turned the car right and spots of rain dotted the windscreen. "You lived there long?"

"All my life." She didn't want to talk about her life and childhood, so she grappled for a way to change the subject. "Tell me about the town where you grew up."

He took a moment to answer as if sorting through memories. "It's called Dark Water. Not a huge place but pretty big by small town standards. Inland from the coast a bit, pretty in a green countryside sort of way." He glanced over at her. "You'd like it. I'll have to show it to you. There's a lake. I used to go swimming there when I was a kid." He went on, not waiting for her to comment. "It used to be a coal mine, now it's so blue it looks almost like the Aegean Sea. It's called Fire Lake. God knows why."

She nodded, liking the way his voice sounded—deep and serious. Her eyelids felt heavy; she let them close. The air inside the car was warm and the hiss of the tyres soothing. Mina felt the worry and anxiety of the past week uncoiling. It felt as if something tight had been wrapped around her body and now it was loosening. She listened to Lee talk about Dark Water as they drove through the night.

# Chapter Eight

Andrea heard noises. Crying, sometimes moaning. At first, she couldn't tell if the noises were real or imagined. For a while, she wasn't even sure if the crying was her own. For a long time she stayed huddled on the torn mattress, knees drawn up, trying to make herself as small as possible. She cried long, hard sobs that tore at her chest and left her throat raw. After what seemed like hours, her body shuddered with exhaustion and she rolled onto her side and slept.

When she woke, a weak bar of light shone down from high up on the wall to her left. Judging by its pale grey quality, Andrea guessed it was morning. Her eyes were swollen and the light dim, the details of her surroundings remained vague and shadowy. She spotted a bottle of water. *Was it there all night or did he sneak in and put it there while I was asleep? Maybe he's here now, watching me.* She jumped and snapped her head around, sure he was sneaking up behind her.

She had no way of knowing where he might be lurking. When he'd entered the room the other night, he seemed to roll the whole wall back and pounce on her, giving her no time to turn around. She didn't want to think about that night and what he'd done; the memory too raw and painful to contemplate. He hadn't raped her, for that she was grateful. *Grateful?* When did she become grateful to the monster that had beaten and strangled her?

She leaned forward and groaned with the effort. Her back and shoulders throbbed with the bruises left by multiple blows. Crawling on her hands and knees, Andrea shuffled across the dusty floorboards to the bottle. She sank back onto her butt and unscrewed the cap. The thirst and hunger were almost worse than the beatings. At least when he finished hurting her, she could curl up and wait for the agony to recede, but the need for food and water bit at her like a rabid dog.

She tilted the plastic bottle to her lips and took a swallow. The cool liquid felt good, washing over her injured throat. After a few more sips, she resealed the lid, resisting the urge to keep drinking. She had to make the water last, there was no telling when or if he'd provide more.

Another look around the room reassured her that for now, he was nowhere in sight. She was unsure of how long she'd been in this place. A week maybe. It felt like longer. That night at the college seemed like years ago and Andrea a younger version of herself. He'd kept her chained like an animal; leather straps around both wrists attached to a long steel chain, bolted to a thick beam on the wall. In the first days, she'd experimented with moving around the room. The chain had given her enough slack to reach two or so metres left and right, but not all the way to the far wall.

It hadn't taken her long to realise the far wall was the way out. It looked to Andrea like some sort of huge rolling metal door; something enclosing a giant freezer. That's how he came and went. If she could reach that door, there might be a way out. She had to think, try to focus on getting her hands out of the straps. But his fists had left her body aching and stiff, and lack of food and sleep robbed her of energy, concentration.

She tried to remember when she'd last eaten. After he had choked and beaten her, he had left a mandarin and one slice of white bread. Since then, she'd woken to a muesli bar and another mandarin on what she guessed was the fifth morning of her captivity. Thinking about the food made her stomach spasm with hunger, the feeling swelled with a ferocity she'd never experienced.

Andrea moved crab-like on her knees back to the mattress, clutching the bottle to her chest. The smell from the plastic bucket she used as a toilet hung in the air, polluting the room with the overpowering stench of human waste. Beneath the foul odour was the faint smell of something sweet and cloying. She curled on her side, face pressed against the mattress, and forced her mind to work.

The rolling door was a way out. *It's locked*, a small despairing voice in her head warned her against hope. *No. I'm chained up, he might think there's no need to lock the door.* It made sense, Andrea wanted it to be true. If the door was unlocked then the only thing standing between her and getting away were the leather straps around her wrists. *What about him?* Her thoughts faltered. *He's probably on the other side of the door.*

*Don't think about him*, she told herself. *Just concentrate on getting out of the cuffs.* It seemed better to only think in small steps, letting her mind go no further than the first hurdle. Finding something to shred away at the leather was a thought to hold on to. A purpose. Hope. Her mind latched onto it with the desperation of a frightened child. She sat up and tucked the bottle under the mattress. If he came in while she was sleeping again, she didn't want him taking it away from her.

Next, Andrea scanned the room. The three walls she *could* reach were brick, but high up, lengths of wood ran between the brick and the roof. The bars of light that filtered in came from gaps in the timbers. The light wasn't much, barely enough to chase the blackness away. She tried to take inventory of her surroundings, but her mind kept jumping back to the way he'd pounced on her... the feel of whatever he'd wrapped around her throat. She'd thought it was the end and in some ways hoped it was. The fear and the hunger were almost worse than death because they never abated—torturing her even in sleep.

The image of her mother's face materialised in her mind, vivid and clear like a snapshot. She looked worried and tired. *Does she think I'm dead?* No, Andrea knew her mum would never give up on her. Nor would her father. *They'll drive themselves crazy with worry. Make themselves sick, but never give up.* Her parents babied her, Andrea knew that. She'd never had to make decisions, plan for things. Her mum and dad always stepped in and sorted everything out. She felt a tiny push of anger.

"Why didn't you make me think for myself? If I was stronger, more independent, I wouldn't be in this mess." Her lips, dry and cracked, stung. She realised she'd voiced her thoughts aloud and immediately felt ashamed.

It wasn't her parents fault she was weak and stupid. They'd worked hard all their lives to give her everything they could. In high school a group of girls bullied her for being fat, when she told her parents, her dad sold his boat so she could go to a private school. *They should have told me to lose weight,* she thought and pounded the mattress with her fist. *Those girls were right, I am a baby pig—dumb and greedy.*

Tears ran down her face and fell in drops onto her chest. Her bowels clamped and groaned. The realisation that she needed to use the bucket again made her cry harder. Crouching over the foul-smelling mess horrified and repulsed her. She drew her knees up to her chest and hoped the urge would pass. Instead the pressure increased.

In the end, Andrea gave up and crawled the three or so metres to the bucket. Crouched above it with her track pants around her ankles, she could smell the contents so intensely her stomach lurched. *If I vomit, it'll smell and I'll be stuck with it.* Besides, she thought it might be important to keep the water she'd drunk in her stomach. She felt light-headed so she was probably dehydrated.

When she made it back to the mattress she was huffing as though she'd been jogging, and her head buzzed with a static-like noise. The idea of curling up on the mattress and sleeping tugged at her mind like a tap dripping over and over, the word *sleep* echoed in her head.

"I'll just rest for a while," she spoke as if someone else were in the room with her. Her mother maybe. *Yes*, Andrea smiled, stretching her cracked lips over her teeth. She could almost see her mother's face, glasses perched on her nose, and hair clipped in a messy bun. Andrea lay her head on the mattress, ignoring the stiff grubby feel of the fabric. She was on the couch at home with the TV chattering in the background. Her eyelids drooped and she slipped into sleep.

# Chapter Nine

"Mina." Her mother's voice snapped her from sleep as though she'd spoken in her ear. She sat up in bed, eyes still heavy. In spite of everything, she'd expected to see her mother standing over her. It had been eighteen months since her death, but Irene Constantine's presence filled the house. Every cushion, every dish lovingly placed; her mother had been determined to make the place—once their prison—a home.

Mina dropped her head into her hands. The voice had seemed so real—an urgent whisper next to her ear. Her nightmare was now always the same: running through the tall grass with thunder roaring overhead; the red building, impossibly large, looming towards her; something pulling her towards the structure— a nebulous force she felt powerless to resist. In the seconds between sleep and waking, Mina had felt her mother's hair brush her cheek.

*I can't go on like this.* She ran her fingers through her hair and swung her legs out of the bed. She'd been looking forward to today, seeing Lee again. But now the remnants of the dream hung over her like a heavy blanket, and her mind turned to Andrea. Where was she? Alive or dead? Suffering? The questions plagued her. *She's not my responsibility*, Mina told herself over and over again. Some of the time she believed it. But the constant nightmares contradicted her.

Lee was due to arrive at nine, she had less than an hour to get herself ready. Forcing her mind away from thoughts of Andrea, she headed for the shower.

\* \* \*

After the way she'd behaved Thursday night, Mina wouldn't blame Lee if he didn't show up. She'd made a real fool of herself when he drove her home. First, she'd fallen asleep while he was telling her about his home town and then, when he'd walked her to the door, she'd vomited over her mother's flower bed. In the end, Lee had to help her inside and put her to bed on the couch. Mina remembered the way she'd doubled over near the front door, vodka mixed with bile spewing out of her mouth. She took a sip of coffee and groaned at the memory. The hot, sweet liquid soothed her nerves.

*I'm nervous.* Whether it was because she hadn't been on a date in more than two years or being close to someone set off jolts of panic, Mina didn't know. She emptied the dregs of her coffee in the sink and looked out across the backyard. The sunlight, weak as it struggled to break through the clouds, fell across the lawn. *At least I'm feeling something.*

The doorbell chimed, echoing through the soundless house. Mina crossed to the kitchen table and picked up her bag. When she opened the front door, Lee was half-turned looking towards the driveway. His face in profile struck her as almost frail. He was attractive, good looking even. But standing in the sunlight—face in repose—a disturbing quality hung about him, one Mina couldn't quite identify.

"You ready?" He smiled and the look vanished.

Mina nodded, she felt a little off balance. The morning air smelled of damp grass and wood. The clean, familiar odour took the edge off her jitters. He held out his hand and without thinking, she took it. He led her to his car and opened the door for her. Neither of them spoke until they were on the road and heading south.

"I wasn't sure you'd show up." Mina hesitated. "Not after the spectacle I made of myself on Thursday."

He shrugged. "It's not like I've never had too much to drink. The vomiting part *was* pretty gross though." He gave her a sidelong glance.

"Oh God," Mina covered her face with her hands. "I hoped you'd forget that bit."

"No. I'll never forget that." He smiled at her, the wrinkles around his eyes deepened. Mina couldn't help smiling back. "You have a beautiful smile, Mina. I'd like to photograph you."

"Let's just see how today goes." The words came out sounding harsher than she'd intended.

He stopped smiling and looked back at the road.

"Sorry. It's just a reflex," she paused, trying to find the right words. "I don't know why I'm so standoffish with people." It wasn't like her to try and explain herself, but making Lee understand seemed important. "It's a defence mechanism I suppose."

"It's okay." He reached over and covered her hand with his. She liked the feel of his skin against hers. "You don't have to explain yourself." He glanced at her. "I get it. But you can relax, I'm not trying to push myself on you."

Unsure how to respond, she focused her eyes on the windscreen. The marble-grey sky held a stiff wind, chilling the air. Mina had dressed accordingly in jeans and a grey jumper. Despite the thickness of her clothing, she was intensely aware of his hand and its proximity to her thigh. She tried to think of something to say.

"How long did you say it would take?"

"To reach Dark Water? About two hours, maybe two and half." His hand still rested on hers. "It's been—" He frowned. "It must be nearly two years since I've been back. I hadn't thought about it till now, but it's been a while."

She couldn't remember exactly what led them to plan the drive to Dark Water. All she knew was that she'd been drunk, and a two-and-a-half-hour drive to look at Lee's home town sounded like a good idea. Now she wasn't so sure. She was attracted to him, that she couldn't deny, but visiting his home town seemed like rushing things. The other night, she'd thought Lee would go home with her and that's where it would end, only that didn't happen and now it seemed like he wanted more from her. More than she could give.

"I thought we could drive out to Fire Lake first, then I'll give you the tour of the town."

"Sounds good." Mina could hear the enthusiasm in his voice; it worried her. She wanted to say something, tell him this wasn't the start of a relationship. Instead she found herself wondering if maybe it could be. *Why can't I have some happiness? Why can't I just forget the past and enjoy this* … her thoughts faltered. How long could it last if she was incapable of letting him get close to her? He seemed like a nice guy, did she want hurting him to be on her conscience too?

She thought of telling him she didn't feel well. Asking him to turn around and take her home. Then give him the brush off with a vague promise to call. She could imagine the disappointment on his face. The wounded look in his eyes. It would hurt but be kinder than if she let things drag out.

The words were already forming in her mind when he spoke.

"You look worried. Am I coming on too strong?" He sounded playful, but she could hear the undertone. An edge of doubt as if preparing himself for the rejection.

"No. No, I'm fine." *It can't hurt to have one nice day, can it?* "I was just thinking it might rain."

He let out a breath. "I think we'll outrun it."

"How old are you?" The question had been bouncing around in her head since Thursday night. He was good looking, kind, and funny so why was he single?

"I'm thirty-three and before you ask, there's nothing wrong with me... Well not that I'm aware of." The playful tone was back, only this time he sounded more relaxed. "I was married—once. It didn't work out."

"I'm sorry." Mina could imagine the heartbreak that went with divorcing so young. "It couldn't have been easy."

"It was a long time ago. I'm well and truly over it." He kept his eyes on the road. "But after the divorce, I moved around a lot for work so I never really had time for another relationship." After a brief pause, he continued. "What about you?"

"How old am I? Or, have I ever been married?" It occurred to Mina that this was the longest conversation she'd had with anyone in a long time.

"Both," he said with a chuckle.

She took a deep breath. "Twenty-nine and no, never."

"Okay," he said. "I guess we know enough about each other. Now let's talk about the Kardashians."

Mina let out a bark of laughter. She heard herself make the unexpected sound and couldn't help laughing again. It felt good. Better than good, it felt normal.

They turned off the highway around eleven o'clock. The road leading into Dark Water was a wide, grey expanse of low-grade bitumen lined on both sides by thickly packed trees. The July weather remained too cold for the wildflowers to be in bloom, but the bush had a look of lushness brought by winter rains. Mina liked the feeling of being so far from the city, the isolation offered anonymity—peace. She thought of voicing her feelings, but the trip had been fun. After the initial awkwardness, they'd chatted and joked, steering clear of anything heavy or too personal. She didn't want the mood to change, so she kept her thoughts to herself.

"Here's the turn off for Fire Lake." Lee indicated and pulled onto a narrower road that cut a straight line through the dense bush. They drove for another five hundred metres before the road curved and ended in a broad expanse of orange pea gravel.

Lee pulled the car to the left and the water came into view. Mina climbed out, eager to get a closer look. It was unlike any lake she'd ever seen. The crystal blue water was edged with soft white sand and surrounded by grassy banks that, in some areas, jutted out like jade islands.

"I can't believe this place exists." She trotted across the pea gravel enjoying the cold breeze that ruffled her hair.

"I used to come here when I was a kid." Lee stepped up beside her and took her hand. "We'd swim and kayak." He continued leading her down a grassy slope until their shoes crunched on the damp sand at the edge of the water.

Mina's hands were cold, Lee's skin warmed her and she had the sudden urge to press herself against him, seek out his body heat. Still holding his hand, she stepped closer, resting her shoulder and hip against his body. He let go of her hand and slipped his arm around her. They both watched the water ripple under the push of a breeze. For a while neither of them spoke.

It was a moment Mina thought she might store up and use when darkness threatened to overwhelm her. A new happy place to visit when sorrow and guilt covered her. Without speaking, Lee turned to look at her. His eyes like stormy seas, intent and searching. The look of frailty she thought she'd glimpse earlier that morning was nowhere in sight. He dipped his head and kissed her, his arms sliding around her back.

His lips felt full and soft against hers. He tasted like mint with a hint of coffee. The kiss, gentle and sweet, lasted only a few seconds before he pulled away. Mina felt a rush of sadness as his lips left hers. Her heart fluttered. Then he pulled her closer and encircled her in his arms.

With her head laying against his chest, she could hear his heart beating through his heavy jumper; a steady drumming that reminded her of the thunder in her dreams.

"I'm glad we came here." His voice sounded hoarse yet peaceful, reverberating in his chest. There was a finality there, as if the kiss had sealed something between them. Mina felt it too; a sense of bonding. She let herself consider what it would be like to press herself against him, their bodies naked, stripped bare of everything that separated them. A spark of excitement ran through her, making her shiver.

"Are you cold?" he asked, sliding his hands up and down her back.

"No. I'm fine." She tried to keep her voice even, but a tremor betrayed her.

"Come on." He pulled away from her, taking her hand and leading her back to the car. "Lunchtime."

They ate at a pub that looked nearly a century old with stone walls and wrought iron railings enclosing the beer garden. The food, tasty and generously portioned, washed down with pints of beer, left Mina feeling lethargic and heavy-eyed. Sitting in a weathered leather armchair in front of an open fire, she watched Lee drain his glass with a sense of contentment that seemed alien, yet enticing. *I could live like this*, she thought. *Sharing my time with this man and enjoying a life free of memories*. The more time she spent with him the more tangible the dream became. Maybe there could be a life for her outside of solitude.

"You look sleepy." Lee's eyes travelled over her as if searching out every curve and rise of her body. She could feel that shiver of excitement building again; she welcomed it.

"I guess it's time for the tour." She stretched, lifting her arms above her head, enjoying the way he watched her movements.

"If you feel like a nap," he said, picking up his empty glass and studying the beer dregs. After a pause, he put the glass down and met her gaze. "There's a hotel behind the pub. We could rent a room and you could... lie down for a while."

Mina kept her expression neutral, drawing the moment out. She could see colour rising in his face and flushing his cheeks. He looked younger suddenly, unsure of himself for the first time since she'd met him.

"Will you lie with me?" she asked, leaning towards him.

* * *

Fifteen minutes later, they entered a spacious, if basic, ground floor hotel room. The curtains were open, spilling gloomy grey light across the queen-size bed. Mina took off her jacket and tossed it over the chair in the corner. Outside, birds trilled and the occasional hiss of wheels came across the bitumen. The languid feeling she'd experienced in the pub had vanished. Her body filled with energy, all jittery and hypersensitive.

Lee didn't bother to turn on the lights or draw the curtains. He crossed from the door to where Mina stood at the foot of the bed and pulled her into his arms. This time when he kissed her, she felt the urgency. He ran his hands down her back letting them come to rest on her hips and then pulling her against him with a jerk that made her groan with anticipation.

Mina pulled back and pushed his jumper up revealing the skin on his stomach. She bent and pressed her lips against the muscle above his jeans savouring the salty taste of his flesh. Lee gasped, pulled his jumper off and tossed it to the floor.

In seconds, they were both naked; bodies pressed together on the bed. His hands roamed over her skin. With each new touch, Mina felt her body jolt as if her blood had been replaced with electricity—the sensation almost painful in its intensity. All coherent thought melded into a haze of heat and urgency as the pressure of his mouth on hers intensified.

Later, the room melted into darkness and Mina slept with Lee's arm locked around her waist. It was a deep slumber undisturbed by sound or dreams.

When she woke, the room was in darkness and Lee no longer lay beside her. Even without the light, she immediately became aware of the strange surroundings; the unfamiliar bed. A door creaked and light fell across the room. Mina sat up, clutching the sheets to her chest. Lee stood in the bathroom doorway, a towel slung around his waist, and things suddenly made sense.

They were in the hotel room and night had fallen. Pearly lines of moonlight spilled through the window, bathing the room and washing the bed in greyish light. Mina let out a breath and pulled her hair over her shoulder. The sheet she'd been clutching dropped to her waist.

"Want to order room service?" he asked, his eyes wandering over her naked breasts.

She nodded. For a moment she'd thought he'd gone, leaving her alone in a strange town. Why she'd been so quick to think he was capable of such behaviour, she couldn't say, only that anticipating other people's actions wasn't her strong point. *No*, she corrected herself. *I'm too busy worrying about myself to notice what other people are doing.* Her mind turned to Andrea. *She was afraid, if I hadn't been so fixated on keeping my distance, she'd be home now—safe.*

"I'm starving."

Lee clicked on the lamp and sat on the bed. He leaned back, laying his head on the pillows and touched her shoulder. "Are you okay?"

He looked peaceful, content; his right arm was curled under his head. She wondered how he'd react if she told him about Andrea. She imagined the shock in his eyes. She could almost hear his voice, *how could you just leave her standing there? What's wrong with you?* Disgust and loathing turning his usually kind voice into something deep and unrecognisable.

"I'm fine." Mina laid back against the pillow so that their heads almost touched.

"You sure?" She could feel his breath against her cheek when he spoke.

"I was just a bit thrown by waking up in a strange bed. I'm fine now, really." She inched off the pillow and onto his shoulder. He kissed the top of her head, a gesture so affectionate and familiar Mina felt tears blurring her eyes.

"Okay, so you're not regretting what happened? Because I'm not." His voice resonated and she felt the vibrations through his chest. "You're the best thing that's happened in my life in a long time and I don't want to do anything to mess that up." His words came out in a rush as if he'd been holding them back, waiting for the right moment.

Mina rolled onto her stomach pressing her breasts against his chest. His skin felt cool, almost chilled. Shadows cast by the glare of the lamp hollowed out his features. The look of frailty she'd caught a glimpse of earlier was back, making him look tired and haunted. Her mind threw up a memory, but she couldn't quite take hold of it. She felt a rush of affection towards him, a need to protect him from whatever demons plagued his mind.

"I don't have any regrets." She kissed the cool skin on his chest. "I'm exactly where I want to be. I feel..." She searched for the right words. "I feel the happiest I've been in, well, I can't tell you how long."

The look of relief on his face sent a wave of pleasure through her body. She pulled herself upwards, her skin brushing against his. She spoke with her lips only centimetres from his mouth.

"I didn't think I could feel this human again."

She dipped her head and kissed him—a soft kiss, her lips almost closed. He clasped her face in his hands and soon they were lost in each other again. Later, they ordered steaks and a bottle of red wine which they consumed while chatting about nothing important. The steaks were tender and well-seasoned and, to Mina, the wine the best she'd ever tasted. When they finally slept, it was with a sense of peace she hadn't experienced since childhood.

* * *

With Lee sleeping soundly, Mina grabbed her clothes and ducked into the bathroom. Checking her watch, she noticed it was later than she'd thought; almost nine o'clock. Usually still bleary-eyed and half-asleep in the morning, today she felt uncharacteristically alert. Before leaving the room, she paused and watched Lee's unmoving form. She barely knew him, but already the curve of his shoulders and the taut muscles tapering down to his waist were familiar. The draw of his warmth almost pulled her back to the bed, but instead, she took her bag and slipped out of the room.

The streets were bustling with cars and pedestrians yet despite the buzz of activity, the small-town vibe remained. In this tiny corner of Western Australia, her house and all its memories seemed distant, no longer the things that defined her. Mina stopped for a moment and tried to remember which direction to take. She recalled seeing a coffee shop when they drove along the main street so she headed right and hoped for the best.

Caffeine wasn't the only thing on her mind. Being with Lee, sharing a bed with him, stirred up feelings that she didn't know she was capable of. She needed to sort through her emotions, figure out what was real.

Without realising it, she walked too far and was standing at an intersection outside a real estate office. She was about to turn back when she noticed the glossy posters in the window advertising houses for sale or rent. The only home she'd ever know was the house in Civil Park. A house bought by her father, with his stamp indelibly branded on every inch of the place. With so much in her life on the verge of changing, she couldn't help wondering what it would be like to choose her own place. Start with a clean slate and make something truly hers.

"Some great properties." The voice startled her out of her reverie. Until he spoke, Mina hadn't heard the man approach. "Buying or renting?"

She kept her eyes on the posters and jammed her hands in her pockets. "Neither." In the window, she watched the man's reflection, hoping he'd give up and go away.

"Yes, no problem." He shifted slightly, but didn't move on.

Mina felt a spark of resentment. Until the agent invaded her morning, she'd been enjoying her walk. Even dreaming about buying a new house, but now she'd have to either tell him to find someone else to pester or turn and walk away. Both choices would be rude and kill the pleasant buzz she'd been relishing only moments earlier.

"Still," he continued, "it's nice to dream about what a new start might look like."

Half turned, Mina stopped. His choice of words took her by surprise and the blunt brush-off died on her lips. It was probably his standard patter, but he'd managed to verbalise her thoughts. Still lost for words, she turned and stared up into the agent's welcoming face.

"I'm Terry." He pulled a square of paper out of his pocket. "Here's my card."

There was something earnest and open in his expression that made her feel guilty for being so dismissive. The man was just doing his job and trying to make a living. *What's happening to me? One night in a small town and I'm becoming a pushover.*

"Thanks, but I'm not looking to buy anything, just walking past." She forced her features into what she hoped was a polite smile. "Could you point me in the direction of the nearest coffee shop?"

He nodded. "Just down that way about thirty metres." He used his business card as a pointer. "Great coffee, very friendly place."

Mina pressed her lips together, trying not to laugh. He really was a good salesman. "Thanks." She turned to go, but he wasn't done.

"Don't forget this." He held the card up. "In case you change your mind or know someone who's looking."

She took the card and shoved it in her pocket, then looked at her watch. "Okay. Bye."

By the time she reached the coffee shop, it was almost 9:45 a.m. She bought two coffees and hurried back to the hotel, worried Lee would wake and think she'd skipped out on him.

# Chapter Ten

The streets of Dark Water were quiet, few cars passed them and most of those were utes stained with orangey dust. A sprinkling of rain dotted the windscreen, but the clouds quickly dispersed revealing a brilliant blue sky. Mina watched the buildings go by with a feeling of weightlessness, as if the burden of being alone had been a physical weight, now lifted and cast off allowing her to breathe more deeply.

"That's the primary school." Lee pointed to an open area ringed with waist-high cyclone fencing. The buildings behind the fence were scattered amongst play equipment and patches of veggie gardens. "That's where I went to school. Not very exciting."

"I bet you were a wiz on the monkey bars," Mina teased.

Lee chuckled, a deep hearty sound. "Oh yeah, I could miss a bar. I was just that good."

They drove through town, Lee pointing out the police station, town hall, and buildings of interest. Shops and offices lined either side of the main street with a petrol station at the far end of town. A smattering of people milled along on the pavement, no one seemed to hurry.

Within minutes they left the town centre and drove through streets where homes were scattered on large green blocks. Some of the houses looked ancient with weatherboard walls and tin rooftops, while others appeared to be new builds. Mina watched the structures spin past wondering what it must be like to live in such a place. There seemed to be a sense of ease in the town as if openness and tranquillity were what these people had found.

They passed a woman riding a white horse up the centre of the road. The creature looked incredibly tall and muscular, its hooves clopping on the bitumen as it trotted alongside the car. The rider, an elderly woman in a brown, quilted vest barely glanced their way as the car edged past.

"This is the house where I grew-up," Lee said as he eased the car to a stop on a narrow dirt access road. "See? Over there, on the other side of that field."

Across a wide field populated by a few sheep and a goat, a sprawling brown brick building sat amongst a cluster of gum trees. Mina could see a washing line hung between a shed and the rear of the house, sheets flapping in the breeze. She tried to imagine Lee as a little boy, chasing the sheep across the field; his chubby legs visible beneath grey school shorts.

"Where are your parents now?" It hadn't occurred to her until she'd seen Lee's home that he hadn't suggested they visit his family. It seemed strange that they drove all this way and he hadn't even mentioned his parents.

"My dad died when I was seventeen." He let out a long breath. "Cancer."

"I'm sorry." His arm rested on the steering wheel. Mina reached out and touched it. He flinched as if startled.

"Thanks." His voice sounded stiff, as if he were speaking to a stranger; someone he'd bumped into while stepping off a bus. Mina withdrew her hand not sure what to say. "My mother's remarried now. She lives in Brisbane."

"Oh." It was all she could think to say. She thought of her own house and the ghosts that dwelled there. She could understand how seeing his former home might bring back memories so vivid, they had the power to snatch his previously happy mood away. Wasn't it only yesterday she'd sat on her bed caught between sleep and waking, confused enough to believe her mother was calling her? Even now, the thought of returning to her empty house filled her with dread.

"We'd better get going." He sounded brighter, too bright. *Forced* was the word that popped into Mina's mind. *He's lucky*, she thought. *He gets to leave his memories behind.* It was in that moment she first began to consider selling her house.

As they drove out of town, the idea took root in her mind. She'd sell the house and put the past to rest. Or at least not have to relive it every day. It seemed so simple, so logical she wondered why she'd never thought of doing it before.

Just before the turn off for Fire Lake, they passed a mailbox. Not much more than a tin box on a short crooked stake, almost hidden amongst the tangle of natives that surrounded it. But what caught her eye was the sign next to the old box swathed in vines and faded by the sun: *For sale or lease.* Had it been there when they drove into town? She didn't remember seeing it, but that didn't mean it wasn't there. She'd been so flushed with pleasure after their first kiss, she'd have missed an elephant if it were walking up the road.

"Did you see that?" She turned in her seat watching the sign disappear.

"What?" Lee slowed the car. "Was it a roo?"

"No. No. Not a roo. That sign. There's a place for sale. I didn't see it when we drove in. Can we go back and have a look?" She could hear the excitement in her voice. *What am I thinking? Selling the house is one thing, but moving to the country?* It was crazy, she knew she'd never do it, but something about the crooked old mailbox called to her and it seemed important that she see where it led.

Lee turned onto the road for Fire Lake and pulled over. "There are dozens of places for sale in Dark Water. It's a country town, people are always trying to sell. Since the mine's been struggling, people are moving out in droves." There was an edge to his voice, not quite impatience, more nervousness. *Maybe he thinks I'm asking him to move in with me,* Mina thought and tried not to smile.

"I just want to have a look. I'm not planning on moving to Dark Water if that's what you're worried about."

With the engine still idling, he turned to look at her. His expression unreadable. "Good. I don't want you moving away from the city." He hesitated. "I mean we've only just met and I don't want to have to drive two hours every time I want to see you."

"It's nothing like that, I'm just curious." The truth was, she didn't know why she wanted to see the place that belonged to that mailbox. It just seemed important. She waited for him to respond, unsure why he seemed so hesitant.

"Okay. We'll go and take a look."

The access road was little more than a dirt track partially hidden by overgrown natives and a scattering of twisted banksias. Mina expected the ride to be bumpy, but the ground seemed surprisingly even and tightly packed. Still, Lee drove slowly taking care to keep the wheels in the ruts. After a couple of minutes of dense bush, the area opened onto an expanse of long grass that waved and undulated under the breeze. The house, a ramshackle weatherboard structure, sat under the bare limbs of a large jacaranda tree. There was an abandoned feeling to the place as if no one had set foot there for years.

Lee pulled the car up next to a section of rusted wire fence that separated a cluster of mandarin and lemon trees from the front of the house. Mina climbed out and walked towards the building, her shoes crunching over loose gravel. The cloying smell of rotting citrus fruit hung in the air. She stopped at the steps leading to the front veranda and looked back. Lee remained near the car as if unwilling to approach the house.

The place was clearly unoccupied, but the thought of climbing the three wooden steps seemed like trespassing. Instead, she walked towards the back of the house taking big awkward steps through the long grass. There was another veranda at the rear of the building and a small shed about twenty metres away. A Hills Hoist turned a few centimetres in the breeze, squealing with rusty resistance. Further back, almost obscured by trees and natives, a glimpse of red brick; Mina guessed it was another shed.

"Have you seen enough?" Lee's voice startled her. She let out a yelp of surprise. She hadn't heard him approach and wondered how he'd tromped through the thick grass without a sound.

"You scared me." It came out a little more accusatory than she meant.

"Sorry." He took her hand and turned, leading her back to the front of the house. "You ready to go?"

Mina allowed herself to be guided back to the car. In the distance a bird squawked—a lone, mournful sound. She opened the car door, but before getting in took one last look at the house. It felt familiar somehow as if she should know this place but didn't. She shook her head and slid into the car.

"Have you ever been here before?" she asked, securing her seatbelt.

Lee was already reversing across the gravel, loose stones clattering against the outside of the vehicle. He seemed eager to be back on the road. It wasn't until they were on the main road that he spoke. "The couple who lived here were friends of my parents. My dad used to bring me out here sometimes. Seeing the place just made me think of him." He turned to look at her, the muscles in his jaw clenched. "That was back before he got sick. Seeing the place abandoned like that." He let out a long breath. "It reminds me of how much time has passed and... I don't know, how easily everything moves on without you after you're gone." He tried to laugh, it was a dry humourless sound. "Deep, huh?"

"I'm sorry. I wouldn't have made you go back there if I'd known." She reached out and touched his leg.

"No. It's okay." He laid his hand on hers. "It was good to see the place. Sad, but okay, if that makes sense."

Mina nodded. She wanted to ask him about the couple who owned the house; what they were like and if they had kids, but sensing his discomfort, she decided to let it go. By the time they reached Perth, things had returned to normal. Lee turned on the radio and sang along with a couple of pop songs, getting the lyrics mixed up and laughing at himself. Mina pushed the empty house to the back of her mind, enjoying the moments before the trip ended.

# Chapter Eleven

The sound of a car door thudding snapped Andrea awake. She pulled herself up and pressed her back against the cold brick of the wall. The mundane slamming of a vehicle door was enough to plunge her back into the memory of his last visit. He appeared without bothering to do so quietly. She'd heard his van approach and grumble to a halt. The door had rolled open to reveal the man who'd torn her from her life and turned the world into a place of pain and fear.

He was tall, or at least he seemed to be from her position crouched against the wall. Behind him, she saw a glimpse of a grey… what might have been the outside, but shut off from view too quickly to make out any details. He'd rolled the door closed and stood breathing in and out, a garbage bag pulled over his head, eye and mouth holes just large enough to be functional. A brown cord fastened around the bag at his neckline, giving him the appearance of a scarecrow.

Andrea screamed and pressed herself into the wall. "Please don't hurt me." She'd managed to form the words that came out in a rush of tears.

He stepped towards her, his arms hanging loosely at his sides. He held something; it dangled near his knee but in her panic she could see only his eyes—as if distorted by a watery film, they shone inside the plastic holes. "No. No. No." She cringed and curled into herself.

He watched her. The only sound came from Andrea's sobs until somewhere outside a bird sang, a happy twittering sound. After what felt like hours, he turned and walked towards the bucket. It was only then that she realised what he carried: a yellow plastic pail identical to the one she'd been using as a toilet.

He dropped the clean bucket and picked up the used one. She could hear the contents sloshing against the sides as he crossed the room and placed it next to the door. Her sobs diminished into hiccupping breaths. Her mind tried to fathom what was happening.

*He hasn't come to kill me; doesn't the clean bucket prove that? If this should be the end, why would he bother to change it?* The realisation brought relief. There'd been times during the endless hours when she'd thought death might be better than the torture of living in fear. Dread and panic knotted together in her stomach, never giving her a minute's peace. Yet the relief she felt when he replaced her toilet bucket told a different story. She wanted to live and would endure the gnawing pains in her stomach and the humiliation of her captivity and, yes, the agony of the beatings just for one day back with her parents.

He came towards her. His hands wrapped around her ankles, his fingers cold and dry pulled at her legs, drawing her away from the wall with frightening strength. His breathing was so loud it blocked all other sound. She wanted to pull away, snatch her legs from his grasp, but knew better than to resist him.

His hands slid upwards, claw-like and determined, pushing the filthy fabric of her track pants up around her knees.

"Please don't hurt me." He seemed surprised by the sound of her voice, pausing in his movements. It was as if he'd forgotten she were alive. His eyes met hers. She sucked in a shocked breath. The glassy orbs shone with excitement and something else—pleasure.

With a fast, jerky movement, he flipped her onto her stomach and in spite of all she had learned, Andrea struggled and used her elbows to lurch forward, the chains digging into her ribs. A punch landed on her shoulder blade with enough force to knock her arms out from under her. Her face hit the mattress and a wail burst from her lips. His weight dropped on top of her, mashing the air out of her lungs. Dry fingers pulled at the neckline of her fleecy top. Something wet touched her skin. Andrea whimpered and then his teeth sunk into the soft flesh of her shoulder. A scream filled the room, its pitch so tortured and desolate she barely recognise it as her own.

She felt the smooth cloth slip over her head, skim her face and draw tight around her throat. Her body bucked and for a second, his weight lifted. Another blow landed in the soft tissue of her waist. The choke hold tightened and Andrea's vision blurred. She could hear him panting, feel his body pumping against her, pounding her with a violent beat. He slapped her with his free hand, a stinging blow that sent spirals of pain through her head.

She gagged and spittle hit the wall ahead of her. Dimness crept into her vision, she felt herself sliding into blackness. He grunted, a guttural sound that a pig might make, and then the tension around her throat eased. The air rushed into her lungs burning the inside of her mouth. Her windpipe spasmed and Andrea continued to gag and cough. His weight lifted, making it easier for her to breathe.

It was over.

She'd survived another attack, but how many more could her body endure? She remained on her stomach, now propped up on her elbows sucking in air and trying not to vomit. Behind her, the sounds of movement, his shoes scraping across the gritty floor and the plastic whispering. Something hit her in the back and seconds later came the familiar sound of the door rolling open. She closed her eyes and counted. Six seconds later the door rolled shut, its final clang echoing like thunder.

She heard her own heartbeat with surprising clarity. Andrea raised a tentative finger to her throat, the area around her windpipe felt covered with grazes. She winced and pushed herself up into a sitting position, something slipped from behind her and bounced on the floor with a dull clatter. Fruit, nut, and yoghurt energy bars. Three of them. Her eyes filled with tears, this time not from misery but anger. He'd choked and beaten her. He'd come close to killing her all the while enjoying some kind of freakish sexual gratification, and in return, he'd left her three energy bars.

She wanted to fling them across the room, smash the bars into pulp. But in truth she'd do no such thing because part of her *was* grateful. The food meant a few more days of life. He'd left it not as payment for what he'd done, but as a means of keeping her alive so that he could continue to use her. She was nothing but a means to an end in his eyes. *My God, his eyes.* The gleeful viciousness shining out from the holes in that black bag sent chills through her like bolts of terror.

She'd wished not for freedom, but something smaller; a blanket. Something soft in a world of harshness. Something warm she could wrap around herself and disappear into.

Her mind then turned to her bedroom; she'd come to spend a great deal of time picturing her home. It had become a way of passing the endless hours, keeping fear if not at bay, then at least from consuming her. She saw her bed; a king-single with a vibrant yellow quilt cover, the pattern a field of daisies. On the bed, a scattering of cushions in yellows and whites. Resting amongst the daisies, a large stuffed penguin. In her mind's eye, the white blinds on her window were open, spilling a stream of sunlight across the bed.

Andrea smiled and raised her hand, reaching for the brightly coloured fabric. She could almost feel the soft fuzz of Mr Beaky, the penguin, before the image dissolved under the tearing hunger that never left. She'd let out a cry that sounded as dry as dead leaves under heavy boots. The energy bars. Why had she wasted time dreaming when her body cried out for food? *Because I'll go mad if I let my mind stay in this hell hole.* Her imagination was all she had, but lately it threatened to take over. She couldn't let herself slip into a fantasy world while her body lost strength.

She leaned forward and grabbed up the bars. The sight of the nutty creamy bar through the clear wrapping made her mouth water. She wiped her face on her sleeve and swallowed. Even forcing saliva over her injured throat made her wince. What chance did she have of getting the energy bars down her throat? Her eyes searched the room as if the answer might be hidden somewhere on the dirty floor. She spotted a bottle of water near the toilet bucket. He must have put it down before he left.

She had a bottle under the mattress containing only a couple of mouthfuls. Andrea took out the bottle using her left hand, the blow he'd landed on her right shoulder made her arm feel heavy, almost numb. She'd sat the bottle in her lap and unscrewed the cap, resisting the urge to hurry. Even with a full bottle now in reserve, she couldn't afford to get careless and spill what little she had.

When she had the cap off, she lifted the bottle to her lips and took a small sip. The water felt wonderfully cool, but swallowing was like forcing a knife over the soft tissue of her throat. Her stomach cramped with impatience. She picked up an energy bar and ripped open the packet. The smell of nuts and sugar made her woozy with hunger. When the sugar hit her tongue, she groaned with satisfaction. Swallowing was painful, she took another sip of water and managed to get the food down. Repeating the process, this time grinding the pieces between her fingers until the bar was little more than a pulp, Andrea demolished the first bar. She'd licked the packet and then every one of her grubby fingers.

She'd finished the food days ago. Since then, she'd been alone. Shivering through the freezing blackness of night and the endless gloom of day. Sometimes she wondered what would happen if he were killed in a car crash. Would she lie on the mattress growing weaker, listening to the sound of her heart winding down to complete failure? In those moments she felt panic spinning in her gut, intensifying with each turn.

"I'm Andrea Fields. My mother is Maureen and my dad's Norman. I live on Waverly Road and I work at the Busy Buy. I'm going to be a writer and buy a big house near the river." Her voice rasped over the soft, damaged tissue in her throat. In spite of the pain, she found comfort in repetition. Whispering the same words over and over until her mind lulled itself into a state of mistiness.

Now, with the thud of a car door the panic returned. Her breathing grew raspy and her hands shook. Part of her wanted him to return. The energy bars were long gone and hunger clawed at her insides. The beating and choking would be a nightmare of pain and fear, but then he would give her food. *If I live, I'll never tell anyone that part*, she thought with a rush of shame.

She sat forward, listening for him. Her vision narrowed, seeing only the door and then she heard something startling. A yelp. Distant but clearly female. Andrea pressed her fingers to the sides of her head winding them into her tangled hair. Had she really heard a woman's voice? She waited, straining to pick up any sound from the outside world. Is it a trick? Is he testing me? Caught in a tangle of indecision, she stumbled to her feet, the chain clinking between her legs.

"Help!" The word came out as a thin, wavering cry. She sucked in a breath and tried again.

"Help!" Her voice cracked with the effort. She coughed and cleared her throat.

"Help! Help! Help!" The words built until she was screaming. She ran towards the door forgetting the chain until it snapped up and pulled her back. Andrea slipped forward and hit the floor with a thud that sent a jolt of pain through her elbows.

"Help!" She continued to call until her voice faltered and the words were nothing more than sobs.

# Chapter Twelve

When Lee looked at her, Mina didn't see a monster reflected back in his eyes, just a woman. Being with him made it possible to believe there was more to her than the terrible things she'd done.

She picked up her wine glass and took a sip. Around them, voices raised in conversation, and the sound of laughter coalesced into a buzz of life and happiness. For once, she felt included in the energy; caught up in the mood of the little beachside restaurant.

"I told you this place was noisy, are you sure it's not too much?"

She had to lean forward to hear, her head almost touching his. "It's fine, really."

Lee smiled and rubbed his hand along her thigh. She could feel his fingers through the fine fabric of her dress.

This was the first time they'd been together since returning yesterday from Dark Water. She'd spent the day worrying, terrified that the feeling of lightness she'd experienced during their time together might vanish and she'd find herself anxious and guarded in his presence. But her fears turned out to be unfounded. She felt relaxed and happy, grateful to be with a man who didn't push and probe.

"Have you finished?" he asked, nodding towards the remnants of the pizza.

"I couldn't eat another thing." Mina had to raise her voice to be heard over the din. "Do you want to take a walk?" As much as she enjoyed the liveliness of the restaurant, she was eager to be alone with him.

They crossed the road holding hands like teenagers and walked along the path that led to the beach. The tangy, salty smell of the sea reminded her of a day she'd spent there with her mother. It had been their secret thing to do during the summer—only possible when her father had a busy day at the office. Then her mother could be sure they'd be free to spend a few hours without worrying about his constant phone calls. Those days on the hot sand running towards the cold shock of the Indian Ocean had been the most carefree of Mina's life. Usually, thinking about those moments made her feel heartsick with loneliness. But with Lee holding her hand, she found herself smiling at the memory.

"You look happy."

"I was just thinking about when I was a little girl and my mum would take me to the beach." She breathed in, letting the clean, chilled air fill her lungs. "I couldn't get enough of the water. We'd spend hours in and out of the surf." She hadn't meant to share her thoughts, but now she'd let her guard down it felt natural to talk about her happy memories. *God knows, I don't have many.*

"You miss her, don't you?"

The question surprised her. It wasn't what she'd expected. But then, she realised she hadn't had many personal conversations in her life. Of course, she'd shared her thoughts with her mother, but there hadn't really been anyone else.

"Yes. Every day." Lee let go of her hand and slipped his arm around her shoulder, pulling her close to him as they walked. Mina felt safe—protected. She wanted to lean on someone. Let her guard down and just be.

"What about your dad?" Mina felt her body stiffen. She hoped he didn't notice. "Didn't he go to the beach with you and your mum?"

It was an innocent question. Mina knew Lee meant nothing by it, nevertheless she felt a prickle of annoyance. Everything had been perfect and then he'd mentioned her father.

Her first impulse was to snap at him and end the conversation. But she bit her tongue. Lee had no way of knowing her father had been a brutal bully, looming over every moment of her life until... She closed her eyes and stopped walking.

"He... he worked a lot." She could feel her hands clenching into fists. She wanted the conversation to end. She didn't want to talk about her father. Not with Lee. Not with anyone. "What about you?" She tried to keep her voice relaxed, but she could see by the way Lee was looking at her that it wasn't working. "I mean, do you like the beach?" It came out sounding forced.

"I'm a country boy, so I did most of my swimming in a lake. The ocean sort of scares me." He laughed, a relaxed sound that soothed Mina's nerves. Maybe he hadn't noticed her reaction. *No, he's just kind.* "I guess that makes me sound like a wuss."

"A little bit," Mina teased. "But I'll still let you take me home." She took his hand and they continued along the path towards the parking lot.

\* \* \*

Lee woke her early. Mina could hear magpies warbling outside the window. She lay in her bedroom, the light breaking through the blinds was sparse and dreary. Lee was already dressed, holding a cup of instant coffee which he placed on the bedside table. Mina watched his movements from the warmth of the bed. She felt hazy, only half awake.

"I've got to go." He bent and kissed her on top of her head. He smelled minty as if he'd just brushed his teeth. Mina wondered briefly if he'd used her toothbrush. "I've got a job this morning and I can't be late."

"You're leaving?" Her tongue felt thick, forming words was difficult.

"Sorry to rush off, but I've got an appointment. I should have said something last night." He moved towards the door in a hurry to leave. Mina sat up and rubbed her hand over her eyelids trying to make sense of what he was saying. "I'll call you later."

"Okay, but—" He was gone before she could finish. A few seconds later, she heard the front door open and then close with a rattle of glass.

Mina threw back the covers and crossed the room. She flipped a slat open on the blinds. The front yard, still shrouded in mist looked bleak. She watched Lee jog towards his car and open the door. He paused for a second and looked around. Mina, standing naked at the window, shivered and wrapped an arm around herself. She wondered if he'd look up and see her watching. Maybe he'd wave and smile. He did neither. With a dipping feeling in the pit of her stomach, she watched him climb into his car and drive away.

\* \* \*

Around midnight, Mina gave up waiting for Lee to call. Possibilities and excuses whirled around in her mind. Maybe he'd lost his phone and with it her number? Whatever he was doing went on late and he didn't want to call after ten. The urge to drink came and went, then returned and settled over her like a heavy blanket. She went as far as opening the fridge, hand out, almost touching the bottle, but then pulled back and slammed the door.

*What am I doing? This isn't me.* Getting hung up over men was for others. Pathetic women who could only function if they had a man in their life. Girls like Andrea; needy and clingy. She knew it was wrong to think that way about the girl, but that was how she saw her. Wasn't that why she'd been so repelled by her? It was Andrea's weakness that Mina hated, not her plump body or crooked teeth.

Mina moved through the house turning off the lights. Thinking about Andrea left her feeling edgy and hot as though she'd been caught doing something criminal. Upstairs, she kicked off her slippers and crawled into bed. She could smell his scent on the sheets, a mixture of aftershave and sweat. She could almost imagine him in the bed next to her, his body warm and comforting.

Telling herself she was being ridiculous, Mina turned off the bedside lamp. He'd call tomorrow and there'd be a reason for his disappearing act. If not, then so be it. She'd gotten by on her own for a long time and would continue to do so. She'd done harder things than wait for some guy to call. *Not just some guy*, she thought. *He's more than that, isn't he?* Laying in the dark, listening to the familiar sounds of the house settling around her, she drifted off to sleep.

* * *

"Hi." Mina waited. It had been two days. She almost didn't answer the phone when it finally rang. Standing in the kitchen listening to the frantic buzzing, Mina had the urge to dismiss the call—end the nonsense before it went any further. She didn't like games, felt angry at herself for letting him have this power over her. Yet her heart rate kicked up a notch when she heard his voice.

"Mina, I'm sorry I haven't called." He sounded tired. "I've had a lot going on." He paused, waiting for her to speak. She gave him silence. "It's family stuff. My mother," he continued, "I have to go to Queensland. I'll be gone for a while."

He was lying. She knew it by the distracted way he said her name and the finality in his voice. He was brushing her off, making excuses.

"When will you be back?" The hopeful note in her own voice made her angry. Angry with him for being so spineless and herself for still wanting to believe him.

"I... I'm not sure. Months probably." There was silence on the line, not even the sound of traffic or voices. "I'm sorry."

Mina felt her hand tighten around the phone. "Don't be sorry." Her voice came out tight with anger. "We had a good weekend. You didn't make any promises, so you're free to do whatever you want." She wanted to yell at him, call him a liar. A stream of invectiveness bubbled up her throat. "Have a nice life." She bit off the last words struggling to keep hold of her temper. It was a childish thing to say. She heard him suck in a breath and felt a flicker of satisfaction. Her choice of words hadn't been that stinging, but his reaction told her she'd hurt him.

"I didn't mean to—"

"Bye Lee." She hung up before he could finish. It was a small victory, petty and empty. Mina looked at the phone and noticed her hand shaking. He'd used her; it burned like a hot blade to the heart, but the real pain came from the angry screw turning in her stomach. Was she that lonely, that desperate? It took only a few kind words and a sympathetic smile, and she'd fallen into his arms dreaming of their future together.

She placed the phone down on the counter and took a breath, then another, deeper this time. Finding a sense of calm in times of turmoil was a skill she'd developed—a coping mechanism. When her father beat her mother, Mina held the tears in check through focus and breathing. To cry or scream would only make matters worse, for her *and* her mother. And her father could always make things worse: a kick to the kidneys as she shuffled past or his hand twisted in her mother's hair dragging her across the room.

Mina turned from the counter; her gaze fell to the kitchen floor. It always came back to this place. Of all the days of torment, one etched in her mind so deep it had a life of its own.

\* \* \*

Pale grey streaks of light filtered through the kitchen window casting shadows across the cheap linoleum flooring. Mina ignored the chill in the air and bustled around the room helping her mother prepare breakfast. Her father liked toast, medium brown with a thin spread of butter; a warm hard-boiled egg and white coffee sweetened with two spoons of sugar.

Thomas Constantine entered the kitchen, his breakfast ready on the table with the daily newspaper neatly folded next to his coffee.

"Good morning," Thomas waited for both Mina and her mother to respond with their own "Good mornings," before seating himself at the head of the table. The morning ritual had been in place for as long as Mina could remember, with the exception of Sundays, when her father liked his egg fried. No variations allowed.

With the formal greetings over and Thomas seated, Mina and her mother took their places on either side of the table. Her mother sipped tea while Mina nibbled on a piece of toast and stole covert glances at her father as he ate his meal and read the paper. He didn't speak once he began, nor did his wife or daughter. Not until his plate was empty and the last drops of coffee drained did Mina dare break the silence.

"Dad, I'd like to apply for a part-time job at Thrifty's. Just one evening a week so I can earn some pocket money and—"

"No." He cut her off without a glance. "Irene, I'm finished," he said with mild reproach.

"Yes. Sorry, Thomas," her mother apologised and cleared his plate and cup away.

Mina looked down at her plate and chewed her bottom lip, biting back words she might regret. Her father's reaction came as no surprise. In order to maintain strict and total control over the two women in his life, Thomas had always done his best to isolate them from any outside influences. His wife had never been allowed to work outside the home, and socialising with other women was forbidden. Cut off from friends and family, Irene and Mina were prisoners of fear and circumstance.

Irene stood over the kitchen sink, hands submerged in dirty grey water. Mina noticed her mother's shoulders slump. She knew Mina desperately wanted a part-time job. It would be the first step in getting her daughter out of Thomas' grasp. They'd discussed it while her father was at work and decided that the best time to ask him would be after breakfast. For some reason, known only to him, he always appeared happiest in the mornings. *Happiest*, Mina wondered if he'd ever really experienced a happy moment in his entire, miserable life.

"Dad, I won't let it interfere with my schoolwork and I'll–"

"I said–"

Irene turned from the sink, frustration branded across her face. Mina caught her mother's gaze and shook her head, but Irene ignored her and broke one of Thomas's cardinal rules, she interrupted him.

"Let her do it." Her voice lilted light and coaxing, but Mina could see her eyes shining with determination. Mina winced, as if physically struck by her mother's words. Irene's desperation to free Mina, if only in small steps, had forced her to cross a dangerous line. She could see by the look in her mother's eyes, she knew it too.

Thomas leapt from his chair and was on her before she could turn around. His large hand grabbed her around the back of the neck. He pushed her head into the sink.

The shock of the water made Irene gasp. Mina watched in horror as her head disappeared into the dirty liquid. Irene's body bucked as she tried to pull her head up, but his hand held her in place.

Desperate for air, she tried to twist her head to the side, but his iron-like grip held her in place—a desperate, fluttering bird. Her movements weakened, then stopped. Mina could see her mother's ankles bowing out as if her weight were sinking. Things spun out of control. Mina wanted to scream for him to stop but her body stiffened, her throat constricted. When he finally pulled Irene's head out of the water, her mother sagged in his grip. All the years of punches and sprained wrists, everything narrowed to this moment. Her mother dead in his arms because she tried to give her daughter a chance at a normal life.

There were no tears, Mina closed her eyes and watched a kaleidoscope of images. Her mother taking the blame for Mina's sloppiness making the bed. Irene tearing Thomas off her daughter, begging him to forgive her teenage rudeness only to take a beating herself. All the cries and sobs these brick walls had absorbed echoed in Mina's head.

A slap, wet and jarring broke the spell. Irene spluttered out a breath and then gagged. A stream of water ran down her chin like an invalid drooling soup. Mina felt no relief that her mother had survived, only the lead weight in her gut that told her it was only a matter of time. Her father was losing control of himself and his family. He'd kill Irene, and Mina had no doubt, her too. If not today, then soon.

Irene tried to rub the soap out of her eyes with the backs of her hands, her arms trembling while Thomas shook her like a rag doll. Mina stood and crossed the kitchen.

"Never interrupt me when—"

"Let her go," Mina said through clenched teeth.

She held the point of a large kitchen knife against her father's throat. One minute she'd been sitting at the table watching him attack her mother, the next a knife was in her hand and at his throat.

A cold wind that seemed to come from every crack in the floor and ceiling, blew across her face. Her heart rate slowed. Her clothes seemed tight as if they could barely contain her body and the power flooding her muscles. She felt strong, calm; she almost wanted him to resist so that she could slice him open and watch the blood run down his perfectly ironed shirt.

Thomas moved slowly, he kept his hand on his wife's neck and he turned his head to look his daughter in the eyes. She could see a vein at the side of his temple, throbbing; his pale grey eyes glazed with anger. His lips had turned blue and were drawn back in a grimace. She'd never seen him look so crazed, but rather than frighten her, something about the loss of control pleased her.

"Let her go or I'll push the point all the way in." Her voice remained calm and even; her hand as steady as a rock.

Thomas blinked several times in quick succession and, just for an instant, she saw something flicker. Fear? He dropped her mother and let his arms fall to his sides.

"Mina... please don't." Her mother's voice, scratchy from coughing, broke the spell. Mina stepped back, but kept the knife up. She looked past her father and saw her mother, slumped over the draining board, hair plastered to her head, the front of her dress soaking wet where her father had held her under water. And suddenly, the reality of the situation hit and her hand shook. The adrenalin that had flooded her body dissipated. The knife felt heavy and her knees trembled.

"Put it down, love," her mother said softly, and took a shaky step towards her.

Her father hadn't moved. He stood next to the sink watching her, his face now unreadable. She knew she'd gone too far. What had just happened had changed their lives. That momentary shift in power would have terrible consequences. She turned and put the knife on the table and braced herself for what was to come.

Everything happened in a split-second. Her father lunged, knocking Mum out of the way. Mina stepped back and stumbled into the fridge. He loomed over her, large and terrifying. His pale eyes bulged with outrage, a ghastly contrast against his blood-red face. Mum grabbed his shoulder and tried to pull him back.

Mina braced herself, and in that moment one clear thought invaded her mind, *if I survive, I'll never let anyone do this to me again.* She closed her eyes and waited for the blows to reign down, promising herself she wouldn't beg.

Then silence.

She opened her eyes and saw her father's face only a metre or so from hers. He still looked terrifying, but something had changed. The grimace was clearly from pain, not anger, and his eyes bulged with shock.

Her mother still had hold of his shoulder, but he seemed to sink under her grasp. His shirt ripped, the sound of tearing fabric impossibly loud. Thomas' knees hit the floor and his hand flew to his chest. He let out a groan and fell sideways.

"I'm... I... help me."

He rolled onto his back and curled his shoulders inwards as if his chest contracted.

"Oh God, I think he's having a heart attack," her mother said, standing over him.

She looked at Mina. Their gazes locked. Mina shook her head; it was a small movement that conveyed a world of unspoken meaning. They both knew that all they had to do was wait, and soon all their suffering would be over. For a second neither woman moved. The only sound in the house came from Thomas' laboured groans.

"Irene, help me!" His words came out around short gasps.

Irene gave her daughter a pleading look. "I'm calling an ambulance."

Mina nodded. She knew no matter what this man had done, her mother couldn't let him die. In a way Mina was relieved, not because her father might be saved, but because she knew her mother wouldn't be able to live with the guilt if she stood by and watched him die.

"You go call. I'll wait with him." Mina sat down on the cold linoleum next to her father. Thomas gasped and gripped his chest as if trying to push his fingers through the skin in order to clutch his ailing heart.

Her mother left the room, Mina waited and listened, counting off a few seconds in her head. The clatter of running footsteps on the hallway floor told her the coast was clear.

There was only one phone in the house, an old-fashioned type with a keypad and attached handset. Another instrument of Thomas' absolute control. Any calls made or received took place in his study, where he could monitor what was said. For once, she was glad her father had resisted modern technology; it meant her mother would be in the study for at least five minutes giving Mina some precious time alone with her father.

She sat up on her knees so she could stare into his eyes. His lids fluttered revealing bloodshot, watery orbs. With his dramatic widow's peak, he'd always reminded Mina of Dracula, but right now he just looked old. She put her mouth to his ear.

"Why did you have to be so fucking crazy?" Her words were soft, barely more than a whisper.

His eyes snapped open. They were raw looking. When he saw her face something else crept into his gaze, a hint of fear.

"Mina… my heart—"

She shook her head.

Things could have been so different. All her life she'd wanted him to be normal, like her friends' fathers; but that was never going to be. She took a deep breath and felt the cold on her face, it seemed to blow away her doubts. She pinched her father's nose with her thumb and forefinger and then used her other hand to clamp his jaw shut.

His body arched. His hands came up to grab her shoulders. For a second, his grip was strong. He almost managed to pull her off him, but she held fast and his strength soon ebbed.

As Mina stared into his eyes she could see the panic and confusion; her identical grey eyes filled with tears. She hadn't wanted it to come to this. She'd planned on saving money and running away, then sending for her mother when she had a place for them to live. She heard her mother's footsteps approaching and took her hand away from his mouth. She continued to hold his nose closed and put her mouth over his.

When her mother entered the kitchen, Mina was crouched over her father giving him mouth-to-mouth.

"He's not breathing, Mum. Go call them again and tell them he's stopped breathing," she said over her shoulder.

Her mother hesitated. "I can take over," her voice high and anxious.

"No. It's better if I don't stop," Mina said between breaths.

When her mother left the room, Mina put her hand over her father's mouth. She hadn't been breathing into him, just making puffing noises, but it had been enough to convince her mother. She took her hands away and put her ear to his mouth, then his chest.

Nothing.

She felt for a pulse in his neck... It was over. All those years of oppression and fear were at an end. She didn't feel released, she felt sick. Bile rose up in her throat, she turned her head and vomited. When the retching stopped, she put her head on her father's chest and gave in to the tears.

* * *

Her thoughts came back into focus. She'd relived the past so many times, it had become almost comforting. The last moments of her father's life were lived in this kitchen. He'd struggled for breath under her unflinching hands. Was it any wonder she couldn't hold on to happiness? Maybe Lee wasn't to blame. Could it be that a few days with Mina had left him feeling cold?

She pushed away from the counter and pressed her fingers into the corners of her eyes. It would be night soon; tomorrow held little appeal. With Lee, she'd had a spark of hope, something to look forward to. What now?

She'd planned on leaving the house, moving out and putting the memories behind her. It occurred to her that maybe now more than ever was the time to go.

"There's nothing here." She spoke to the empty house and a feeling of fatigue washed over her. It was as if she'd been awake for weeks. The urge to retreat to her bed, leave the thinking for another day, almost tempted her enough to turn from her course of action.

She resisted the pull of exhaustion, filled the kettle with water and flicked on the switch. With each movement, a feeling of purpose returned. Whether the feeling was real or not didn't matter. A hot cup of coffee in hand, she headed for the study. It took her less than a minute to get the laptop up and running. With nothing to hold her, she could go anywhere: Melbourne, Sydney. She could even try Hobart.

Releasing herself from the only home she'd ever known had other advantages. The penguin clip hidden in the sandwich maker was reason enough to go. The Magician knew where she lived. For a while, she'd pretended none of it had happened, but maybe Lee *had* done her a favour. She needed to get her head out of the clouds and do something before the freak who took Andrea decided it was her turn.

Money wasn't a problem thanks to her frugal, business-minded father. After his death, her father's solicitor gave Mina and her mother the good news. Unbeknownst to either his wife or daughter, Thomas Constantine owned two rental properties, both mortgage free, as well as the family home and accounting business. The properties and business, together with a sizable life insurance policy and superannuation pay-out, meant that Mina could choose to live just about anywhere, within reason.

Mina ran her index finger over her upper lip. On impulse, she dashed back to the kitchen. Searching through her handbag, she found the real estate agent's card tucked in the side pocket. Once back at the computer, she placed the card on the desk and typed in the web address.

She had no solid reason for deciding on Dark Water, just a feeling that something important was happening. The sensation made her pulse quicken.

Mina found what she was looking for on the first page. The heading read, *Country Cottage*. The house in the picture didn't look very cottagey; with a tin roof and walls the colour of dry mustard, the place looked too sensible to be anyone's idea of a cottage. Even so, something about the place made her skin prickle with gooseflesh. The cottage was similar to the derelict house she had stopped at with Lee but, smaller and in much better shape. Barely glancing at the property details, she fired off an email to the agent asking if he would be available tomorrow for a viewing.

With the message sent, Mina pushed back her chair and headed for the kitchen. She made herself a chicken sandwich, which she ate at the table, washed down with a glass of orange juice. Chewing and staring into space, she made a mental list of the details that would need addressing before she could leave the house in Civil Park. The gas and electric could be left on, for now. There'd be packing, but she decided that for the time being, she could manage with very little. *I'm really doing this*. The thought took her by surprise.

She should have been wallowing in self-pity thinking about Lee. Maybe getting drunk and crying herself to sleep. Instead she felt a flicker of excitement, not quite happy, but close enough. A crash would come, but for now Mina chose to push such thoughts to the back of her mind. Maybe her motivation was tied up with the night she'd spent in the town with Lee. She'd been happy there, even if it was only for one night. She wanted to believe she could recapture that feeling.

The mail would have to be redirected. She raised the second half of her sandwich to her mouth. *When did I last check the mail?* The bread slipped out of her hand and landed back on the plate. Mina glanced over at the window. The early evening light had almost melted into darkness. She hadn't collected the mail since the day she received the hairclip. How long had it been? There was no need to count the days. A week ago. Fourteen days since Andrea disappeared, yet that night seemed distant.

The flap on the back of the mailbox clanked open. The box was not as overflowing as she'd expected. *Reclusive behaviour has its advantages*, she thought, flicking her tongue over her suddenly dry mouth. Glancing around, she was struck by how silent the street seemed. In the windows, lights flickering behind closed curtains and blinds were the only sign of life. With the stack clutched to her chest, Mina turned and hurried up the path.

A glass-rattling *clang* echoed and the front door slammed behind her. Another envelope, identical to the last. The same rich texture *and* an odour. She tried to identify it but all that came to mind was polish of some sort, maybe wax. Had the smell been on the first note? Mina dropped the packet on the table and sat.

It wasn't over.

How had she ever convinced herself it was?

She let out a long breath, surprised at how laboured it sounded. *I could throw it away. If I don't look, I won't have to know.* Her mind raced through possible scenarios. *Maybe this time the Magician would give details. A location.* Mina pulled her hair over her right shoulder and twisted it around her hand.

She picked up the envelope and tore it open. Once more, a single sheet of paper, thick and grainy. Before unfolding it, she shook the envelope and a second penguin clip tumbled out. A soft noise somewhere between a sigh and a gasp escaped her lips. The clip bounced on the table and then lay still. Mina had the urge to sweep the little plastic clip to the floor and crush it under her foot. Instead, she unfolded the paper.

This time the message was longer, but no less disturbing.

*The gift that keeps on giving.*

The large sloping letters were unmistakably written by the same person. Mina stared at the words trying to see more than what appeared on the page. *What does he mean? And more importantly, where is this going?*

Six words. Enough to send a trail of sweat running down her spine.

She put the page on the table alongside the clip and focused on one word, *keeps*. Did that mean Andrea was still alive? Maybe he was trying to tell her something? But why her? In movies, the killer often sent taunting notes to the police or the hero. But this was no movie and she was as far from a hero as a woman could be.

The light drained out of the day, reflecting darkness into the kitchen. She had the eerie sensation of being watched: someone hiding outside the house, peering in the windows. She had the urge to turn and look out of the kitchen window, but the fear that she might actually see a face pressed against the glass kept her from looking over her shoulder. She needed light to chase the shadows away.

Half out of her chair, the shrieking of her phone erupted. The noise was so shocking in the darkening room that Mina slapped her palm on the table in surprise. The phone was on the counter where she'd left it after Lee had called. She stood on numb legs and reached for it, keeping her eyes off the window.

"Hi." A male voice. For a split second, she thought of Lee. But then as the voice continued, she realised her mistake. "Am I speaking with Mina Constantine?"

She glanced back at the note and could only make out the creamy lightness of the paper in the gloom.

"Who's this?" Her voice cracked. She could feel her heart pounding up high, near her throat.

"This is Terrance Briggs from Reliance Real Estate." There was good humour in his voice as if he were smiling. Mina felt her body sag and let out a sigh of relief mixed with irritation. He must have heard the sound because his next words were less cheerful.

"Sorry, I hope I'm not interrupting anything?"

"No. No. It's fine." Mina flicked on the lights and walked through the hallway to the study, glad to leave the letter behind.

"Okay. Great." The cheerfulness was back. "I received your email and thought I'd give you a quick call. The property you asked about is available immediately." He paused and Mina realised it was her cue to speak.

"Okay. That's good." She sat down at her mother's desk and turned on the lamp. Her mind had trouble jumping from the note and all its possible meanings to the normality of the phone conversation.

"Well, you said you wanted to view the place as soon as possible. I can show it to you tomorrow." He stopped speaking. Mina could hear a slight echo on the line as if he were calling from a tunnel, but it could have been that he was sitting in his car.

"Um." Things were moving quickly. She thought of the penguin clip and the letter. This was a real chance to put some distance between herself and everything that had happened since Andrea's disappearance. "Tomorrow works for me."

"Okay. Great." He sounded positively exuberant. "What time suits you?"

# Chapter Thirteen

By nine-thirty, she was on the road along with an overstuffed suitcase and her laptop. Both items were flung in the boot to be retrieved *if* she decided to stay in Dark Water overnight. A smattering of rain cleared to reveal blue sky and the promise of a crisp morning. She'd arranged to meet the agent at noon, giving herself two and a half hours to make the drive from Perth. A steady stream of traffic flanked her for the first hour, then thinned out to a trickle by the time she reached the Forest Highway.

As the soulless roadside bush skipped by, she couldn't shake the feeling she was driving away from something rather than towards it. Would her life be any better in Dark Water? Or, would she merely be hiding in a new setting? Whatever it was about her that invited a killer into her life would still be there, no matter where she went. If Mina wanted a better life, she'd have to change herself, not just her location.

*Fine plans in capable hands*, she thought, remembering one of her mother's favourite sayings. But was she capable of change? *Time will tell*, another Irene Constantine maxim. What would her mother think of her daughter moving to a little country town? *She'd think I should take the notes to the police, maybe try and help Andrea.* Mina spotted the turn off for Fire Lake and her chest tightened. Less than a week ago, she'd been here with Lee.

Mina checked the navigation map on the dashboard. According to the display, the property wasn't far from the lake. A right turn took her around to the west of Fire Lake and onto Stilltree Road. With twenty minutes to spare before her meeting with the agent, Mina turned and drove up the crushed gravel driveway.

The house stood amongst overgrown native shrubs and bare rose bushes with an expanse of lawn in front. A silver-grey Hyundai was parked under the blue carport that leaned against the right side of the house. On the left stood a shuttered garage skirted by yellow weeds. The place reminded her of the one she'd visited with Lee, only this had a lived-in feel. It reminded her of a film she'd seen about a family in the depression. A comfortable but serviceable home.

The agent, Briggs, said the house was vacant so she guessed the Hyundai belonged to him. Mina stepped out of her car and slammed the door. She rubbed the base of her spine which, after two plus hours of driving, ached. The odour of damp grass and wood smoke hung in the air.

The front door opened and a man dressed rather formally for the country setting stepped out. "Hi. Nice to see you again, Miss Constantine. I was just making sure everything's shipshape before you arrived." He let the screen door swing close behind him and bounded down the handful of steps that led from the narrow porch to the lawn.

*Shipshape?* Mina resisted the urge to laugh. Briggs looked to be in his late thirties although she'd never heard anyone under sixty use the term. He offered her his hand and then shook hers vigorously enough to make her shoulder jump.

"Now, before we go in, I'll just give you the run down." His tone, still cheerful became businesslike. "The house sits on two acres of mostly bushland. There's a dirt track around the north side that leads to a service road at the rear." He motioned to the side, reminding Mina of a flight attendant indicating the emergency exits.

She pressed her lips together and nodded.

"You've got the garage at the side of the house." He pointed to the left. "That was added on about ten years ago. And round the back, there are two sheds. One aluminium, pretty modern, and farther back a brick building. Good for storage if you need it."

"Okay. Good." Mina doubted she'd be storing anything, but tried to sound enthusiastic.

"I'll show you the inside and then, if you like what you see, we can have a look at the outbuildings."

Inside, the house looked to be in better shape than she'd expected. Clean fresh paint on the walls and blond timber flooring gave the place a rustic feel that Mina immediately liked. It was smaller than her house in Civil Park but probably from the same era, the 1940s.

"The kitchen's been modernised," Briggs spoke over his shoulder as he led her down the narrow hall. "There's air con and cable television if you want it hooked up." His voice seemed to be getting louder. Mina guessed leasing houses in a small country town wasn't easy. Even so, she wanted to go outside where his enthusiasm would be buffed by the wind and the open air.

Mina ran her fingers over the speckled grey counter top. The kitchen was narrow with a small dining table and four chairs at one end.

"What about the furniture?"

"Good question." Briggs nodded. "The place comes partly furnished. Anything you don't want can be moved out to the shed. Just let me know and I'll have it taken care of."

The tour, inside and out, took less than half an hour.

"Okay." Mina tipped her head up so she could look Briggs in the eyes. "If I fill out an application, how soon can I move in?"

For one terrifyingly awkward moment, she thought Briggs was going to hug her. He took a half step forward and raised his hands as if reaching for her. Mina took a step back, ready to push him away. He must have sensed her defensiveness *or* caught himself before he did something crazy, because he clapped his hands together and nodded. It was a clumsy rescue for a strange situation.

"Why don't you follow me back to the office?" He fished his keys out of his front pocket and headed for the Hyundai. "Once the paperwork's done and I check with the owners, you can pick up the keys tomorrow."

\* \* \*

After leaving Reliance Realty with a copy of the rental agreement in her hand, Mina left her car and walked down the main street. It was as she remembered, clean and wide. She made a mental note of the location of the supermarket and post office. *I'm really doing this.* She'd opted to lease, knowing full-well this was a crazy idea at the best of times. Still, she was doing it. Mina noticed the coffee shop she'd visited on her last trip to Dark Water, sandwiched between a gift shop and what looked like the town hall.

*Blue Smoke* had a modern look to it and a few clusters of tables set out on the pavement. All were occupied. It was well past lunchtime so she decided to grab a coffee and a sandwich before heading over to the hotel. There was no point in driving back to Perth until she'd secured the house and had the keys in her hand.

The café was, as she remembered, surprisingly cheerful—decorated with an eclectic mix of vibrant artwork and ancient mining artefacts. Mina's first impulse was to order something to takeaway and be in and out as quickly as possible. Instead, she sat down at a small table near the window. If she planned on living in Dark Water, snubbing the locals wasn't the best way to start.

"Hi. Have you had a chance to look at the menu?" The woman standing beside the table had short blonde hair, tousled in messy spikes.

"No. Not really, but I know what I want." Mina ordered a smoked salmon salad sandwich and a flat white.

"Are you moving in?"

"What?" The question startled her, it took Mina a second to work out what the woman was asking her.

"You've got a rental agreement from Reliance." She pointed her pencil at the paperwork laying on the table. "Sorry. I don't mean to be nosy." She smiled and dimples appeared on either side of her rather sharp face. "That's not true, I am being nosy, but." She waggled her pencil. "This is a small town so we're supposed to know each other's business."

The old Mina would have told her otherwise but, new life: new attitude. Besides, there was something about the woman that reminded Mina of her mother—a much younger version. "Yes. I'm moving into town. I just rented a house."

"Huh." She looked thoughtful.

"What?"

"You're an improvement on the usual," she looked around and dropped her voice. "Retirees. It's good to have someone under sixty-five move in."

Mina laughed. It felt good—real. "Are you here with your husband?" There was a glint of mischief in the blonde's eyes. Mina couldn't believe she was asking such personal questions and, even though part of her wanted to clam up, she found herself answering.

"It's just me." Mina kept her voice light.

The blonde waitress nodded. "I'm meeting some friends in the pub tomorrow night, you should come. They do a great pizza and pint special on Saturdays." She started writing something on her order pad.

"Um…" Mina thought of making an excuse about being too busy, but stopped herself. She'd taken a chance with Lee, and even though it hadn't led to anything more than a fling, it felt like a step in the right direction. She'd made the decision to uproot herself and start something new, maybe it was time to take another leap. "Okay. That sounds good."

"Here's my mobile number." She tore a scrap of paper out of her pad. "My name's Robbie by the way." She put the paper on the table and offered her hand.

Shaking hands seemed formal, Mina couldn't help chuckling. "I'm Mina."

# Chapter Fourteen

He sat on the dusty floor and leaned back against the wall. He felt safe—untouchable. Everything was as he wanted it to be. The Dolly was the best yet, compliant, soft yet durable. This one would last. He'd learned from his mistakes. The trick was balancing the food and the games. Just enough food to keep her alive, but little enough to sap her strength and urge to escape.

He could hear her on the other side of the rolling door. She seemed to be talking to herself. He couldn't make out the words and didn't care to listen. His thoughts were now elsewhere.

*Mina.* From the first moment he saw her, he knew they were the same. She'd sensed him there in the car park. He saw it in the way she'd stopped, her body tensing. For a terrifying and thrilling second, he thought she could see him. She seemed to be looking right at him. He recalled the moment and felt himself become aroused. He sucked in a breath and bunched his hands into fists.

The Dolly was different; a lifeless thing compared to Mina. Only metres away on the other side of the door, he couldn't even visualise her face while Mina's filled his mind. Since the moment he saw her, he knew his life would change. They would be together and she would understand. *No*, he stopped, his thoughts pushing and crashing into each other. She wouldn't just understand, Mina would embrace his games.

An image, one he found himself reliving more and more frequently, came to mind. Mina, dressed in a flowing gown, trailing her long fingers over the stark white skin of a naked woman. Bruises, dark and angry running over the body's flesh like blood-filled flowers against a wintery sky. Mina's head, veiled by her long black hair, turning so that her face revealed itself slowly. This was how it would be. She'd savour his work; thrill at his superior ability to detach from the mundane and do things others would shrink from. They'd come together in a way that was more powerful than anything either had ever known.

He relaxed his hands and reached for the hood. His heart tore a deafening beat through his chest. He pulled the dark plastic down over his face and fastened it at his throat. Soon, he'd have Mina and they'd make the games last longer and reach frantic heights. He lunged to his feet and flung back the door.

\* \* \*

There was blood on his hands. He frowned and tore at the hood. The cold air slapped his face drying the sweat on his cheeks. He couldn't remember how the blood came to be on his hands. He could hear the Dolly crying on the other side of the door, a feeble sound that reminded him of his auntie's cat. He held his fingers up in front of his face and watched the light shine through the blood. *Dishy*, the cat's name was *Dishy*. *Stupid ugly thing stank like a rancid corpse.* He let out a long sigh and tossed the hood to the floor.

He'd tell Mina all about Dishy when they were together. God, how that cat howled when he'd pushed its greedy ass into the fridge. The smile that creased his face faded. When the thing was finally dead, he took it outside and threw it in the bushes. He could almost feel the weight of it, heavy in his small hands, difficult to open the back door with the furry load clasped to his chest. In his eight-year old mind, it made perfect sense; once he got the cat out of the house, he'd pretend he knew nothing about it. His auntie would think it had been bitten by a snake or something. But he didn't think about the mess in the fridge. Not about the piss and fur that coated the butter and was left on the pork chops and cheese singles. Not about the broken jars and spilled cordial.

When his auntie got home, the first thing she did was call the cat. His lips had stretched back into a grimace as fresh sweat rolled down his face. He remembered hearing her voice flat and deep like a man's. She'd stalked around the house, her wide hips rolling like two pigs on a see-saw. He kept his eyes on the TV, pretending to be watching cartoons, the colours jumping and moving, making no sense. She didn't bother to speak to him, not that he cared.

After a few minutes he heard her grunt and head for the kitchen. He kept his face blank. He wanted to giggle—the sound building like a tickle in the back of his throat, trying to push past his lips until he slapped his hand over his mouth. The fridge opened with a rattle. Not until that hollow clanking of jars and bottles rang out did it occur to him that he might be in trouble.

"What have you done?"

He didn't need to ask who she was talking to. They were the only two people in the house and besides, the sick realisation that he hadn't thought to check the fridge spread through him like a bout of stomach-flu. He forced his legs to move, slipping off the couch and heading for the front door. If she got her hands on him, it would be worse than the time he'd shoved a stick up the next door neighbour's budgie's ass.

He rounded the doorway and headed down the hall, but she beat him to it.

"Where's Dishy?" Her face looked puffed up and shiny like she'd swallowed something hot that was burning the inside of her mouth. She reached out her fleshy paw and grabbed his shoulder, her fingers digging into the skin between his bones. "Did you ..." The words seemed to catch in her throat. "Did you do something to Dishy?"

He shook his head. "No. No, I didn't. I didn't do anything, I promise." He tried to make his face serious but all he wanted to do was get around her and out the front door. If he could do that, he'd be able to hide until she calmed down and then he could come up with a story about the cat. But her grip on his shoulder tightened and she was pulling him towards the kitchen.

Even though he knew what would come next, it didn't make the pain any more bearable. His auntie, a big woman with muscular arms built from years of cleaning houses, threw him over the kitchen table. She pressed his face onto the speckled wood veneer.

"You're a disgrace to your mother." He heard a drawer open and cutlery being tossed about. "I don't know how to make you stop. It's like you're possessed by the devil." He could hear her breathing, a thick heavy sound.

"I didn't do anything. I'm sorry." He could hear his own voice, high and panicked. "I'm sorry, I won't do it again. I didn't mean to."

She used an iron spoon. The first blows landing on his shoulders and neck with a wallop. He shrieked and bucked, twisting his head from side to side, but it was no use. She outweighed him by at least fifty kilos, and her dense thighs were pressed to the back of his legs pinning him to the table.

That evening he crept to the bedroom window, his back hunched like an old man's, wincing at every movement. He watched her bury the dirty old tom cat. She was crying. In the flat dusky light, he could see her shoulders quivering as she shovelled dirt over the hole. He watched her pause over the mound, her whole back jerking with grief, he smiled and decided the day hadn't been a complete loss.

*  *  *

In a detached and dreamy way he massaged his jaw, wondering why it ached. The Dolly was still crying. The sound reminded him of his auntie and the way her fat jiggled when she cried. He had the urge to roll open the doors and put a stop to the wailing. But that would mean no more games, at least until he found a replacement. He didn't want to waste time hunting, not when he needed to concentrate on Mina.

The letters were only the beginning. Being close to her had been everything he'd imagined—and more. He stood and picked up the bucket. The stink made his eyes water. The Dolly really disgusted him. The crying and begging, not to mention the filthy muck that came out of her. Still, she did make the games fun and that was more than he could say for the last Dolly. He walked out of the shed and turned left. The bucket sloshed at his side as he headed for the hole.

He tipped the contents into the pit and tossed the bucket aside. A few shovels of dirt covered the mess and, with each layer, he felt a calmness spread over him like a soft cloud. His life was comfortable now and soon he'd know what it meant to be joined with someone. The relationships he'd always had were strained, at least for him. Smiling and agreeing with mindless chatter about a world he barely noticed. That's not what he wanted. Mina would change all that. In some ways, they'd be each other's saviour.

He noticed a bird sitting in the tree above the hole. It ruffled its greyish-brown feathers looking non-descript, as if nature had forgotten it. He tipped his head to one side and watched the creature hop along the branch. He wondered if it had a mate.

# Chapter Fifteen

Mina dumped the box she was carrying on the sofa and elbowed the front door closed. The house still looked a bit of a mess with boxes littering the lounge room floor. A part of her couldn't believe she'd done it. In only a few days, she'd packed up and moved to Dark Water. Everything she needed, at least to begin with, was piled up in the kitchen and lounge of her new home.

Yesterday, she'd driven back to Perth and loaded the car before returning to Dark Water. Just being back in the city seemed strange, as if she'd already left and was now just a visitor. She hoped it meant she'd made the right decision. *No going back now*, she thought, and inched a box of sheets towards the coffee table using the toe of her shoe.

The house was in order, Briggs had made sure everything was ready for her. She had to admire his zealous approach to the rental business. When she dropped by the office that morning, the keys and a list of contact numbers were waiting for her in a large brown envelope, which his receptionist handed over along with a complementary fridge magnet. He'd thought of everything, including leaving her a bottle of red wine on the kitchen counter. Now all she had to do was unpack and start a new life.

All the lights were on, even in the bedroom. An odour of dried paint and dust hung in the air, suggesting the place had been empty for some time. She thought of opening the windows and airing the house out, but glancing outside at the purple light bleeding into orange, she decided to wait until morning. She could put up with the stale smell for one night. God knows she'd coped with worse.

The house came partly furnished, which meant there were some pieces of ancient furniture, including a wrought iron-framed double bed. Mina walked around the master bedroom inspecting the mattress. It looked clean—well, unstained anyway. There didn't appear to be any bedbugs. She sat on the edge and gave it a bounce deciding it would do until she could order a new one online.

Once she'd put clean sheets on the bed, Mina closed the curtains and thought about the rest of her evening. She could continue unpacking, but the thought of tackling more boxes brought on a wave of exhaustion. It seemed like she'd been moving constantly over the past week, pushing herself without stopping to think. Maybe her mind didn't want to linger on Lee or Andrea. Both loomed in her thoughts for different reasons.

She sat on the bed and listened to the sounds of the house creaking and settling. In time, each new noise would become familiar, perhaps even comforting. However, as night crept closer, the rattles and bumps unnerved her. Usually resigned to her own company, Mina found herself craving voices and distraction. She left the bedroom and went in search of her handbag and the scrap of paper with Bobbie's number on it.

She hesitated, sucking in her lips while staring at the screen. She barely knew the woman and here she was plunging into a meeting with Robbie and *some friends*. Some friends could mean two or twenty people. The thought should have worried her, but for some reason it excited

Mina instead. She hit send and drew in a breath. *Fine plans in capable hands.*

Her phone buzzed. Robbie seemed happy to hear from her, explaining that the group was meeting at the Dark Water Pub at seven-thirty. Mina checked her watch, she had time for a quick shower and a change of clothes.

After towelling herself dry, she dressed in black jeans and a pale blue turtle neck jumper. Grabbing her jacket and bag, she was on her way into town by a quarter-past seven.

\* \* \*

Mina stepped through the heavy swinging door grateful for the blazing fire that chased the July chill away. A couple occupied the table she'd shared with Lee; the woman, bundled in a woollen wrap, leaned across the slab holding her phone out to her male companion. Mina looked away. She gave herself a moment to take in the rest of the pub, noticing the clusters of people around the bar.

She spotted Robbie standing over a table holding a pint and talking to Briggs. Mina was a little surprised to see him with Robbie. He seemed a little too uptight for her. Robbie, dressed in faded jeans and a long woollen jacket, looked over and caught Mina's gaze. She waved her free hand in a beckoning gesture.

"You know Terry." Robbie took Mina's arm and gave her a hug. A quick one-armed embrace that felt natural and breezy, as if they'd been friends for years instead of just meeting yesterday.

"I rented Mina the Hammer place." Terry looked relaxed. Mina decided the manic cheerfulness had to be an estate agent thing he did when showing houses. He was still dressed rather formally, white shirt and black pants, but the tie was pulled loose and he'd rolled his sleeves up. "How's the move going?"

"Hang on." Robbie held up her hand. "Introductions and drinks before you start discussing light switches and cupboard space."

"What'll you have?" Briggs smiled. He wore his dark hair cropped very close to his scalp making him look quite severe.

"I'll have whatever you're all drinking." Mina nodded to the drink in Robbie's hand.

While Briggs wandered over to the bar, Robbie made the introductions. "This is Tom and Laura. Tom's dad owns Blue Smoke, so I have to pretend to like him."

Tom shook his head and offered Mina his hand. "How's it going?"

After shaking hands with Tom and Laura, Mina took a seat at the table. The smell of melted cheese and fried bacon permeated the air. Her stomach rumbled in response. "Something smells good."

"We've ordered a few pizzas," Laura said. "I hope you're not a vegetarian, we've asked for extra bacon *and* cheese."

"No. I'm definitely not a vegetarian."

"So, what do you think of Dark Water?" Robbie waved her arm gesturing to the room behind her. "It's a bit gloomy during winter, but once spring arrives, things get pretty exciting."

"Yeah," Laura joined in. "The annual wood chopping championships will blow your mind." Both women laughed.

"Don't forget the school fetes. Those things go off." Tom added with a dead-pan expression.

Mina smiled. "I don't know if I can handle that kind of fast-paced living." Maybe it was the feeling of leaving her old life behind or the friendly banter, but she realised she was enjoying herself. Doing something different and meeting new people had started off as a way of closing a door on her past, but now it felt like something new was *beginning*. Something positive—fun. She'd expected a

111

change, but had never really thought she'd make friends. Maybe things were looking up.

"What did I miss?" Briggs asked, placing a pint of lager in front of Mina. His confused expression only made the four of them laugh harder.

The group broke-up around eleven o'clock. Briggs—who everyone called Terry—had an open house in the morning. Tom and Laura were driving to Margaret River the following day to visit Laura's parents so Mina and Robbie were the last to leave.

"Thanks for a great night." Mina wondered if she should hug Robbie. It was a bit of an awkward moment. Pearly light from the pub's windows spilled onto the pavement encircling the two women in a warm glow.

"I'll walk you to your car," Robbie's voice echoed in the empty street. Mina felt a chill run up her spine. The words hit her like a shock of cold water. She thought of Andrea and suddenly her mouth felt dry. If Mina had been as kind as Robbie, the girl might be at home now, safe. Robbie hadn't thought twice about the offer. This was what decent people did for each other.

"No." It came out too quickly sounding harsh and dismissive. She noticed Robbie flinch. "I mean. Okay. Thanks, but let me drive you back to your car." Mina hesitated. "Just to make sure *you're* safe."

Robbie's face relaxed. She slipped her arm through Mina's and they began to walk together.

"I'm just around the corner." Mina pointed to the left. Soft music followed them from the pub mingling with the clack of their heels on the damp footpath.

"What do you think of Terry?" Robbie asked. "I mean he's sort of a geek, but in a nice way. If that makes sense."

Mina considered the question. She hadn't really given him much thought. He'd been more relaxed tonight, less pushy. He did seem like a bit of a geek, a little awkward but kind of sweet.

"He's nice, I suppose. Are you and he…?"

112

"That's a good question." Robbie turned to look at her as they rounded the corner. In the moonlight, her sharp features looked shadowed and stark. "We're sort of off and on. I've known him for years, since school." She pulled Mina's arm tighter. "I don't know. Sometimes I think I want to take things further, get serious and then…" Her words trailed off. "Something holds me back. It's hard to explain."

"Mmm. Relationships are difficult." Mina thought about Lee. Things felt so right, as if she'd found where she was supposed to be, and then it was over. "When are two people ever on the same page?" Mina stopped walking. "Here's my car."

Mina unlocked and opened the driver's door, but Robbie made no move to get in the other side. "You don't have to drop me around the corner. I've lived here all my life, it's pretty safe."

Mina leaned on the open door and glanced around the darkened street. A fine sheen of mist hung in the air blurring the surrounding houses and gardens.

"It's really no problem." Mina kept her tone light. She even managed a smile, one that she hoped would disguise how desperately she wanted Robbie to get in the car. "I'd like the company."

"In that case," Robbie rounded the car and got in. "Are you okay?" Turning in her seat, she narrowed her blue eyes and frowned. "You look a bit… a bit startled."

Mina let out a long breath. "I'm fine. Really. It's just…" She hesitated, not sure if she should tell Robbie about Andrea. She hadn't discussed what happened with anyone, not even Lee. Trusting people wasn't her way, yet she felt she *could* trust Robbie. She could tell the woman was waiting for her to continue. "Have you seen the news stories about that guy? The Magician?"

Robbie nodded. "You'd have to be living on the moon to have not heard about him. What a sicko."

113

Mina ran her fingers through her hair, pulling it over one shoulder and tucking it into her jumper. "Something happened a couple of weeks ago. When the last girl went missing." The air inside the car smelled rubbery and damp. Outside, rain peppered the streets, splattering the windshield with large droplets. The story came out in a rush. She told Robbie everything, holding back only the part about the notes and hairclips. She couldn't share that, not ever.

Mina paused her story only once, when she got to the part about refusing to wait with Andrea. She heard Robbie suck in a shocked breath, but other than that, she didn't speak. By the time Mina finished, the rain had petered out. The only sounds inside the car came from their breathing.

She watched Robbie, trying to read her face for signs of disgust or anger. Mina half expected her to get out of the car and slam the door. She wouldn't blame her if she did.

When Robbie finally spoke, she said something Mina hadn't been expecting. "That must have been hard for you. Dealing with something like that. I can't even imagine what that's like."

Mina realised she'd been gripping the steering wheel as she spoke, clenching her fingers so tightly the tendons in her wrists ached. She let her hands slip off the wheel and into her lap. "Hard for *me*?" Mina shook her head. "What about Andrea? I'm responsible for what happened to her." She could hear her voice rising, and lowered her head, breathing through her nose.

"No." Robbie's voice was flat, certain. "You're not. The bastard who abducted her is responsible. Mina, ninety-nine times out of a hundred, nothing would have happened to that girl. You were both in the wrong place at the wrong time. Jesus, Mina. You could've just as easily been the one he targeted."

Mina suppressed the urge to shudder. He *was* targeting her. "Then why do I feel so guilty?"

Robbie made a clicking sound with her tongue. "Because you're a nice woman and you did something a bit careless."

Mina wanted to believe her. Especially the part about being a nice woman. But was she nice? She'd done some very bad things. If Robbie knew the half of it, would she still think Mina was nice? Probably not. If she told her about the notes, the hairclips, she'd probably insist Mina take them to the police. She couldn't risk the attention, not to mention the questions about why she'd waited. No, it was too late to do anything about the notes.

"Promise me you're not going to let this eat you up." Robbie paused and then surprised her by chuckling.

"What's so funny?" Mina asked, a little taken aback.

"I had you pegged for a bad break-up. I mean that's why I thought you were in Dark Water. You know, putting the ex behind you with a fresh start or something."

Mina grimaced. "Yeah, there's that too."

"Jesus." Robbie shook her head. "You really have had a rough time."

"You could say that."

It was nearly eleven-thirty when Mina dropped Robbie at her car. The lights were out, leaving the pub standing in a mist of grey moonlight. "Why don't we meet up this week? Go into Busselton and have lunch?" Robbie had the passenger door open and one foot on the bitumen. Cold air rushed past her and flooded the car.

"Okay. That would be nice." It seemed that even after everything she'd told Robbie, the woman still wanted to be friends. Mina felt a rush of gratitude.

"My cousin's coming to town tomorrow so I'll probably be roped into some family stuff, but I'll text you on Monday."

Mina watched Robbie get in her car and drive away before heading home.

# Chapter Sixteen

Andrea lay slumped on the mattress. Pale slivers of moonlight seeped in through the cracks in the wall. Her life had become nothing more than a series of light changes. Pearl in the morning, yellow in the afternoon, then black. She missed the stars and that feeling of vastness that came from looking up at the sky. Her face throbbed, the rhythm beat in her ears like the constant hum of a blow-fly around her head.

Her cheek felt swollen, puffy, like it was stuffed with cotton wool. She'd been working up to this point since he left this morning. *I can do it*, she told herself. *He's hurt me in so many ways, it can't be that hard.* But it was.

She balled her hands up and rubbed her eyes. A sob caught in her throat making her head jerk. The loose incisor moved in her gum, tipping inwards with a sickening creak.

She had to pull it free, it was the only way. When he choked her that morning, he'd hit her in the jaw. The blow so sudden and violent, spots of green light had flickered behind her eyes and she felt her tooth shift as if it actually bent. Now it leaned against her tongue moving up and down with each breath like a small gritty stone. With each tiny movement, the stalks of flesh that still tethered it to her gum tore and pulled, making every breath painful. If she left it hanging from her swollen gum, it might fall out while she slept and choke her. *Maybe I should just let it happen. I'm not really alive anymore.*

He'd stripped everything from her. The beatings were more violent with each new attack. He was losing whatever small semblance of control he possessed. Soon he'd reach the point of no return. He'd choke the life out of her or beat her to death. Either way, if she didn't do something, the end was coming. Maybe it would be easier to meet death on her own terms?

Could she do that? Could she let death take her? Andrea pulled herself into a sitting position, the chains rattling on her arms. Head bowed, she closed her eyes and tried to look inwards. She pushed past the pain and the hunger, strained to grasp the essence of herself, how she had been that night before the world fell away.

It seemed they were now two separate people. The person she used to be: awkward yet happy, filled with dreams of a future as a writer. Parents who loved her; even her crappy job seemed bathed in a rosy glow of fond memories. Then there was the Andrea who used a bucket as a toilet: a starved and beaten creature that lived in the dark. If she let go, which life would she be shrugging off?

Andrea made herself count to three, breathing through her nose with each second that passed. When she pulled, a gurgle of saliva and blood bubbled over her lips. She felt something stretch then snap and the tooth was in her hand. She could feel its smooth slippery surface between her fingers.

Laughter built in her throat but came out sounding more like a wail. She held the tooth up so a shaft of moonlight played on its edges. It looked like a pearl shimmering under dark seas. Her relief turned to something darker. For the first time since the hood was thrown over her head, Andrea felt anger.

She wanted to hurt the man that had brought her so low. He'd done things to her that made her skin itch with disgust. He kept her chained like an animal—starved, beaten. After all those tortures, it was the tooth that tipped her over the edge.

If she gave in, her whole life would be reduced to a scattering of teeth and bones. She'd be nothing but remnants lying undiscovered in this room or buried somewhere no one would ever find. She had to get out. She would get out or die fighting.

The tooth fell from her hand with an almost soundless click. Standing, the world tipped slightly and darkness, deeper than that of the cell she inhabited, blossomed and then dissolved. She tasted blood, metallic and sour oozing from the empty socket in her gum. She took the water bottle from under the mattress and allowed herself one swallow. It wasn't much, not enough to slake her thirst, but for the time being, her mouth tasted cleansed of blood.

She'd spent years trying to diet and mostly failed, but the past weeks of starvation had taken their toll on her body. The fleecy pants, at first snug on her thighs now hung around her hips like a filthy nappy. The old Andrea would have been giggling with pleasure at the weight loss, but the new version regarded her frailer body with grim calculation.

She used her right hand to turn the leather cuff on her left wrist, noticing the ease of movement. Repeating the process with her opposite hand, Andrea found the cuffs had loosened considerably. If she could get her hands out, the only thing between her and freedom was the door. *It's locked*, a warning voice whispered in her head.

"Maybe." Andrea's voice sounded loud in the silence. It had been a long time since she'd been spoken to. Like the stars and the night sky, she missed the sound of voices. "If it's locked, I'll find another way." She liked hearing her own voice, it reminded her she *was* still alive.

She grasped the left cuff and pulled with her right hand while the other moved up and down against the leather. She worked slowly, inching the restraint over her skin. She managed to work the cuff past her wrist, but then found it jammed against her thumb.

"Come on." Despite the cold air, a sheen of sweat broke out on her forehead.

A few more minutes of straining and her face and neck were bathed in perspiration. She almost stopped to swipe at her face when an idea froze her movements. She pushed the cuff back up her wrist, losing the precious and painful centimetres of progress she'd made. Dropping back down onto the mattress, she wiped her left wrist across her face and neck. It came away slippery with sweat.

Knowing she had no time to waste, Andrea began the process of pulling the cuff and rotating her wrist. With her skin slick with perspiration, the leather slid over her hand. It still lodged around her thumb, but this time a little farther along than the last.

Andrea stopped pulling and started pushing from the other side of the cuff. The skin on her hand bunched closer to her knuckles like a wrinkly glove. She could feel something tearing, as if her flesh were being bitten by a million sharp needles.

Blood seeped from under the cuff and smeared her skin. "Hah." Andrea grimaced and pushed the cuff forward, giving it a slight twist. A combination of blood and sweat acted as the lubrication needed to slide the restraint past her thumb and over her fingers. The cuff dangled from the chain, a ring of dark leather dripping with blood.

Andrea gasped and lay back staring at the black ceiling. Her breath came in exhausted gasps, like an athlete who'd just crossed the finish line. She felt drained of strength, but satisfied. She'd taken the first step. Cradling her left hand to her chest, warm blood trickled from her wrist and soaked through the fabric of her top as Andrea fell into a fitful sleep.

# Chapter Seventeen

He'd taken care with his appearance, tonight would be a special evening for both him and Mina. Starting their life together would be difficult at first. He wasn't stupid, she'd be resistant to the change. He inspected his hair in the mirror and found a few strands of grey appearing close to his right ear.

"Fuck." He flipped open the cabinet and found the tweezers. The greys grew coarse and wiry, he had to yank on the tweezers to shift them. The stray hairs drifted into the sink. For a while, he watched them—transfixed by the pattern they created on the porcelain. His eyes fluttered closed and he saw his hand, blood staining his fingers. Then his head snapped up and he regarded himself in the mirror.

He frowned then smiled. The frown made him look thoughtful—caring. But the smile, that was the clincher. Sincere with a touch of mystery, she loved that look. He saw it in the way her eyes moved over his face. Mina would pretend to be shocked by his lifestyle, but he'd soon show her how to embrace the power. She had a taste for it, he could almost smell it on her. It might take time, but she'd come around.

He flashed the smile again only this time his lips drew back further. "I'm a patient man."

He left the bathroom and headed for the kitchen. There was work to do, preparations to make. He checked the cupboards under the sink, ignoring the flaking paint and overflowing basin. Counting the lines of canned food soothed him. One of the reasons he'd been so successful was his attention to detail.

Next, and most important, Mina's room. The bolt he'd fitted to the outside of the door looked startlingly shiny against the faded and chipped paintwork. He pushed the door, it opened to bare wood floors, unpolished and patchy with age. Planks covered the window, four nails a piece. He pulled on each board knowing they were secure, but still re-checking. A forgotten detail could ruin everything he'd worked and planned for.

A single bed, bolted to the floor and dressed in a simple set of white sheets with a grey blanket folded at the foot, stood in the centre of the room. The space looked monastic, stark. Chains hung loosely from the head of the bed, held in place by padlocks. He ran his hand over the cold metal. It wasn't how he wanted their life together to begin, but it couldn't be helped. The room would be temporary, a transitional place where they would develop a deep bond.

He clicked his tongue against the roof of his mouth. "Can't forget the bucket." He dashed from the room, returning with a red plastic bucket much like the one he'd left with the Dolly. Placing it next to the bed, he nodded and turned around. A smile, very different to the one he practised in the mirror, lit up his face.

# Chapter Eighteen

A new routine was beginning. Mina woke at seven and made herself a slice of toast and a cup of instant coffee. Despite the dreams, she felt alert and rested. Unburdening herself to Robbie hadn't exactly taken the guilt away, but she certainly felt lighter.

Dressed in faded jeans and an oversized T-shirt, Mina puttered around the house unpacking and putting things away. There wasn't much cupboard space, but she hadn't brought a lot with her, only the essentials. She'd need to drive into town to pick up a few groceries and some things from the hardware shop. When she returned home the night before, she'd noticed the gate at the front of the property swinging open and decided she'd feel a hell of a lot safer if she could lock it at night.

Mina put a stack of folded towels in the linen cupboard. The house still smelled musty, she made a mental note to open the windows when she got back from town. But before she could leave the house, she had a few final jobs to take care of.

She left the sandwich maker in a box on the kitchen table. Just touching the thing made her uncomfortable. She pulled it out of the container and sat it on the table.

Rubbing her fingers across her lower lip, she tried to think of a hiding place. Maybe hiding it wasn't a great idea. It would probably be less suspicious to just shove it in one of the cupboards that ran along the left side of the room. *Less suspicious, no one's going to be searching my house, why would they?* Still, Mina put the sandwich maker in the cupboard behind a stack of plates.

Brushing her hands together as if there was dirt clinging to them, she picked up her phone. One last thing to tick off before she could relax and enjoy setting up house. Herbert Longfellow answered on the third ring.

"Mina, nice to hear from you. Are you coming in to the office this week?"

She'd dreaded making the call. Herbert was a kind-hearted man, why he'd ever be friends with her father she'd never been able to work out. "No. That's why I'm calling."

"Oh?" He managed to make the word a question.

"I've… I've decided to move. I need a change."

He took a second to respond. "Good idea. You've been alone in that big house for too long. There are some nice apartments in Subiaco, if you like I can come with you to look at them?"

"No. But thanks for the offer. I've already moved." Mina wondered how she could explain the sudden tree-change without sounding crazy. "I've rented a house." She gave a forced laugh. "I'm just unpacking now."

"That's…" he hesitated. "That's sudden. Do you need any help? May and I could–"

"No. The thing is, I've moved out of Perth. I'm in Dark Water." When he didn't respond, she rushed on. "I like it here, Herbert. I don't know how to explain it, but it's what I need. To put some space between… Between the old memories."

"Well, you sound brighter. If it makes you happy, then I'm happy for you."

"Thank you. And with the office, I thought you could just email anything I need to sign and I could have it couriered back."

"Yes. Yes. I'm sure we can work something out. You know it just occurred to me that I'll be down your way next weekend. May and I are planning on spending a few days in Wonderup. Why don't we stop by for lunch? You can show us around."

Mina knew what he was doing. He wanted to make sure she hadn't lost the plot completely, it was sweet really. She'd always been so busy keeping him *and* everyone else at arm's length, she'd never stopped to appreciate his kindness. "That would be lovely. Why don't you text me with the details? I know a great café in town."

Mina dropped her phone in her handbag. She had two lunch dates lined up for the coming week, more social activity than she'd seen in a year. The thought of interacting with people still made her stomach flutter, but even that was starting to pass. Taking hold of the zip, ready to close her bag and pick up her car keys, she noticed the knife. It had been in there since last week. She shook her head and put the blade in the top drawer next to the sink.

One other bonus of moving out of the city was that the Magician wouldn't be able to find her. It occurred to her that she had no idea how he'd found her the first time. The only obvious answer was that he'd followed her home. The thought made her skin prickle with goose flesh. Another thought popped into her head, *could he have followed me here? No.* A voice in her mind warned. *Don't do this to yourself, not when everything's going so well.*

There'd been no notes, but she *had* only been in Dark Water for two days. Mina put her hand on the drawer that contained the knives and then just as quickly drew it away. He would have no idea she'd moved. Not unless he'd been watching the house. It was possible. Who knew what the crazy freak might do.

"Possible, but unlikely." Mina picked up her keys and headed for the door. She'd lived in fear for the first seventeen years of her life, she wouldn't go back.

* * *

It took longer than she expected in the hardware shop. Once she was inside, the options seemed endless. In addition to the length of chain, she bought two torches, one heavy duty and one slimline, as well as a few padlocks and a pair of secateurs. She stopped at the gardening section and considered buying some seedlings, maybe starting a vegetable garden. The young man that worked in the shop was eager to help, explaining that tomatoes, capsicums, and squash keep providing each season.

"The key is to start out small."

Mina noticed his badge: *My name is Leon, ask me about gardening.*

"People get excited and plant too much, then they end up wasting a plethora of produce."

"Okay, maybe I'll just think about it for a while." The air in the gardening section was heavy with the smell of fertilizer which, to Mina, smelt like wet dung.

"Well, I recommend a spot with plenty of sunlight, that way the plants will bear more and won't be as susceptible to insects." Leon scratched his ginger beard and regarded the row of seedlings from behind wire-framed glasses. "Most vegetables do best in moist, well-drained soil."

"You know what, I'll just take some tomatoes." Mina grabbed two pots eager to end the conversation and be on her way.

"Okay, do you want me to help you chose some planting mix?"

Mina plonked the pots on top of the other items in her trolley and began heading for the checkout. "No. But thanks." She kept moving, hoping Leon wasn't about to chase her down with a pair of gardening gloves and a trowel. Despite the assistant's over-enthusiasm, she couldn't help smiling. *God, they breed them cheerful in the country.*

Her next stop was the supermarket which was surprisingly large. Mina bought a steak, a ready-made salad and a few other essentials. When she put her items on the conveyer belt at the check-out, she was thankful the plump teenager working the register was disinterested and surly. *Finally, someone normal.* Mina almost laughed. She couldn't remember when she'd felt this upbeat. Certainly not in the last eighteen months.

Thinking about the steak dinner she intended to cook, Mina didn't notice the man walking towards the entrance as she moved to the exit. Instead of watching her surroundings, she looked up at the sky noting the gathering clouds. She'd half-planned to eat on the tiny deck at the back of the house, but it seemed the rain was on its way.

"Mina?" She knew the voice, recognised the timbre; it stopped her mid-stride.

She almost didn't turn. She could see herself walking away and never looking back, but as much as she wanted to escape, part of her was desperate to see him one more time.

"Lee." The plastic shopping bags swung at her side. She had the urge to reach up and smooth her hair, but her hands were full.

"I thought it was you." He looked surprised, unsmiling. She couldn't blame him. It had to seem weird running into her in his home town. "What... what are you doing here?"

"I could ask you the same thing." She shot the words at him with more anger than she'd intended. The pained look on his face should have given her some satisfaction. Instead, it only reminded her of the way Andrea looked when Mina left her standing alone in a deserted parking lot.

"I'm just visiting for a while." He moved his arm as though to touch her but then lowered it. "I never wanted it to be like this."

She wanted the encounter to end. Hearing his voice, being next to him, was almost more than she could bear. In the last few days, she'd found a small measure of happiness and now she could feel it slipping away.

"What *did* you want?" She tried to keep her voice under control, but a tremor of anger or grief, she didn't know which, crept in.

"I'm sorry. It's all I can say." His shoulders slumped. For the first time, she noticed the change in him. It had been less than a week since she'd last seen him, but he looked different—older. His hair seemed faded and his cheeks hollow, as if he'd lost weight. Maybe he *was* feeling guilty about ending it with her. *Good*, she wanted him to suffer. God knows he'd caused her enough needless pain.

"I really don't care what you have to say. Getting involved with you was a mistake, but at least it was a quick one." She could feel her throat tightening. If she didn't get out of there, the tears would come and that would be the final humiliation—standing in the street crying over a man that had used her then dumped her like a day-old newspaper.

He opened his mouth to speak but Mina had already turned away. She made it to her car and dumped the shopping in the boot. By the time she got behind the wheel, she'd regained some control over her emotions. After all, she had plenty of practice putting on a stony face.

\* \* \*

Being so close to her had nearly broken his resolve. He'd wanted to touch her, make a move. Sweat broke out on the back of his neck, it trickled down his spine while he kept his arms at his side. He had a plan, one that he knew would work. If he acted now, in the heat of the moment, things could go very wrong. Besides there were too many people around. All of them gaping like idiots. No, tonight would be better. Darkness always worked best.

He could go to the Dolly. Work out his frustrations. The thought appealed to him. He opened the door and slipped in behind the wheel. Instead of driving away, he sat and watched Mina put shopping bags in her car. Her movements were smooth, languid. The wind ruffled her long black hair. He let his hand drift into his lap and pushed at his erection, feeling it spring back against his hand.

Mina disappeared from view, he let out a long breath. All thoughts of the Dolly slipped from his mind. A burst of conversation brought him back to the moment. An old woman, bent over a silver walking frame, moved past the window. Holding her arm was another woman, large with pendulous breasts pushed against the thin fabric of her black shirt. The older one looked like a walking corpse with knotted blue veins running like dark worms up her legs. Loose cotton socks hung around her swollen ankles. He had the urge to start the van and drive into the women, watch them bounce and break. *The big one would probably dent the front grill*, he licked his lips and continued to watch their slow progress across the parking lot.

*  *  *

Mina dumped the groceries on the kitchen table. Seeing Lee brought everything back with a jarring thud. She was angry, with him *and* herself. With Lee for using her and then lying, but mostly with herself. She'd slept with him, that didn't really bother her. She'd enjoyed it; well, maybe more than enjoyed. What really stung was how much she'd opened up to him. The tough skin she'd built up over years of abuse and then guilt, dropped away like a paper shell when he turned on the charm.

She'd let Lee see her loneliness. It made her feel exposed, like standing naked in a crowded room. Her skin itched with the humiliation. She stared at the shopping, not really seeing it. In her mind's eye, she saw Lee's face: tired and pale. Something played around the edge of her thoughts and then slipped away before she could touch it.

Leaving the groceries on the table, she went to the bathroom. It was a small space, old-fashioned with a pale green tub and shower over-head. Mina stripped off her clothes and turned on the water. She stepped under the jet wanting to scrub the feeling of vulnerability off her skin.

Twenty minutes later, the water turned from hot to warm then freezing. Mina stepped out of the tub shivering and dried herself. She felt calmer, but the optimism she'd experienced that morning had vanished, and no amount of washing would bring it back.

"Fuck him," she said aloud, and pulled on her clothes.

With sunset came a breeze strong enough to sweep the curtains out in billowing lengths across the lounge room. Mina pushed the flapping fabric aside and slammed down the window. Outside, the sky cast a marbled shadow over the front yard. Closing the windows that had been open all afternoon, she noticed only a faint trace of the musty smell.

The wind rattled the house, shaking panes and jostling doors. Mina put her laptop on the kitchen table and looked through her playlists. She wasn't in the mood for love songs. Instead, she chose something upbeat—pop songs from the eighties. With the sound of Wham! playing softly in the background, she turned on the cook top and heated up some oil in the only pan she'd bothered bringing with her.

As the steak sizzled in her mother's heavy cast iron pan, Mina's thoughts returned to Lee. Now that the initial shock at seeing him had died, she couldn't help but wonder why he'd lied about going to Queensland. If he'd wanted to end their brief relationship, why not just say he was going out of town? Why an elaborate lie?

She flipped the steak, barely noticing the rich, meaty smell coming off the pan. Another thing bothered her, he'd said he hadn't been home in almost three years. If that were true, why had he rushed back to Dark Water as soon as he stopped seeing her? It could be that their trip together made him realise he missed his home. It was plausible. But that still didn't explain why he lied about going to Queensland.

*Maybe, he thought I was so crazy about him I'd follow him to Dark Water.* She thought of their meeting outside the supermarket and screwed up her face in a grimace. Wham! gave way to Prince, the beat changed, slowed—became more soulful. Mina grabbed the salad from the fridge and tipped it onto a plate, then opened a bottle of red wine.

Sitting at the table, ploughing her way through the steak, her thoughts kept coming back to Lee. Seeing him hurt more than she'd have thought it would. Yet, above the pain, questions lingered. The way he'd just appeared at the shops, it seemed like more than just a chance meeting. Had he been watching her?

Mina picked at her dinner, not really tasting it. Half-way through, she gave up and pushed the plate away. She was being paranoid. If anyone looked like a stalker, it was her. At least that's how it must seem. As if summoned by her thoughts, her phone beeped. She pushed back her chair and grabbed the wine glass.

She didn't need to look at the screen to know who'd texted her. The message would be from Lee. She couldn't say how she knew. Just a feeling in the pit of her stomach. A certainty. She took a swallow of wine and winced at the way it hit the back of her throat. The phone beeped again reminding her there was a message.

*I'm sorry about today. We need to talk.*

She dropped the phone on the counter and sipped her wine. Outside the window, the sun had almost disappeared leaving only smudges of orange draped in grey clouds. What could he possibly have to say? Did it matter? She wanted the answer to be no, but part of her wanted to hear him out, let him explain why he'd treated her so badly. The phone beeped again and her heart fluttered in her throat.

*Please?*

If she responded, she knew anything he told her would be enough. She wanted to believe his excuses. Since he'd ended it, she'd rushed around looking for a distraction so she wouldn't have to acknowledge how much she missed him. She put down the wine and wrapped her arms around her body. The temperature seemed to have dropped at least five degrees. Rain began to hammer the tin roof making a sound like coins being dropped from a great height. The noise drowned out the music and almost blocked out the rap of the knocker slapping against the front door.

*Lee?* Had he been sitting outside messaging her? A flicker of excitement burned in her stomach or maybe it was the wine mixing with the steak. She headed for the front door telling herself she'd take things slowly. Just because he wanted to see her, didn't mean anything had changed. He was still the same guy who'd used her and then disappeared.

She put her fingers on the door handle, the old circular knob felt icy. How did he know where she lived? It almost hadn't occurred to her. When they met at the shops, they'd barely exchanged a few words. Dark Water was a small town, but not so small that everyone knew where the new arrivals lived.

Another rap on the door, louder now. She almost let go of the knob. There was no peep-hole in the door. Whoever was on the other side remained completely hidden from view.

"Who's there?" Her voice sounded gruff, unwelcoming.

The clatter of the rain muffled the response, but she was sure she'd heard her name. Mina licked her lips, it would be risky to fling open the door when she was alone and had no idea who waited on the other side. She flicked on the outside light and stepped to the side so she could look through the window.

The angle was all wrong. She could make out a shoulder, judging by the height, definitely male. She stepped back behind the door and pressed her face close to the wood. "Hang on." She waited a second, but couldn't hear if he answered.

Mina jogged back to the kitchen and opened the cutlery drawer. *What happened to never living in fear?* she asked herself as she pulled out the knife. "There's a fine line between fearless and stupid." Her voice didn't sound fearless. In fact, it came out as a breathless whisper.

Back at the front door, she held the knife behind her back and turned the knob with her left hand. A gust of cold wind blew back her hair and plastered her T-shirt to her body. The glare of the outside light blinded her for a second before the familiar face became clear and she relaxed the arm behind her back.

# Chapter Nineteen

The skin on the backs of Andrea's hands was shredded and bloody, but she was free. The second cuff slipped off with a wet slurp and now the restraints sat piled on the dirty mattress. She stepped away from the filthy bed. The absence of the ever-present clanking of chains was a sweet silence so new and precious, it was almost worth ruining her hands just to experience the nothingness.

She crossed the room in a few long steps and grasped the side of the door. Her heartbeat ratcheted up until it hammered in her ears. Pushing back the door could do two things: get her killed or set her free. *No,* she corrected her thinking. The door might be locked and then nothing. The third option seemed almost worse than the first.

It had taken so much of her will and strength to tear off the cuffs, she couldn't let the fear of failure sap what little she had left. Her insides felt as shredded as her hands. Her arms trembled, she had to try.

"Please. Please." Her voice sounded high and childish, as if she were begging her mother for an ice-cream instead of pleading for her freedom.

She pushed sideways, wincing at the ribbons of pain that blossomed across the backs of her hands. The door moved a few centimetres. A shock of relief zig-zagged through her chest. In that second, she could see herself running from the torture chamber she'd been trapped in for so long. She could almost feel the warmth of the sun on her face. The door shuddered to a stop with a metallic *clunk*.

"Urgh." The sound that escaped her lips was more one of disbelief than defeat. She shook her head splattering the door with sweat. Closing her eyes, she whispered, "It'll work." Andrea gave the door a push, rocking it back and forth ever so slightly. There could be dirt in the runner causing a jam.

She coughed and shivered at the same time. Her fingers gripped the side of the door where bloody handprints now stained the faded white paint. She pulled, but the door refused to budge. It was locked. There was no way out. A beaten-down defeated part of her had known all along the door would be locked. It would have been a miracle if he'd kept her captive with an unlocked door.

She let go of the metal and stared at her hands. The skin on the right one was bunched and torn around her thumb, revealing a patch of pink flesh that was starting to crust over. The left looked much worse. Trails of flesh were gouged open in lines that ran from her knuckles to just above her wrist, the skin flapped like a red glove. Blood oozed from the streaks in dark bubbles. The thumb was swollen to twice its normal size and had taken on the colour of an over-ripe plum. She tried bending it and cried out at the pain.

Her knees buckled, sending her sinking down to the dusty floor. She wrapped her arms around herself and pressed her hands against her ribs. Another fit of coughing seized her, rocking her body forward. She'd put all her hopes into getting the door open and in the process destroyed her hands. *Now what? Wait to die?*

It would be easy to crawl back to the mattress and close her eyes. Her body felt alien in its weakness. Every part of her wanted sleep, but what then? He'd come back and see what she'd done. She didn't want to think about what he'd do to her. Her shoulder twitched where the bite he'd left on her skin burned.

"No. I got out of the cuffs. *I* did that. There's got to be a way." She liked the sound of her voice in the empty room. It sounded older, like that of a woman who'd lived a hard life and wouldn't be beaten. She could be that woman. "I pulled my own tooth out." The words, spoken aloud, fed the spark of self-belief that flickered inside her chest.

She'd hidden a half-bottle of water and one energy bar under her mattress. Stashing food away had become her habit. Sometimes he didn't come for two days, so she'd learned to make the meagre rations last. She crawled back to the bed, not wanting to waste energy standing. She decided to eat half of the bar and take three sips of water. Maybe with something in her stomach, she'd be able to think clearly and come up with another idea.

The energy bar tasted dry and woody, as if even through small things he enjoyed punishing her. In spite of the taste, she attempted to wolf down half the bar in one bite, wincing and coughing. Her injured throat forced her to eat slower, savour the sensation of food in her mouth, while her stomach lurched up and demanded satisfaction. She washed the crumbs down with a few sips of water, doing her best to ignore the ooze of blood from the empty socket in her gum.

The golden stream of afternoon light morphed to a dull grey. Soon it would be almost impossible to see. She had to think of something now. Her gaze landed on the cuffs. If he came back before she'd escaped—her thoughts stuttered. She wondered if she'd ever leave this hellish room. As the doubt crept in, she could feel herself losing focus. Her mother would be at home—waiting. Waiting and wondering where her daughter had gone. *Do they know someone took me away?* She almost hoped they thought their daughter had disappeared to follow a secret boyfriend or reinvent herself in another state.

Her hands throbbed, especially the left one. Her gaze kept coming back to the cuffs. She picked them up, hating the stiff feel of the leather. They reminded her of a dog collar. She pressed her lips together in a thin line. She'd slipped her collar and had no intention of ever being chained up again. It occurred to her that if she pushed her hands through the cuffs, just up to the knuckles, he probably wouldn't notice she was free. Unless he wanted to beat and grind on her, he barely glanced her way. He treated her very much like a dog—an unloved mutt that didn't even deserve a word. Well, she'd broken free now and, maybe, she'd get the chance to bite the hand that fed her.

It wasn't much, but it made her feel stronger. Having made progress in some way, even taking back something small, like the freedom to move around the room, gave her a tiny shred of control over her life. She had a secret that she could keep from him. Something that was hers. A smile creased her hollow cheeks.

She decided to walk around the room while there was still enough light. It felt good to move her legs more than a few steps to the toilet bucket. Outside the rain began to fall, she could hear it pattering on the tin roof. Andrea shivered. The cold had become similar to the hunger—a constant. During the night, the temperature would drop with a viciousness that often woke her from sleep. Moving helped.

She crossed the room and examined the door. There was something odd about it. From across the room, she hadn't been able to see it but up close there was a peep hole. She pulled her face back and grimaced. Even after everything he'd done to her, the realisation that he spied on her sent a sickening quiver through her stomach. She imagined him on the other side of the door watching her crouch over the bucket; tears of shame blurred her eyes.

She'd never really hated anyone before, not even the girls at school who bullied her. She disliked them, envied their slim bodies and pretty faces, but never felt the black poisonous taste of real hatred until that moment. Her wounded hands clasped in fists, she leaned against the door.

Whatever lay beyond her cell was steeped in darkness. Andrea pressed the right side of her face to the door, feeling the chill of metal kiss her skin. The possibility that he might be on the other side, maybe even looking back at her, made her catch her breath. It was impossible to see what might be lurking on the other side. A sense of disappointment mingled with relief. She felt sure he wasn't there.

For now, she was safe. But safe to do what? Andrea let her forehead dip and lean against the door. A wave of fatigue pulled at her like a strong rip trying to drag her from solid ground into muddy thoughts and half-sleep. She coughed, covering her mouth with her dirty fingers. Judging by the dull quality of the light, she had maybe twenty minutes before darkness drove her back to the mattress.

*My mother knows I haven't run away.* Andrea pushed herself off the door and forced her body to move. From her spot on the mattress, the corners of the room were always in shadows. When she'd used the toilet, she'd always been so focused on getting the vile task over with, she'd never taken the time to look around. Now, with the freedom to move and the knowledge he wasn't listening outside the door, she worked her way around the room.

The building had been used for some sort of farming purposes. That was as much as she could come up with. It had a dusty wooden floor, and brick walls that ended about a metre short of the roof, the gap filled by widely spaced boards. Taking in as many details as possible, she made her way to the far corner. As she moved, her fingers trailed the wall just as they'd done when she was a child running along the front fence of her nanna's house. Only then, she'd known kisses and Tim Tams waited for her when the front door opened.

Without realising it, she hummed a long-forgotten song. Something her nanna taught her on one of those Saturdays when her parents were both working. Andrea reached the corner and stopped. There was something bundled up against the wall.

She reached out a hand, half expecting a rat to jump from the pile and scurry up her arm. Instead, her fingers found coarse fabric, maybe an old sheet. She pulled the bundle and it unfolded with a cloud of dirt and dust. The taste of the powder in her mouth set off another coughing fit, only this time, her chest clenched with each breath.

The filthy fabric turned out to be an ancient yellow curtain. At least it might have once been yellow. Now it was more the colour of dry porridge. Holding her breath, she shook the curtain sending up another cloud of dust then threw it around her shoulders like a cape. The curtain stank of age and dampness and the fabric felt grimy and stiff, but the added warmth was so wonderful on her shoulders, she laughed out loud. For the first time in what seemed like months, she stopped shivering.

The rain fell in an urgent rush, tapping the tin roof like dead fingers on a coffin lid. Up close, she could see rivers of water leaching in through the gap between the roof and the wall. Maybe the mouthful of food gave her the boost she had needed or it could be the new feeling of hope that came from being close to warm, but Andrea had an idea.

She scampered back to the mattress and grabbed the water bottle. If she angled it right, the rain should run in through the neck. It wasn't the freedom she'd dreamed of, but a few extra sips of water could mean the difference between life and death. All she had to do was hold the bottle at a forty-five-degree angle as close to the top of the wall as she could reach—simple.

Her arm quivered with the exertion, and the torn-up skin on the back of her hand made holding the bottle for longer than a couple of minutes excruciating. *I can do it*, she told herself through fits of coughing and cramps that burned her shoulder like a blow torch. And for a while, she was right. The water trickled into the plastic bottle at a surprising rate. Within minutes, it went from half to three-quarters full.

The rain fell with growing intensity. The bottle, now slippery with rainwater slid though Andrea's fingers. Lightening-quick reflexes stopped the plastic container from dropping from her grasp. Clasping the bottle to her chest, she slid sideways and down the wall; her behind hit the floor with a solid *thump*.

A laugh that sounded more like a squeal echoed in the empty room. "I didn't run away." She raised the bottle to her lips and took a sip. The water tasted rusty and cold on her tongue, like drinking from an old tap. It was the sweetest thing she'd ever drank.

Andrea held the bottle like a prize trophy. She'd found a way to extend her water supply that didn't include the monster who snatched her up and tortured her. All the taunts and cruel names that had plagued her since school fell away. She wasn't the *Baby Pig*, the *Blubber Roll*. She didn't deserve to be hurt and bullied. She'd never hurt anyone, never used spiteful names to make herself feel big. None of this nightmare was her fault.

The thought of being on the other side of the room when darkness fell drove her back to the mattress. Tucking her legs under her and stashing the bottle back in its hiding place made her feel grounded—safe. *There is no such thing as safety*. She understood that now. There was only survival and, today, she'd proved to herself she could be strong. She'd freed herself from the cuffs and found water, tomorrow she'd find a way out.

The short trip around the room left her exhausted and panting. As darkness settled over the room, the rain dwindled to a light patter. With the curtain pulled up to her chin and the cuffs tucked under her arm, just in case, Andrea slept.

# Chapter Twenty

"Terry?" She couldn't hide the disappointment in her voice. Even though she'd brought the knife with her, she still wanted to believe it would be Lee at her door.

"Hi." He looked anxious, maybe even worried. "Sorry to bother you, but it's…" His shoulders slumped. "It's Robbie."

Something was wrong. She could see it in his posture, hear it in his voice. She barely knew him, but it was clear the man was troubled. Robbie was the first friend Mina had made in years. The thought of something happening to her struck a deep chord of concern, washing away all thoughts of Lee and a passionate reunion.

"What's happened? Is she okay?"

Briggs shook his head. Mina picked up on his obvious distress and felt a wave of panic hit her. "Please, Terry, just tell me."

"Can I come in?" The outside light cast a glare around his head, bathing him in a dazzling halo. Mina had to squint to see his face.

"Yes. Yes, of course. Come in." She opened the door wide and stepped to the side so he could pass. The knife dangled at her side, concealed by the loose folds of her oversized T-shirt. She closed the door behind him.

He walked through the lounge and into the kitchen. It struck her as strange that he didn't stop in the lounge and wait for her to direct him to sit. But fear of the bad news that might be to come, quickly swallowed up the thought.

Mina followed Briggs into the kitchen. He wore a black jacket zipped up to the neck. His hair was damp and a fine mist of raindrops glistened on his shoulders. In spite of socialising with him, for some reason she still thought of him as *Briggs* rather than Terry. He stopped walking and stood near the fridge. She had to step around him to enter the room. It was an awkward manoeuvre where her shoulder brushed against his arm. For some reason, the way he lingered near the kitchen entrance annoyed her. She felt a fleeting push of anger. It seemed selfish, almost deliberately obstructive. *I'm being ridiculous, he's awkward and upset*. She wished that just for once, she could be patient and empathetic instead of always thinking of her own frustrations.

"Do you want a cup of coffee?" She stepped away from him and stood next to the sink. She turned her back so he wouldn't notice the knife dangling at her side.

He let out a breath. "Thanks." She waited for him to say something else, but there was only silence. She wished he'd speak. Spit it out, whatever it was. Anything would be better than the unknown.

An upbeat pop track played in the background, something about sunshine. Mina slid the knife onto the counter and picked up the kettle. She glanced over her shoulder and hesitated. He seemed different, bigger than when she'd last seen him. Their eyes locked and she realised he'd seen her staring. She turned back to the kettle, filling it with water and turning it on.

When he'd shown her the house and when they'd met again at the pub, he'd been stooped over, his shoulders curled in slightly. That's what was different. Now he stood with his back straight. She could hear his breathing over the music. There was something off about him. Shock, or maybe grief?

"I hope instant's alright, it's all I've got."

"Mmm." The seconds drew out and the moment seemed uncomfortably long.

She spooned coffee into a mug, regretting offering him a drink. She wanted him to give her the bad news and get out of her house. *For fuck sake, just tell me*, the words were on the tip of her tongue. But Mina thought of Robbie. She'd want her to be kind to him.

Swallowing her impatience, she struggled to think of something to say. "I should get one of those coffee machines. You know the ones that make cappuccino." She tried for a laugh, but it came out sounding more like a sniff.

"The gift that keeps on giving."

The nape of Mina's neck tingled. The words hung in the air while the music changed from upbeat pop to a slow ballad. Her sight narrowed to tunnel vision and fixed on the coffee mug. She didn't blink. Her breathing grew shallow. Every cell in her body poised on edge. She forced her hand to keep moving, spooning more coffee into the cup.

In six words, he'd revealed himself. She'd been so consumed with worry about what others might see in her, she'd looked at Briggs and saw only a cheerful overzealous salesman when a monster had been lurking in plain sight. Trying to deny what she'd heard in his voice would be a deadly mistake. Whatever she did next would most likely decide her fate.

As the seconds ticked by, the air seemed charged with energy as if something was about to explode. The smell of coffee granules coated the insides of her nostrils. Her phone lay on the counter to her right, alongside the stovetop. The back door stood just a few metres farther. The knife was closer.

144

An echo of an old familiar feeling emerged. Calm in the face of fear. It saw her through the blackest days of her life. In her mind, she pictured her father looming over her, eyes bulging and fists clenched. She heard her mother's muffled sobs as she tried to suck in air after it had been punched from her body. In those moments, Mina learned to hold her nerve, ride out the storm.

"I think we should go." His voice startled her. The tone so casual, as if there were an unspoken understanding between them. It was more chilling than the silence.

She put the spoon in the cup and placed her hands on the counter, inching closer to the knife. Had he seen it when she let him in?

"Where will we go?" She spoke slowly, each word carefully placed, not yet ready to turn around.

"I know you don't want to come." The floorboards creaked as he stepped towards her. "But we're the same— once you see that, we can do anything we want."

He stood behind her, not quite touching, but close. She made herself turn, keeping her body in contact with the counter and sliding slightly to the left. His watery blue eyes travelled over her face. She'd been this close to evil before, but her father had been a familiar monster. Terrance Briggs was a new and unknown threat.

They were less than a metre apart. Briggs stood over her and for the first time she noticed his odour: musky and sickly sweet. Up close, the skin on his face appeared porous. At one hundred and eighty centimetres, Mina was rather tall for a woman, but she had to tilt her head to look into his eyes.

He let out a breath. "You're so beautiful, but you know that, don't you?" His lips were thick, almost feminine. "You're a tough one, Mina. But you know that too." He took a breath, inhaling deeply, absorbing her smell. She resisted the urge to shrink away from him. Something told her that showing fear would be dangerous.

"I'm expecting someone." Even as the words came out, she knew they sounded unconvincing.

"I don't think you are." His voice was soft, almost a whisper. "You shouldn't lie to me. Stupid lies are for the weak." He shook his head. "I want to be patient with you." He brought his hand up quickly as if to strike her, but waggled a finger in her face instead. She winced and moved to the left. She could see by his expression that her reaction pleased him. "But there are too many liars in the world and my patience only stretches so far."

"Where's Andrea?" She snapped off the question like a gunshot.

He frowned. The pleasure that lit up his bland features changed to confusion.

"What did you do to her?" She could hear the tremor in her voice.

He tipped his head to the left. "Ah, the gift that keeps on giving. She's doing…" He hesitated. "As well as can be expected."

"Where is she?" Mina's voice trembled with a combination of fear and anger. He didn't even recognise the name. Andrea was so unimportant to him that at first he didn't even know who she was talking about. To him, women were just things to be used and forgotten. No, worse than that, he viewed them in the same way her father had, bags of skin to be beaten and terrorised.

"You seem concerned, but when you gave her to me, it looked like you found her distasteful." He smiled, one side of his mouth jerking skywards. His face took on the look of a mask, clownish and stretched over sharp bones. It was as if she was really seeing him for the first time. Why had she never noticed how freakishly clown-like he looked when he smiled? *Because he kept that smile hidden.* The smile Briggs showed the world looked cheerful and harmless; he'd practiced it and knew when to use it to fool people. She wondered fleetingly how she could possibly know that about him, but the truth was, she'd studied her own face often enough with the same question in mind: *do I look normal?*

"I didn't give her to you. You took her." She could feel something building in her stomach, stretching and growing. Moving sideways, Mina tried to push past him and in the process reach backwards and grab the knife.

His reflexes were fast. He grabbed her right arm and jerked her back in place so that she was pressed against the counter. She curled her fingers around the knife's handle and held it at her side. He pressed his body against hers, pinning her in place.

"Do you think I won't hurt you?" The glare of the overhead lighting reflected in his eyes making them glitter. "I will if I have to." Still grinning, he leaned in and pressed his mouth against hers; his lips parted so that he created a seal over her entire mouth. "Mmm," he murmured.

Her gut clenched with revulsion. She closed her eyes and tried to turn her head, he clamped his hand on the back of her neck, pushing her towards him She could feel the wetness of his mouth sucking at her skin. In the background the pop music banged in a jarring beat. Mina brought the knife up, blindly searching for a target. The angle was wrong and her grip clumsy, her only hope was the back of his neck.

With his mouth still plastered to hers, she opened her eyes. She could feel him growing hard against her and panic threatened to swallow all thought.

She had to act.

Holding the knife behind his shoulder, she pivoted her wrist to get a better angle. Something alerted him, maybe the slither of her arm against his shoulder. He opened his eyes just as she stabbed downwards. The blade made contact. It caught the collar of his jacket.

She pushed down with as much force as she could muster with her left hand and on such an awkward angle. The tip of the blade moved and there was a sliding sensation. Briggs pulled back. A hiss of air escaped through his clenched teeth. He took hold of her arm just below the elbow and plucked it away from his neck.

"Very nasty." He sounded almost pleased.

There was blood on the knife. She could see it still clenched in her fist, the blade tipped with red. He shook her arm trying to jiggle the knife from her hand, but she held on.

"Let go." His tone remained pleasant, with a hint of admonishment. When she refused to comply, he chuckled and pushed his hips against her. "You're sexy when you're angry. I knew you would be." His eyes, still trained on her face, seemed to be unnaturally fixated.

His closeness made her skin crawl. He seemed to be all over her, filling her field of vision and pressing against her body. Even though she clung to the knife, she knew she'd missed her chance. She could think of no other way of hurting him, so she pulled her head back and spat in his face.

Her spittle hit him just above the mouth, dripping off his nose and upper lip like a frothy, white milk-moustache. His expression changed from amusement to anger so fast it was as if the fury had always been there shifting below the surface.

Briggs made a noise, a harsh sound somewhere between a howl and a gasp. He grabbed Mina by the upper arms and lifted her off the floor. Gathering momentum as he turned, he swung her with ease like she was no heavier than a child. She felt her body leave the ground and, for a second, she seemed to be spinning.

Her back hit the kitchen table. She heard herself grunt as the air rocketed out of her lungs. Her head hit something sharp and the sound of braking crockery pierced the air as the table shook under the force of the impact.

Sprawled flat on her back, Mina's eyelids fluttered and then the ceiling came into focus. She couldn't see Briggs but could hear him moving around the room. The music had stopped and the only sounds that remained were her laboured breathing and the crunch of his shoes on broken china. Something slapped against the side of the table with a rubbery hiss. Her back ached from the violent collision with the table and her lungs seemed to shudder with the effort of breathing.

Groaning, she pushed herself up onto her elbows. The room rocked slightly and then her equilibrium returned. Briggs stood at the end of the table. He held the cord from her laptop, letting it dangle from his right hand. His head was turned away, searching for something. In profile, his nose looked pointed. She could see a smear of blood on the side of his neck from where she'd stabbed at him.

One glance told her what he meant to do. He'd use the cord to tie her up and then she'd be at his mercy. The feeling of something growing inside intensified until her whole body seemed to expand. A breeze, curling its way under the kitchen door, caressed her face, cooling the fear until only stillness remained.

Briggs turned and stooped, his head disappearing from view. Mina moved with liquid speed, pulling her legs up to her chest, pivoting and sliding off the table. Before she knew what she intended to do, her hand gripped the heavy cast iron pan. The smell of cooked meat juices wafted up as she lofted it across her body, like a tennis player preparing for a backhand.

Briggs held the extension lead that ran from the side of the fridge to the socket. He must have heard her approach because he turned towards her and straightened up. His mouth hung open, lips still damp from the wet kiss he'd forced on her, or maybe from her spittle.

"You kn—"

Mina swung the pan, cutting off whatever he was about to say. The flat side of the fryer hit him just above the ear with a ringing clang. His head jerked sideways and his left leg slid out from under him, scraping across the floorboards.

He tried to regain his footing, but his right leg trembled and gave out. He turned his head towards her, his lips moving as if trying to form a word. "Thuludge." Whatever he'd been trying to say came out as a nonsensical sound.

Mina raised the pan, this time above her shoulder; ready to pound him down if he tried to get up again. He lurched forward and flopped onto his belly. She waited, listening to the sound of her own rapid breathing and watching Briggs' still form.

He was unconscious or dead, she didn't really care which. The only thing that mattered was that he didn't get up, at least until the police arrived. The pan suddenly felt like it weighed fifty kilos. Her arm trembled with the effort of holding it. She couldn't stand over him until help arrived nor could she risk allowing him to regain consciousness. There had to be another way.

Using two hands now, she lowered the pan and set it on the table. The feelings of strength and certainty that had driven her to overpower him ebbed. She had to keep moving, keep the adrenalin working for her. Her mobile phone was on the counter, the most obvious course of action would be to call the police.

Her mind raced with possibilities: leave Briggs, take her phone and drive away; she could phone the police from her car, or better still, drive to the local police station.

Time was ticking, he'd been on the floor for at least two minutes. She had to move, yet her feet remained glued to the spot. If she left, he could get up. He'd have time to disappear. If that happened, what would become of Andrea?

Mina wrapped her arms around herself. He'd implied Andrea was still alive. *As well as can be expected.* If she left him, she'd be risking the girl's life. On the other hand, if

150

she stayed with him till the police arrived, he might try to get up and attack her again.

Mina looked around the kitchen taking in the smashed plate laying on the floor and the food scraps from her dinner littering the table. There had to be a way of ensuring he didn't escape. Her gaze fell on Briggs' body sprawled in front of the fridge.

The scene was all too familiar.

Instead of calling the police, she stared at the man on her floor. Her father had fallen in a similar position, only Briggs lay on his stomach with his face turned to the side and her father had been staring up at her. Was it a coincidence that these things always seemed to end in the kitchen?

She recalled the wide-eyed look of panic on her father's face as he realised what was happening. Had it been terror in his eyes or realisation? She'd never been sure. In his final moments did he recognise the same cold, cruelty in her as in himself? She could almost feel the way his fingers gripped her shoulder, fighting against her unrelenting hands. She'd lived with the guilt of what she'd done for so long, it wasn't until this moment that she recognised the sense of release and satisfaction she'd drawn from killing her father.

Thomas Constantine was a monster, similar in many ways to Briggs. When she'd killed him, the world had become a better place. A safer place for Mina and her mother. She reached out her hand and touched the pan. It would be easy to finish what she'd started. One or two solid blows and it would be over, Briggs would never hurt anyone else. The cast iron pan felt startlingly cold against her fingers. There was a part of her—a big part—that wanted to do it. Maybe that's what stopped her.

She drew her hand away. If she killed him, Andrea might never be found. Even if he was lying and the girl was dead, didn't she deserve to be recovered? Didn't her family deserve the consolation of knowing what happened

151

to her? Mina ran her fingers through her hair and nodded. She'd phone the police and wait, take her chances with Briggs until help arrived.

She noticed the laptop cord on the floor next to his right hand. *I'll only tie him up until the police arrive*, but even as the words raced across her mind, another voice whispered the truth. She had no intention of calling the police.

Touching him was the hardest part. The thought of his wet mouth sucking at her face made her want to run away in disgust. Instead, she crouched next to him and felt his neck. His pulse thumped in a strong, steady rhythm, his skin felt warm. She supposed that was a good sign.

When she pulled his hands behind his back, he showed no sign of movement. His limbs seemed floppy, he appeared to be deeply unconscious. Using the cord, she bound his hands together behind his back. Then following his line of thinking, she crawled over to the side of the fridge and pulled out the plug. The extension cord was long enough to bind his feet together and then attach the remainder of the cable to his hands. When she'd finished, Briggs was almost hog-tied. The only difference being his legs were straight and not bent behind his back.

"Briggs." She raised her voice and spat the name in his ear. "Hey. Do you hear me?" After a moment's pause, she slapped him on the side of the face. Nothing. His breathing came slow and regular like he was in a deep sleep.

She leaned back and sat on the floor. "Now what?" she asked the unconscious man. Even as she asked, a plan took shape.

Grunting with the effort, she rolled Briggs onto his back. Mina grimaced and snaked her hand inside his jacket. The inner pocket held his phone. She grabbed it and put it on the floor. She could see the bulge of his keys in the front pocket of his black pants. She had no choice but to reach her fingers in and fish them out.

"Oh fuck." Her fingers came away damp. He'd wet himself. The thought of having Briggs' bodily fluid on her fingers made Mina's stomach churn. She swallowed and tossed the keys on the floor next to the phone.

She'd need to go through all his pockets, search him. There was no telling what he might be carrying. It took her less than three minutes to go through them all and pat him down. He wasn't carrying any ID or personal items, but she did find a large knife in a nylon sheaf strapped to his calf. There was something evil looking about the black sheaf, the way the fabric curved and hugged the blade. She wondered how many women he'd hurt or threatened with the deadly weapon and grimaced.

When she'd finished searching him, she wiped her hands on the leg of his pants and stood. She dumped the phone, keys and knife on the table and checked the time on her watch 7:40 p.m. It had been less than twenty minutes since she'd opened her door to Briggs and now he lay unconscious on her kitchen floor—her prisoner. Standing over his body, she could find no pity for the man, only a grim determination. As long as she had him, Andrea was safe from harm.

Maybe after everything she'd done in her twenty-nine years, she'd finally managed to help someone—do something good. But then another thought occurred to her, *how long can Andrea survive?* She had no idea what physical condition the girl was in *or* where he'd put her. Mina glanced at the kitchen window. The pane looked black and empty. Andrea could be anywhere. If Briggs didn't regain consciousness, there'd be little hope of ever finding her.

How long had he been out? It couldn't be more than five or six minutes—ten at the most. She couldn't keep him in the house and risk Robbie or someone else dropping by. She had to secure him somewhere and hope he woke up. Her first thought had been the bedroom, but having him in the house with her would be too risky.

Mina tapped a finger to her lips. She recalled seeing a wheelbarrow in the aluminium shed at the rear of the property. She remembered thinking it was in fairly good shape, it could be used to transport Briggs. If she could wheel him the almost thirty metres to the old brick shed, she'd be able to secure him there until she had time to think.

With a plan in mind, Mina flicked on the back lights. The shed keys hung on a hook near the back door. She snatched them off the wall and left the house. Her purchases from that day were stacked under the sloping roof that partially covered the deck. The rain had stopped, leaving the earth damp and rivers of water dripping off the roof. She took the heavy-duty torch, the length of chain, and the padlocks out of the green plastic bags. Next to the bags sat the two tomato plants. She let out a breath and hefted the chain over her shoulder. *Maybe gardening's not my thing.*

A few minutes later, she wheeled the barrow up to the deck. Near the three steps that led down to the garden there was a metre drop off at the edge of the timber deck. She parked the wheelbarrow alongside the drop. If she could drag Briggs out of the house and onto the deck, she'd only have to roll him into the barrow. The hardest part would be wheeling him the distance to the outbuilding. A task that would be made more difficult by the rain-dampened ground.

"Shit." She dragged the back of her hand across her forehead, it came away moist with sweat. Despite the chilly night air, her skin felt hot. An owl hooted from the darkness of the trees, an eerie sound when mingled with the drip of water from the eaves. *What am I doing?* She could still call the police, put an end to her crazy plan. But the real truth was, the moment Briggs revealed himself as the Magician, his fate was sealed. She would deal with him as she'd done with her father. *And Mum,* a voice in her head whispered. Mina pushed the thought away and went back inside the kitchen.

Briggs had moved. Her heart rate jumped, her back tensed as if she were about to be attacked. When she left the house, he'd been on his back with his legs held together by the extension cord. Now he was on his left side, face pressed to the floor. His breathing had changed from deep and regular to nasal. Dipping her head, she forced her shoulders to flex and relax. It would be disastrous if she allowed panic to swamp her. He'd moved, that's all. A good sign. *Dangerous, but good.*

If he was nearing consciousness, she had to get him secured as quickly as possible. Stopping to think about what might happen would only slow her down. She forced her body to keep moving. First lifting his legs, then dragging him across the room. He was lighter than she'd guessed or maybe the adrenalin blasting through her system made her strong. Either way, she had him at the backdoor in a few seconds. She dropped his feet and opened the door, cursing herself for not thinking to prop it open before she started. *I've got to do this right,* she told herself. Mistakes could be deadly.

A few minutes later, she stood next to the wheelbarrow and began the process of shifting his body from the deck to the barrow. She grabbed his jacket with her right hand, just below his shoulder. Then, using her other hand, she grabbed him by the waistband of his pants and pulled. It was like tugging on a dead elephant. He gave a snort and drool ran from the side of his mouth, but his body barely moved.

After a few more gut-wrenching pulls, she realised it wasn't going to work.

"Great." She let her arms drop to her sides and grimaced as a gurgling sound escaped his open mouth.

"Now what?"

"Duh duh."

Mina took a step back. It was almost as if he'd tried to answer her. "Briggs?" She reached out and poked his shoulder. "Can you hear me?"

His face looked almost yellow under the deck lights. She noticed the left side of his head looked swollen as if a large golf ball were buried under the skin.

"Better out than in." She'd heard that somewhere about head injuries. Something about the swelling on the outside being better than on the inside. She waited a beat to see if he would speak again, but the only sound was the rhythmic drip of water as it ran off the gutters.

Trying to pull him from the deck was never going to work, so she scampered up the steps and crouched down beside him. The acrid stench of urine stung her nose. She'd planned to push him but at the last moment, came up with a better idea. Spinning on her butt, she pressed her shoes against his arm and side, and pushed. To her surprise, he slid off the deck like melted butter slipping across a hot pan. The second his torso disappeared over the edge, a dull clang rang out.

Mina muttered a curse and jumped up. His legs were still half on the deck, his black leather boots caught by the heels on the wooden rim. Looking over the edge, she realised the clang came from the back of his head landing in the wheelbarrow. She rubbed her fingers across her forehead and screwed up her eyes. She had to be more careful. If she accidentally killed him, that would be it. Andrea would be as good as dead.

His eyelids fluttered.

# Chapter Twenty-one

It was fully dark when the pulsing pain in her hands pulled Andrea from sleep. For an instant, just before dreaming dropped away, she forgot where she was. But the fetid smell of the toilet bucket and the unrelenting cold brought her back. She clamped her mouth closed and listened: water dripping… a *tap tap* of drops against the roof. The room cloaked in black revealed nothing.

"Is someone there?" Her voice sounded alien, like that of a very old woman. She waited. If he was in the room, he wouldn't answer. But in her dream, a voice had been calling her, singing her name over and over again. For some reason, the woman she'd met at the college the night all this madness started, popped to mind.

The dream seemed so real, her heart still skittered with the memory. She sat up and wrapped her hands around her knees. She could detect no movement in the room. He sometimes came at night, but maybe the rain kept him away. If that were true, she wished for a flood, lashing rain that would continue until the building she sat in washed away. Drowning would be better than this slow crawl towards death.

A cough, deep and wet rocked her body. She pressed her cheek to her knees and tried to recall the dream. There'd been a woman, Andrea could almost see her: pale eyes, wearing a black cloak or hood. She looked like Regina, the girl in Andrea's book, *Moon dance*. Or at least how she imagined the beautiful protagonist would look. Tall, with perfect features set in pale skin. Similar, she realised, to the woman from the college. Regina was strong and resourceful, everything Andrea wasn't.

It was ridiculous, she knew, but nevertheless Andrea tried to imagine what Regina would do in her situation. The young woman in Andrea's book was only a figment of her imagination, but she embodied everything that was strong and indomitable. Regina was the woman Andrea could never be. *She wouldn't lay here snivelling.* Andrea swiped at her nose with the inside of her wrist, taking care to avoid the back of her hand.

*Regina would have never let herself be abducted in the first place, she'd have fought back.* Andrea wondered if fighting would have done any good. He was strong, brutal. If she'd tried harder, could she have broken free? Since the first night she'd spent in that room, she'd gone over those moments. She'd tried to struggle but he hit her so hard. She'd never been hit before. A few girls at school—the ones that called her baby pig—had pushed her, but that had been more of a sly shoulder as they walked past. The way he'd punched her, it shocked as much as it hurt.

It wouldn't do her any good thinking about what she didn't do; what mattered now was what she did next. She closed her eyes and summoned an image of Regina. She could almost see the tall slim figure moving around the room, her dark hair fluttering out behind her like wings. In Andrea's mind, Regina ran her fingers over the walls searching for... for... her mind faltered. She coughed and tasted something thick and sour bubbling up her throat. With a grimace, she swallowed the vile glob. She'd search for a foothold, a way to climb the wall and reach the boards that made up the metre or so between the roof and the bricks.

Andrea lifted her head. The room lay in a darkness so deep, it seemed to push back at her. *There has to be a weak spot up there.* It made sense. During the day, light came in from between the lengths of wood. Rain leaked through the gaps. Her mind raced forward. *Rain and sunlight would have weakened the wood.* She could feel her heart thundering, not with fear but excitement. All she had to do now was wait until morning.

For the first time in what felt like weeks, she had something to hold on to—hope. Once she could see, she'd find a way out.

# Chapter Twenty-two

Briggs mumbled something unintelligible. His blue eyes fixed on Mina's, drilling into her with startled intensity. She stared down from the deck and waited. If he started bucking and trying to fight his way out of the wheelbarrow, there'd be little chance of getting him to the back shed. The seconds ticked by. His lids wavered then closed. She shook her head and took a deep breath.

Now that the moment had passed, she couldn't be sure what she'd seen in his eyes. Fury? Fear? He was hurt and trapped, it would be natural for him to feel either emotion, yet it seemed there had been something else lurking in those unmoving, cold eyes. An emptiness that reminded her of her father. Even as the thought occurred to her, she recognised it for what it was—justification. Doing this thing—taking another human being captive—was easier if she could ignore his humanity. Projecting her hatred for her father onto Briggs was a way of mitigating her actions.

Mina wiped her hands on the front of her jeans. *He's a killer.* She couldn't lose sight of the things he'd done. The rain stopped, but she had to get him to the shed before it started again.

The steps were damp, her right foot slipped and she almost took a tumble on her way off the deck. Righting herself just in time, she let loose a stream of invectives before snatching up the torch from beside the wheelbarrow. The lights from the deck spilled out for five or so metres, but beyond that the property was swallowed by night.

It took longer than she'd expected to reach the back shed. There was an uneven brick path leading to the side of the first shed, but hefting the wheels up and down over the broken stones proved to be almost impossible. After ten minutes spent struggling with the handles, she gave up and steered the cart off the path and onto the grass. The torch, balanced on Briggs' stomach, bounced light off the thick growth of trees that ringed the sides of the shed. To her surprise, the going was much easier. Without the constant up and down she made better time.

It took another ten minutes of spurts of movement and rest stops before she rounded the first shed and headed farther into the darkness. Despite the cold night air, her hair lay plastered with sweat to her face and neck. She set the handles of the barrow down and wiped her face with the edge of her T-shirt. Her arms felt weightless and shaky.

She picked up the torch and turned it on Briggs. His torso filled the barrow. Like an oversized puppet, his butt balanced over the edge, his legs trailing on the soggy ground. During the journey from the house, he'd groaned and mumbled, but gave no signs of waking further. He'd been semiconscious for at least half an hour. She had no idea how long was too long. All she could do was push on and hope for the best.

Using her T-shirt again, she wiped her sweaty hands, wincing at the blisters forming across her palms. She plonked the torch back on his stomach and picked up the handles. This would be her last rest stop. With her strength dwindling, if she put the barrow down again she knew she wouldn't have the will to pick it up.

"Okay," she managed through gritted teeth. "The woods are lovely, dark and deep, but I have promises to keep, and miles to go before I sleep." The words came out as grunts between breaths. She wasn't sure where they came from. A poem she'd read years ago, maybe at university. Somehow the words were clear in her memory as if she'd read it only yesterday. The same lines continued to play over and over in her mind like a mantra. It helped her focus and force one foot in front of the other.

When the back shed came in view, it appeared for less than a second. The bouncing light hit the red brick and then jolted up. For a moment, she thought she'd imagined it, but with the next step came another glimpse of the building.

"Hah," her voice rasped out over dry lips and panting breath. She pushed forward taking the last few steps on burning legs.

The door had been black at some point in the past. Now only jagged scraps of paint clung to the heavy wood. Mina fumbled the keys out of her pocket under the shaky light of the torch. Her fingers, throbbing from the constant weight of the handles, felt numb. The key refused to work, fitting halfway in the keyhole and then jamming. For one terrifying moment, she convinced herself that the key didn't fit and she'd have to wheel Briggs all the way back to the house.

On her third attempt, the key slid in place and turned. The relief took her breath away. If she hadn't been leaning against the doorframe, Mina probably would have toppled to the side. As it was, she let her head rest against the ancient wood and closed her eyes. She wondered briefly if her mother watched over her, but just as quickly rejected the sentiment. If those who loved you watched from the other side, it meant there could also be malevolent forces conspiring to cause harm. She didn't want to image her father's pale dead eyes following her progress.

She glanced at Briggs, his outline black and shadowed. If the dead could influence the living, he'd be in serious trouble. *So would I.* It didn't bear thinking about. The dead were gone and nothing could bring them back. Mina had come to accept that she was on her own in this world, so her only hope was to take care of herself. That's why she'd left Andrea that night, frightened and alone. *Now I'm putting things right*, she told herself and pushed open the shed door.

There was no source of light inside the brick structure. The only illumination came from the torch which broke through the dark to reveal stark brick walls, jarrah beams, and a concrete slab. The smell of rot and rodent droppings hung in the air. The old storage shed reminded her of the prison cells she'd seen while touring the Old Melbourne Jail with her mother. Only the cells had been tiny, the walls crowding in so that spending only moments inside made your skin crawl with the feeling of being trapped. The back shed was wide and cavernous, yet somehow just as oppressive.

Briggs groaned, snapping her back to action. She dumped the torch back on his stomach and jostled the barrow over the thin concrete lip that acted as a threshold. In the last hour, she'd become quite adept at manoeuvring the cart. In seconds, she had the wheelbarrow inside the room.

"Right." Mina nodded at the upright beam standing like a thick bare tree trunk in the centre of the room. "All that's left is to get you set up in here." Her voice echoed off the bricks making it sound like she was inside a cave.

She thought of pitching the cart sideways and letting Briggs roll out, but that would mean risking his head hitting the concrete. She gathered her hair over her right shoulder and tucked it in the neck of her T-shirt. The sweat that had built up on her neck and arms went from hot to icy. She shivered and wrapped her arms around herself. *If only I'd put on a jacket or jumper.* The thought gave her an idea.

Untying him would be the riskiest part. Taking a large swallow, she half rolled, half shoved him onto his left side and untied his hands. If he were faking, now would be the time he'd make a move. The knotted cord took some work, but within seconds, his hands were free. His right arm jerked. Mina hefted the heavy-duty torch over his head, ready to smash the bridge of his nose if he made a move. He let out a groan, but lay still. She let out a breath and relaxed.

Wrestling Briggs' jacket off took work. She couldn't sit him up, instead she used a technique she'd seen in an old film where a nurse had changed the sheets under an unconscious man. It looked much easier in the movies, but by rolling him one way and stripping the jacket half off, then repeating the process on the other side, she managed to get him out of the heavy padded garment. In just a black T-shirt and pants, he looked smaller, less imposing. Or maybe the defencelessness of his posture made him look less of a threat. Either way, Mina didn't intend to relax her guard.

She remembered watching a news program where a shark got caught on a drum-line being hauled aboard a fishing boat. The creature looked pathetic and vulnerable. But turn that same shark loose in the water and it would return to its deadly nature. Briggs was like that shark. A killer. The sooner she had him secured and rendered helpless, the better.

Once she'd wrapped the padded jacket around his head, she lifted the handles of the wheelbarrow and tipped it to the side. His legs hit the floor first, landing with a rustle of fabric and a soft thump. When his shoulder made contact with the concrete, his body bounced slightly and rolled backwards letting his head land with only a slight bump. The noisiest part was when the chain and padlocks tumbled out after him. Mina let out a long shaky breath.

The hardest part was over. She felt the urge to sink to the floor next to the unmoving form and rest her burning limbs.

*I can rest later.* She imagined sliding into a hot bath. If she worked quickly, the last part would be over in minutes. Then there would be plenty of time to rest *and* think. She nodded and shone the torch on Briggs' head, still wrapped in the jacket. It would be easy to pull the fabric taut over his mouth and nose. A few minutes and it would all be over. She wiped her mouth with the back of her hand and smelled urine. Killing him would be easy, but living with the guilt of Andrea's death would eat at her.

She crouched down and unwrapped the jacket. Her fingers brushed the back of his neck and came away bloody. Absently, she wiped her hand on Briggs' T-shirt. His breathing was strong and regular. She could leave him trussed-up like a suckling pig, but if he regained consciousness, she wanted him to be able to use his hands to relieve himself.

"I could let you wallow in your own piss." She shone the torch on his impassive face. "I wonder what Andrea would want me to do. I wonder what you'd have done to me if I'd given you the chance?" She waited for a response, not really expecting one.

His arm fell forward and lay limply over his stomach.

"Jesus." Mina exhaled and rolled him onto his back. Her heart drummed in her ears. She re-tied his hands in front using the same cord, only this time leaving ten centimetres of slack between his wrists. When she was satisfied that the binding was secure, she reached behind and found the chain.

Five minutes later, Briggs hands were chained together, a padlock dangling from between his wrists. Using the two metres of extra chain, she fastened it and him to the upright beam in the centre of the room, held in place by a second padlock. The laptop cord around his wrists would work as a back-up. If by any means, he broke out of the chains, he'd then be faced with the task of chewing through the cable.

Running the light over him one last time, Mina stopped at his boots. Black shiny leather, most likely steel-capped. She crouched and undid the extension cord binding his legs together. Allowing him the freedom to stand was a last-minute decision. The chain would give him about a metre and a half of freedom and as far as she could see, there was nothing he could reach that could be used as a weapon or means of escape. Except the boots. One kick from those steel-caps could do a lot of damage.

She untied the laces and yanked the boots off his feet, leaving him in only black socks. *I should have known he was up to something, he's dressed like a serial killer,* Mina thought with a wry smile. *That or a cat burglar.* One last sweep of the room and she was satisfied. Mina dumped the boots in the wheelbarrow and left, locking the door behind her.

The walk back to the house was remarkably short when not burdened with Briggs. Climbing the three steps to the deck took more effort. Her legs felt thick and heavy. She'd reached the final limits of her strength. The adrenalin that had driven her for the past few hours abated, leaving her body and mind shaky.

There was still so much to do. So many things to be taken care of. Her mind tried to catch hold of the thoughts that spun around her head. Finally, she decided to sleep. The next step would be much clearer once she'd got some rest.

With shaking fingers, she set the alarm on her phone for one in the morning. That would give her four hours of sleep. She didn't remember walking to the bedroom, but found herself sitting on the side of the bed pulling off her filthy trainers. *I'll have to clean them, and hide the boots.* She could smell herself, sweat and blood mingled together to form a cloying stench. She thought of showering, but couldn't find the energy to stand. *I'll change the sheets tomorrow.* As her last coherent thought faded, sleep took her and dreaming began.

# Chapter Twenty-three

Lee flicked off the TV and tossed the remote on the bed. Outside the hotel the sound of voices and car doors slamming signalled the emptying of the pub. The chatter echoed with urgent excitement, bouncing off the empty streets. He envied them their carelessness. He rubbed his eyes with his knuckles, they came away wet with tears.

His fist slammed into the bed. Coming back to Dark Water had been a mistake, seeing Mina made him realise that. There are things you can't out run, no matter where you go. He should have known there was no escaping what was coming. But it wasn't escape he'd hoped to find, just a few days of peace, time to think.

He felt restless, disjointed. With everything spinning out of control, Mina was the one thing that made sense and yet he'd let her go. *I had no choice.* Pulling her into his life had been unfair, even before things got bad again. He stood and pulled his T-shirt over his head and let it drop to the floor. *The heating must be turned up too high.* Sweat dripped down his sides.

He crossed the room and pressed the temperature button—it was broken—then paced around the bed before opening and closing the minibar. *Get it under control, man.*

He pulled back the mustard-coloured curtains and stared out into the street. The wide, flat road looked slick and shiny under the street lights. On the other side of the road, a couple walked huddled close together. Their strides were fast and purposeful; he wondered where they were going this late at night.

In less than a minute they disappeared around the corner and out of sight. Only a week ago, he'd walked these streets with Mina. He closed his eyes and for an instant could almost smell the sweet scent of her skin. In those days spent together, he'd let himself hope that his life had turned around. He'd never known anyone quite like her. She was beautiful, sexy, easy to be with yet, at the same time, so distant and guarded. She seemed separate from the world that buzzed around her. Maybe that was what drew him to her in the first place.

He leaned his forehead against the window pane. The glass felt like ice against his hot skin. The night sky hung above the street, a perfect meld of black and blue. He wondered what Mina was doing. She'd ignored his texts or maybe they'd gone unread. She might be out there somewhere, soaking up the night. He wouldn't blame her if she'd already moved on. They'd only been together for a few days; what did he think she'd do, become a nun?

The unfairness of life had been on his mind so much lately, clouding every moment with blackness. He had to pull himself out of this spiral of self-pity and focus on what needed to be done. Turning away from the window, his eyes fell on the phone. Would it hurt to try again? If she'd been out, she might not have noticed the texts.

It was selfish. Contacting Mina wouldn't change anything, it could only make matters worse. He picked up the phone. The way she'd looked at him tore at his soul. He'd hurt her; the raw injured look in her eyes made that plain to see. He couldn't leave her feeling used and unimportant.

"Damn." He dashed the phone down on the bedside table. He was being a self-centred prick. What did he expect from her? Unburdening himself would make *him* feel better, but what would it do to her?

The air tasted stale—stuffy—or maybe it was the bitter taste of guilt. He'd let her enjoy tonight and try again in the morning.

# Chapter Twenty-four

The curtains were open, she must have forgotten to close them. Muted light dropped through the window, tinting the bedroom with a watery gloom. Mina flung her forearm over her eyes trying to block the sting of the cold light. The movement sent a ripple of pain through her shoulder muscle. Her mind took less than a second to make the connection between the pain and the events of the night before.

A jolt of panic sent her grappling for her phone.

"Damn it." She'd set the alarm for p.m. not a.m. Instead of getting up in the middle of the night to check on Briggs, she'd slept till almost six o'clock the next morning. "No. No, No. Oh God."

She shoved back the throw rug tangled around her stomach and sat up. Another flurry of pain blossomed in her lower back. Clothes were strewn across the floor. Her trainers lay abandoned halfway between the door and bed. Dressed in nothing but a pair of underpants, she dashed out of bed and headed for the open suitcase near the wardrobe.

Desperate to get clothes on and check on Briggs, Mina pulled out a pair of pyjama pants and a red-checked flannel shirt. Every movement seemed to smart, a sharp reminder of the night's exertions. Once dressed, she dragged on her shoes, hopping on one foot then the other. As much as she wanted to race to the back shed, the pressure in her bladder couldn't be ignored.

After a quick bathroom stop and a few sips of water straight from the tap, she was off and running. It wasn't until her fingers were on the back door that she stopped. *What am I doing?* Rushing was the surest way to make a mistake. He'd been in the back shed all night; if he was dead rushing wouldn't change anything. If Briggs had escaped... her thoughts tapered off. If he'd escaped, he'd have done one of two things. Kill her or run. She was alive so that limited his movements.

Letting go of the door, she turned to the fridge. It had been turned off since last night, but the bottles of water she'd put in there yesterday would still be cold. Mina crossed the room and took one out. She unscrewed the cap and emptied three quarters of the water into the sink then put it on the table. Next, she picked up Briggs' phone. It was on and charged.

Pressing the button, she saw it wasn't locked and let out a relieved breath. "Very silly."

By checking his contacts, she easily found a number for the office. Mina scratched her head then fired off a text:

*Hi, not feeling well. Might be flu. Won't be in for a few days.*

She had no idea if it was the sort of thing Briggs would do, but it might buy her some breathing space. She realised she didn't know if he lived alone. There could be someone wondering why he didn't return home. No, a man with his taste for abducting women would need freedom *and* privacy. She couldn't see Briggs answering to anyone or wanting anyone questioning him. If she had to bet, she'd say he lived alone.

The next thing was to be ready for anything. She went back into the bedroom and took her puffer coat out of the wardrobe. Even inside, the air carried a chill, she'd need it for warmth—and the deep pockets would give her somewhere to put the knife.

Back in the kitchen she decided on Briggs' knife; it was longer and decidedly more threatening than the one she'd hidden in her handbag. Unclipping the sheaf from the ankle strap, she stuffed it in her pocket, picked up the shed keys and the water, then headed outside.

* * *

No sound came from inside the back shed. She held her ear close to the door and listened, but apart from the chirpy sounds of birds in the nearby trees, she couldn't hear anything. She wondered if he was dead. She'd hit him pretty hard with the pan. Maybe he had a fractured skull, the injury so severe he never woke up.

The possibilities were many and none were pleasant. Most alarming was the notion that he *was* alive and waiting on the other side of the door. There was a small window to the right, grimy and set high up in the wall. If she could get a look inside, she'd at least be able to see what she was dealing with before she opened the door.

She noticed an old grey milk crate sitting near a stand of peppermint trees. Mina set down the bottle and keys next to the door and retrieved the crate. Turning it over, she tested the bottom. It seemed solid enough. Trying to make as little sound as possible, she set the crate beneath the window and climbed up.

Thick with years of dust and filth, she had to use the bottom of her shirt to wipe the pane until a small patch of glass finally cleared. Inside, the shed looked gloomy and laced with shadows. She could make out the top of the centre beam and what looked like a form lower down near the base. She tried scrubbing away a bit more dirt, but soon realised it would do no good. The only way she'd know for sure if Briggs was still secured was to go inside.

The chill morning air stung her face while at the same time sweat formed on the back of her neck. Once again, she found herself fumbling with the lock only this time her fingers trembled. She took a deep breath and expelled a cloud of warm fog into the cold air. Using her foot, she kicked the door open, letting it creak and swing wide.

A shaft of light cut through the gloom. It took her a second to make sense of what she saw. At first only a dark shape appeared, but as her eyes adjusted to the dimness, Mina realised she was looking at Briggs' back. He was sitting up, resting his spine against the far side of the beam.

If he heard the door, he gave no indication. He made no sound or movement. *He could have sat up and then died,* the possibilities piled up in her mind. Or, he'd freed himself and was sitting in wait. After what she'd seen of him last night, Briggs was the sort of man who'd enjoy setting a trap and watching her terrified reaction.

There was a third possibility, one that made sense and held much more appeal; he'd regained consciousness and was sitting up with his hands still chained to the thick wooden post. Mina rubbed her palms together and watched for movement.

"Briggs?" She hated the reedy quality of her voice. "Hey!" She tried again, biting the word off like a dog barking at the mailman.

His unresponsive stillness seemed to indicate the first or second option. She crouched and picked up the bottle of water, keeping her eyes trained on his motionless shape. Her right hand slipped into the pocket of her puffer coat and caressed the handle of the knife.

"I'm coming in." The words hung in the air, awkward and unanswered.

A few steps in she stopped and listened, hoping to pick up on the sound of his breathing. Her own heart beat a deafening rhythm, making hearing the subtle sound of respiration almost impossible. She had no option but to get close enough to see what he was up to.

At a metre and a half out from the post, she stopped again. If he moved suddenly and lunged for her, she'd be at the edge of his reach. *That's if he's still chained,* she reminded herself. *Of course he's still chained, he's a man not a magician.* Her thoughts halted and the urge to run back to the house took hold of her with an almost irresistible pull. Keeping Briggs here was like playing with a cobra. The sane thing to do would be to call the police. How many times over the last twelve hours had she gone over this? Yet here she stood, in a darkened shed getting ready to face a killer.

A few more steps and she was close enough to see the wound on the back of his neck, a short angular slit crusted over with blood, so dark it almost looked black. She thought she heard him sigh, but the sound could have come from the doorway behind her as the breeze played through the old peppermint trees.

A step closer and she could smell urine as well as something heavy and sour. *If he's been sweating, then he's alive.* The thought offered both comfort and terror at the same time. If not for Andrea, she'd be relieved to see him slumped over, eyes cloudy and skin blue.

She would go no farther, touching him wasn't part of the plan. Once she'd checked if the chain was still secured to the beam, that would be it for now. She'd leave the water and go back to the house. Her eyes travelled over the post, the wood looked aged, but solid. At the base, the chain snaked in a loose circle pierced by the heavy-duty padlock. Satisfied that Biggs was secure, Mina crouched and placed the bottle of water near the base of the post.

A gust of wind kicked through the open doorway flapping her coat to the side. Instinctively, she removed her hand from her pocket and pushed down the hem of her garment. When she looked back towards the beam, Briggs was facing her. His eyes focused on her face with unwavering intensity.

# Chapter Twenty-five

The night seemed unending. When the first rays of pale light broke through the darkness, the sunrise appeared like a mystical phenomenon—something spoken of but astounding to unbelievers. Andrea watched the dawn with tearful happiness. Last night seemed blurry. Had it been a dream or did the woman appear in the room and show her the way out?

Andrea tried to remember if she'd been asleep or awake when Regina, clad in a black cloak, trailed her slim fingers along the walls. The line between what was real and imagined blurred until Andrea was sure Regina was more than just a name on a page. In this desolate place, it was easy to believe there were things that appeared in the night—unexplainable things.

A stab of pressure in Andrea's chest made her gasp for air, clutching her ruined hands to her breasts. Her eyes bulged with the effort of sucking in oxygen. When the air filled her lungs, a deep wet cough bubbled up, rocking her body forward. Something was happening to her, she knew that much. The coughing worsened, the pain in her chest eclipsed the throbbing of her hands.

At first, she thought she might be having a heart attack. The same thing had happened to her nanna. At least that's what her parents told her.

"Nanna's heart just gave out." Her mum tried to make her voice strong, but Andrea had heard the tears building in her throat. There'd been deep dark marks under her eyes. "It's called a heart attack."

Andrea hadn't wanted to see her mum sad, it made her tummy flutter with fear. If something bad could happen—bad enough to make her mother cry—then the world wasn't a safe place. "Will she be alright by Saturday?" Even as she'd asked, her nine-year-old brain could see the truth in her mother's eyes. There were things outside of her mum and dad's control. People she loved could leave her.

A few days later, she'd sat between her parents in church. Her mother wore a black dress that seemed too tight. At least it looked that way because she kept pulling at the hem. Her whole body shook as if she were about to fly off the bench and disappear into the air. Andrea remembered her dad reaching across, his hands were big, the backs covered in golden fluff. He covered her mother's fluttering hand with his, holding it in place with a gentleness that belied its size.

Her mother had turned and given him a trembling smile and, to Andrea, it looked like his touch pulled her back from flying away.

Another coughing fit ratcheted through her and the taste of copper filled her mouth. How she wished her dad could pull her back to earth just like he did for her mum that day in the church.

She pulled the bottle out from under the mattress and unscrewed the cap. *One sip*, she promised and put the rim to her lips. The water slipped over her burning throat like silk, sweet and enticing. Somehow she found the will to cap the bottle and resist the temptation to take another mouthful. Her tongue darted out, licking every scrap of moisture from her lips.

The pain in her chest ebbed to a more bearable jab. It wasn't a heart attack, surely that would have killed her by now? And what about the muck that she'd been coughing up?

"I'm sick." Her voice sounded small and lonely. "I want to go home."

The light crept farther into the room, casting zig-zag lines across the dusty floor. Soon she'd be able to see the walls with enough clarity to start climbing. All she had to do was wait.

# Chapter Twenty-six

Mina took an involuntary step back, hooking one foot behind the other in a clumsy hop. Feet tangled, she stumbled then fell into a crouch, arms wheeling madly for balance. Only fast reflexes stopped her from hitting the floor. All the while the scraping of the chain as it moved over the concrete told her Briggs was making his move.

In the seconds it took her to find her balance, she felt his hand close over her right ankle. She barked out a shriek and kicked like her foot was on fire. His fingers pressed into her Achilles, grappling for purchase. With her left foot firmly planted, Mina managed to pull her ankle out of his grasp and hop back.

Briggs, on his knees facing her, rocked back and sat on the floor. The grubby window and open door let in enough light for her to see the impassive expression on his face. If he was disappointed that his surprise attack had failed or angry at finding himself a prisoner, he gave no indication. The only inkling of emotion came from his eyes, they looked almost amused.

Mina sucked in air and forced herself to calm down before speaking. Even though Briggs was the one in chains, he'd frightened her; and the look in his eyes told her he thought he already had the upper hand. She needed information. It wouldn't be easy making a man like him talk. The first conversation with him as her prisoner had not started out as she'd hoped.

Briggs spoke first. "You want to know where the girl is?"

Mina plunged her hands into the pockets of her coat, letting her fingers curl over the knife's handle. Her first reaction was that he'd somehow read her thoughts, but she realised it was the obvious question; only he'd taken the lead and asked first.

"For now, I'm just happy to see you sitting in your own piss." Mina tried to keep her voice steady and her expression as unreadable as his.

"Good for you." His feminine mouth drew back in a smile that made the hairs on the back of her neck stand on end. "You should act on your impulses, do the things that give you pleasure." He lowered his chin. "We are very alike, probably more than you realise."

"How's your head?" she asked, ignoring his comments.

He raised his hands and she noticed the padlock still in place over the laptop cable. "Nothing a couple of paracetamol wouldn't cure. Do you have any? Thank you for the water by the way." His eyes drifted to the left. Mina followed his gaze. He must have knocked the bottle over when he lunged for her, causing it to roll a metre or so to the side of the post. "Would you mind?" he asked, nodding towards the water.

Holding in an angry retort, Mina turned and walked out of the shed. When she returned a few seconds later, she held the milk crate in her hand. She could see the curiosity in his eyes as he watched her. She set it down with a plastic clack and sat on it. "I think I'll watch and see how thirsty you get." She folded her hands in her lap. "I bet it won't take long before you slither over there and get it yourself."

Something passed over his face. A savage, animalistic fury that appeared and vanished so quickly it left her wondering if she'd really seen the change in him or just imagined it.

When he spoke, his voice was calm, like a man with infinite patience. "I wouldn't think of making you wait." He stood, his movements fluid and steady. Mina thought he might be trying too hard to seem unaffected by the blow to the head.

Briggs walked over, slightly drifting, and picked up the bottle. She noticed the swelling on the left side of his head looking larger than it did the night before. A dark patch of bruising stood out just above his temple that reminded Mina of the way ink bloomed in water. He looked like he'd been kicked in the head by a horse. As much as he tried to pretend the blow had little or no effect on him, she bet his head felt like it had split in two.

He uncapped the bottle and took a large gulp, letting the water trickle down his chin. Watching him suck on the bottle gave her a feeling of grim pleasure. It reminded her that he was at *her* mercy. She thought of what Briggs had said only moments before about acting on her impulses and doing the things that gave her pleasure. The pleasant feeling disappeared leaving a sour taste in her mouth. She wanted to get out of the shed and put as much distance between herself and Briggs as possible. But she couldn't give up, not so soon.

"Where's Andrea?"

Briggs recapped the bottle, taking his time. He turned and walked back to the post. She was at least a half a metre out of his reach yet, with him standing, she felt vulnerable. She suppressed the urge to shift under his gaze.

"She's safe." He put the bottle on the concrete and leaned one arm against the wooden beam. "I'll take you to her if it means that much to you."

"What about the other girls?" She had to ask, even knowing there was no chance any of the others were still alive.

He raised his hands to his mouth and made a kissing motion on his fingers then pulled his hands back and splayed his fingers as if letting crushed leaves go into the breeze. The motion set Mina's teeth on edge. She could feel a tremor building in her stomach, if she didn't get away from him it would rock her body until she broke down and sobbed.

Without a word, she picked up the crate and left the shed. Not until the lock clicked shut and she reached the house did she stop moving. She made it as far as the deck before sinking down onto the steps. With her head in her hands, Mina let the tears fall, racking her aching back with sobs. She wasn't sure who she cried for, the dead girls or herself. Or maybe for the way she felt when she was with Briggs. The image of herself she saw reflected in his eyes sickened her.

He wouldn't give answers easily. It'd take force, but how much would test them both. The tears subsided and her mind began to jump ahead to what had to be done. His vehicle would need to be moved—hidden. The kitchen was a disaster, clearly the scene of a struggle. She wiped her eyes on the back of her hand and stood. Taking action always helped push the doubts away.

* * *

Freshly showered and dressed in clean jeans and a purple jumper, Mina poured herself a glass of orange juice and sat at the kitchen table. The juice was still cold, but with the fridge turned off it wouldn't stay that way. She'd need to replace the extension cord and buy a new laptop cable. The vehicle, like a neon sign sitting in front of the house, would have to be moved before it attracted any attention. For now, that was the most pressing issue, everything else could wait.

The windowless white van wasn't what she'd expected. When Briggs showed her the house, he'd been driving a small silver-grey hatchback. *The scheming bastard thought of everything.* She slipped a knitted black beanie from her back pocket and pulled it over her head taking care to tuck every strand of her long hair away. Why she was taking such care to leave no trace of herself behind was a thought she wouldn't allow herself to dwell on.

Much to Mina's relief, the van had an automatic transmission. There had been a moment, just before climbing in, when fear that the vehicle might be a manual and as such undrivable, ballooned into a full-blown certainty. She'd even had a brief vision of herself pushing the thing down the dirt track that looped into the bush at the back of the property.

"Crazy." Mina sat behind the wheel and listened to the engine idle. The cab smelled of chemicals, most likely bleach with some soapy agent mixed in. Apart from a few grains of sand around the brake pedal, the interior was spotless. Everything so far told her Briggs was careful, smart. *Of course he is, that's how he keeps getting away with murder.*

"Not anymore." She shifted the gearstick into reverse and pulled away from the house, unaware of the smile that played around her lips.

The dirt track turned out to be less hazardous than she'd anticipated. Tightly packed pea stones mixed with sand made the drive bumpy, but not bone jarring. As she veered south, the roof of the back shed became visible in snatches of brown. Within seconds, the foliage thickened and all signs of civilisation dropped away.

She drove on for a few minutes scouring the track for dips or fallen trees. At one point the trail narrowed until thick scrub screeched against the wing mirrors like long dry arms pulling at the van. Mina took one hand off the wheel and wiped the sweat from her upper lip. If the bush overran the trail, she'd have no choice but to leave the van in the middle of the track. It *was* private property so the chances of anyone coming from the other way were slim. Still, she had no idea if there was a gate at the rear.

No, she decided leaving Briggs' vehicle on the trail would be too risky. If she couldn't find a suitable place to pull off the track and hide the van, she'd have to reverse back to the entrance.

"Damn." The thought of twisting around and backing-up for five minutes made her aching shoulders shudder. She arched her back slightly and decided to go a little farther.

Something green dashed out of the trees. It came at the van with such speed and ferocity that Mina only had time to break and duck. The object hit the windscreen with a dead thud and sprang back out of sight. Hands raised, she let out a hollow gasp before looking up again. The trail, alive with crisp morning light, revealed nothing out of the ordinary. A silvery wisp little more than two centimetres long on the windscreen was the only indication that the impact had been real and not the product of her exhausted mind.

She reached out a finger and touched the misty glass. Of course, there was nothing to feel from the inside. Whatever had hit the screen, had done so from the outside. Eyes screwed shut, she replayed the incident in her mind. The flash of colour and then a flutter of wings before impact. It had to be a bird. She leaned her forearms on the wheel and let her head rest on the soft wool of her sleeves.

It was just one of those things, it probably happened all the time in the country, yet her hands trembled and cold air invading the cab made her shiver. The smart thing would be to pull herself together and drive on, but she couldn't. Not without seeing the bird with her own eyes.

There was little more than a half a metre between the door and a scraggy wattle that clutched at her clothes with spindly branches. Mina slammed the driver's door and turned sideways to inch past the front of the van. The ground, carpeted in stones and leaves, crunched underfoot.

On the left of the trail the twisted trunks of young gum trees crowded the van. Mina leaned across the still warm bonnet and ran her finger over the tiny crack in the windscreen. The silver line felt rough, almost jagged. A stab of pain made her pull back in shock and stare at the pinprick bubble of blood on her index finger. Without thinking, she stuck her injured finger in her mouth and grimaced at the coppery taste of blood on her tongue. *What am I doing?* A whispered voice in her mind asked. *Things are getting out of hand.*

A shrill cry startled her out of her thoughts. Turning towards the sound, she spotted a rainbow lorikeet in the low branches of a gnarled tree. Its purple head turned to the side revealing a reddish-brown eye that stared at her with glassy intensity. It had survived the collision, but by the look in its eye, the bird was unimpressed.

"Well, I'm glad you're okay," Mina managed a chuckle. "You scared me as much as I scared you." The bird opened its red beak and let out another cry. The piercing sound made Mina wince. *Jesus, it's really pissed.*

The morning was running away and she stood in the bush talking to a parrot. It occurred to her that the ridiculousness of the situation seemed almost funny, *if* you took the serial killer in her shed out of the equation. Turning back to the van, something green caught her eye.

A few metres ahead, on the right of the trail, a small body lay almost covered by leaves. Mina took her hand off the bonnet and approached the unmoving bird. Above, its mate shrilled.

Its head lay at a strange angle, one green wing still extended as if it had dropped in flight. The bird's eyes were open, already misty with death. The vibrant greens, purples and oranges of it feathers a contrast to the twisted mess of the creature's neck. It seemed everything she touched, she destroyed. The cries of its mate intensified, sounding mournful and accusing.

Mina picked up the small body, still warm yet lifeless and limp. Not really knowing why, she placed the dead bird under a nearby tree and covered it with leaves. It was stupid really, but just leaving it where it fell seemed wrong. When all traces of the bright colours were covered with damp leaves, she glanced back at the spot where the bird originally lay. The impact of the van had bounced the small creature more than two metres through the air. It seemed almost impossible for the thing to have broken its neck and then be projected so far.

A frown creased her brow. The area where the bird landed looked thick with bush grasses and shrubs, but the land behind the long grass looked surprisingly open. She stepped forward, pushing through the long growth and realised what she was seeing. An overgrown side road. Well, more of a dirt track that seemed to dart off to the side of the main trail and then disappear into dense bushland.

The bird continued to shriek, but its cries no longer registered. Mina hurried back to the van. Before opening the door, she thought about the blood on her finger. Only a minute cut, but even the smallest drop of blood could be traced back to her. She pulled her jumper over her head and clamped it between her knees. After tucking a few loose strands of hair back under the woollen beanie, she wrapped the jumper around her hand.

Driving with her right hand bandaged in a thick woollen jumper made movement awkward but, by reducing her speed, she was able to steer onto the overgrown track without too much trouble. When the front wheels hit the side road, a brittle snap came from beneath the vehicle followed by a metallic whine as metal ploughed over wood. The van lurched forward and rolled off the main track.

Mina pushed on and drove into a stand of waxy bushes, inching bit by bit until the bonnet disappeared under the foliage. Pushing the door open took a few shoves, then came the task of scrambling out of the bushes in only a bra and jeans.

Shivering and covered in scratches, she pulled the jumper over her head then spent the next twenty minutes gathering fallen branches and propping them up against the sides and back of the van. *Why do psychos always drive white vans?* Of course, the answer was obvious; to blend in. Service vehicles were usually white and could have access to areas where other cars would seem out of place. Still, Mina couldn't help wishing Briggs had broken the mould and gone for green, it would have been much easier to camouflage.

Back on the main track, she crossed to the left and picked up a hunk of rock about the size of a golf ball, but with a pointed edge. Directly opposite the entrance to the side track stood a tall silver gum. Standing on her toes, she reached up and carved a jagged circle on the trunk then tossed the rock behind the tree.

The long grass and weeds looked flattened out and sparse from where the van had ploughed over them, but in some areas they were already springing back up. Mina pulled the beanie off her head and stuffed it in her back pocket. There was little more she could do to disguise the entrance to the side road. She'd have to hope no one stumbled upon it, at least until she'd got what she needed from Briggs.

# Chapter Twenty-seven

There was nothing left to eat, the energy bar had long since been finished and the wrapper sucked clean. Andrea took a sip of water, noticing the bottle contained less than a quarter of the vital liquid now. The lack of food no longer really bothered her, in fact, the thought of eating made her stomach roil and her throat contract. A few days ago, she'd considered catching a cockroach and eating it— something she would never tell a living soul—and now a chocolate muffin would turn her stomach.

The light never penetrated every corner of the room, but the bars of yellow falling across the walls were an indication that the sun had risen high in the sky, spilling down the best illumination the day had to offer. Andrea rolled forward onto her hands and knees, pausing while the room see-sawed and spots of blue danced in front of her eyes. *I'm getting worse.* The realisation didn't surprise her, it was with increasing certainty that she felt death approaching.

It had been days since the maniac had last visited. At first Andrea spent every moment fearful of his return, now she almost wished for it. If the Magician didn't come back, she'd die of thirst long before starvation could kill her. *No,* she thought. *I'm dying now.* She realised even if he did return, her body couldn't take another beating. Part of her didn't want to survive the pain and horror of his sick attacks.

She'd been thinking about the light, waiting for it, but why? Her thoughts were jumpy, hot. Concentrating on one thing had become like trying to work out a complicated math problem. No matter how much she focused, nothing stayed straight. *What would Regina do?* A face came into focus, pale eyes and dark hair. Andrea shivered and pulled the stained curtain around her shoulders.

How long had it been since she last saw her mother? Her features were fuzzy in Andrea's mind, yet Regina was so clear. It was as if she were in the room, almost touching the wall. Andrea opened her eyes, without realising it she'd flopped forward onto her stomach and drifted into a half-sleep, but now she became fully awake and the memory of her plan came back into focus.

The walls. Wait for the light and search the walls. She raised her head. The dizziness she'd experienced earlier had passed, but getting to her feet took a force of will. Legs like spaghetti, Andrea leaned against the wall beside the mattress. The daylight wouldn't last forever and neither would she. Her health was failing, whatever was happening to her seemed to be gathering strength. The sickness felt like a dragon, heavy and covered with spikes, she could almost feel it crouching in her chest. Its thorny tail lashing the insides of her lungs as it hunkered down, muscles bunched and fierce red eyes glowing. When it stretched its wings and roared, she wouldn't stand a chance.

"I'm climbing the castle wall." She didn't recognise the rasp of voice.

In steps that veered to the right, she moved towards the far wall, the one Regina had her fingers over in the dream. Andrea frowned, *was it a dream?* The room, no more than six metres across stretched out like an endless hallway in a funhouse. The roller door ahead jumped and doubled then coalesced into one again.

The palms of her hands slapped the steel door. Sliding sideways, she followed the slab until brick replaced the metal.

"Okay. Okay, yes." Her lips drew back in a smile revealing the gap in her teeth where a bloody plug filled the gaping socket.

The bricks were uneven and powdery as if the years of damp and neglect had rotted them. What she need was a foothold, somewhere to push off. The row of boards looked as ancient as the bricks, wrenching a few out of place might not be so difficult. *Yes. Yes, easy. I pulled my own tooth out. I can pull those slats off while clinging to the wall.* She laughed at the image, only the noise she made sounded panicked, almost hysterical.

The laugh turned into a cough that rattled something wet around in her chest. She considered going back to the mattress and resting for a few minutes but as appealing as the prospect seemed, the mattress was little more than a giant Venus flytrap tempting her into its fleshy mouth. If she gave in and lay down, the filthy bed would swallow her up and she'd never leave this torture chamber.

Andrea wiped her damp face on her sleeve. "I should have done this at the beginning. Why *didn't* I do this at the beginning?" There was no easy answer. Maybe the simplest explanation was disbelief. Even as the Magician beat and choked her, disbelief bombarded her mind. *This can't be happening, not to me.* She came from a loving home. She'd heeded all the warnings and steered clear of drugs. She never talked to strangers. *This sort of thing happens to other people, not to me.*

The simple answer was her unwillingness or inability to comprehend what was happening to her *and* the childlike imagination of a hero waiting in the wings ready to step in and make everything all right. These were the things that kept Andrea pinned to the filthy mattress, paralysed by disbelief born out of a happy home and view of life formed in a darkened movie theatre. But now those beliefs and disbeliefs fell away, revealing a lust for survival formed out of desperation both dark and instinctual. Her own death loomed larger and blacker than anything she'd experienced. The realisation galvanised her into action.

Andrea kicked something solid and a needle of pain sliced through her big toe. Reaching down to rub her stinging foot, she saw the offending article: a chunk of brick. Still crouched, she looked from the brick to the wall above. Less than fifteen centimetres out from the roller door and perhaps a little over a metre from the floor was the very thing she'd been searching for, a foothold.

In her haste to examine the depression, she stood and immediately regretted the sudden movement. The blue spots returned, this time not so much dancing as spinning in a haze of blue and yellow. Her body swayed, sending her stomach into a sickening dip.

"No. No. No." She gripped the edge of the door and pressed her forehead against the metal, willing herself to hold it together. Behind her something clicked, a sound like insect wings, rigid and slippery fanning out. She felt the urge to glance over her shoulder but couldn't risk letting go of the door. If she vomited or worse, fainted, the opportunity would be lost. Finding the strength to come this far had taken every ounce of determination that she had left.

"You won't stop me," she spoke to the sound, imagining the huge flying creature spreading its wings and baring brown jagged teeth in her direction.

Andrea counted to ten, her voice small and flat in the silence of the room. When she opened her eyes, the spots had vanished. There was no more clicking, only the sound of wheezing which she realised came from inside her. Raising her foot, she found the depression in the wall. By leaning to the right, she managed to push herself up using the edge of the door for balance.

Tilting her chin, she could see the wooden slats less than a body-length above her. Her foot, pushed as far in as the hole in the wall would allow, dipped, dropping her body a few centimetres. She balanced, left foot in the depression, right hip braced against the side of the door and her right arm extended, the fingers gripping the top edge of the metal. In this awkward position, her right toes skimmed the wall searching for purchase.

After what felt like minutes, her big toe poked into a hole, jagged and powdery but wide enough to hold a few more toes. She opened her mouth and an almost comic sigh escaped. The second foothold allowed her to shift to the right and release some of the pressure off her left foot.

Transferring most of her weight to her right foot and hip, she pulled her left foot free, drawing it out, slowly curling and uncurling as it prodded the wall like a blind caterpillar. For a terrifying moment it seemed like the surface had evened out and she'd be forced to lower herself down. *Maybe it's better this way*, a small voice in her head whispered. *I can rest for a while, try again when I feel better.* The voice had a comforting quality, reasonable and enticing.

Her right shoulder on fire with gathering lactic acid and her fingers cramping, the temptation to give in to the voice and slip down the wall seemed irresistible. But just as the impulse to quit almost took hold, her toes slid into a hole big enough to accommodate her entire left foot. With the simple act of securing her foot, Andrea forgot the voice of reason and pushed up until she was able to let go of the door and grasp the edge of the ledge where the wall ended and the wooden boards began.

It may have been her imagination, but the air rushing through the gaps in the slats smelled clean, almost otherworldly. Or maybe it was the first time in weeks her every breath hadn't been laced with the smell of excrement. Either way, Andrea sucked in a gulp of the tantalisingly sweet air and lifted her right foot onto the five-centimetre edge of the roller door.

In some areas, the aging grey wood had splintered and whole chunks had dropped away revealing glimpses of the outside world. Her aching knees and burning shoulder forgotten, Andrea gazed out through the gap getting her first glimpse of the sky. She could see little more than a mass of branches and a patch of greyish-blue sky. A small snap-shot of the world, but draped in golden light and startling green foliage, shot through with pearly blue, it was the most breathtaking thing she'd ever seen.

Breathing in the cool air and feeling the wind on her skin felt like freedom. An unfamiliar feeling in her stomach, a pleasant fluttering, took her by surprise. She realised it was hope and her vision blurred, not with dizziness, but tears.

# Chapter Twenty-eight

Walking at a brisk pace, just short of jogging, Mina made it back to the house in fifteen minutes. Along the way, she barely glanced at the shed. There was still work to be done and no time to waste worrying about Briggs. As long as he remained safely locked up, he could wait.

Once inside, she set about cleaning the kitchen. First gathering up chunks of broken china, and then wiping the food scraps off the table and floor. She filled a plastic carrier bag with the debris and dumped it in the wheelie bin in the back yard. Then she tore up a few moving boxes and pushed those down on top of the bag. Finally, she filled a bucket with hot soapy water and washed the kitchen floor.

When she moved on to the bedroom, Mina felt a growing sense of control. She'd set something in motion and the panic and exhaustion of the night before had turned into energised purpose. For the first time in years, she had a plan. But an underlying feeling of uneasiness still remained, a sneaking sense that someone watched her. Over the years, she'd come to accept that creeping feeling of guilt. She supposed it came with the territory when you took the law into your own hands. An uncomfortable feeling, but one Mina decided she could live with.

Once Andrea was rescued and returned home, none of what she'd done here would matter. How this last part would come to pass had been designated: *things to worry about later*. For now, finding Andrea mattered more than what came later. Tossing the bed sheets, T-shirt, jeans, underwear and the socks she'd worn the night before into the washing machine, she started humming.

Satisfied that all traces of Briggs had been either hidden or eliminated, Mina checked her watch and was surprised to see the morning had all but ended. As if in response to the time, her stomach clenched with hunger. The contents of the fridge were sadly unappealing. In the end, she settled for another glass of orange juice and a cheese and lettuce sandwich, which she devoured standing over the sink. Hiding vehicles and cleaning up crime scenes was, as it turned out, hungry work.

At exactly 1:30 p.m., she pulled on her puffer coat and patted the bulge of the knife under the downy fabric. With the keys in her hand, she left the house and made the now familiar trip to the shed.

On approach, she slowed her steps trying to make as little noise as possible. If Briggs was trying to escape, she wanted her appearance to take him by surprise. Before entering, Mina tipped the milk crate up and stepped to the window. As before, the interior lay in shadows. Only this time, instead of a shape at the base of the post, Briggs was clearly standing with his back to the door.

The rhythm of her heart changed, kicking up a gear. She focused her vision and tried to pick out details but the grimy window, together with the lack of light, made it impossible to tell if the chains were still in place. The thick coat felt heavy and restrictive on her body. If it were not for the knife, she'd have shrugged it off. But entering the building clutching a knife would be a sign of weakness, something Briggs would enjoy, maybe even find a way to use against her.

When she swung the door open, Mina made no move. Instead, she let the light shine in, watching it stalk across the dusty concrete and illuminate the area around the beam. The chain appeared to be in place, but with his back to the door, there was no way of knowing if it was still attached to his wrists. *Of course it is*, she let out a shallow breath. *If he'd broken loose, he'd have smashed the window and climbed out.*

"You breathe loudly." His voice startled her. "Or are you panting with fear?" he asked, still standing with his back to the door.

The sound of his voice and the smell of him set her teeth on edge. She had the sudden urge to slam the door and leave him in the old building. Forget about Briggs, and Andrea, and board up the window. How, she wondered, would he feel when the hunger and thirst started eating at him? Would he scream for mercy?

Instead of fleeing, she stepped outside and picked up the milk crate. Then, as she had done earlier, she placed it in the shed and sat on it. When Briggs finally turned, the padlock clinked against the chains. He moved forward, hands bound in front. When he stopped, there was only a metre or so between them. She could see the bruise on his forehead, stark and purple.

"You look flushed, it suits you." She could feel his eyes moving over her face and body like a swarm of flies. "I didn't want to say anything earlier, but you looked awful this morning. Tired and rough, my old auntie would have said." He tilted his head to the left slightly. "But now, you look radiant."

"You're a real Prince Charming." Mina didn't bother to hide her disgust.

He smiled. Not the crazy stretched grin she'd seen the night before, but a slight lifting of the lips. A sad smile that didn't quite reach his eyes. "I'm not sure all the ladies in my life would agree with you."

The meaning of his words hit her like a shock wave. Goose flesh broke out on her arms and without thinking she wrapped them around her middle. *He's talking about women he's killed.* She thought of her good mood and hearty appetite that morning and almost gagged. This wasn't a game or a new hobby, it was about saving a girl's life. *How could I have lost sight of that so easily?* At least three women were dead, they'd never get the chance to return home. He'd murdered them. She thought of the way he'd kissed his fingers when she asked about the other women. To him, his victims were nothing.

"Where is she?" Mina kept her voice even.

Briggs turned and walked back to the post. "Do you wonder about all this?" He spoke over his shoulder. "How you came to be here, of all the places in the world... end up in *my* town?" He sat on the concrete and leaned his back against the wood. "When I saw you at the college that first time, I knew there was something special about you. You couldn't see me, but you felt me, didn't you?"

It was true, that night she'd felt something. That first moment when she'd parked the car and stepped out into the darkened lot, she remembered the familiar sensation of imminent danger. He'd been there, watching her. The very thought of him crouched in the bushes like an animal made her skin crawl.

When he answered, his voice was calm and unhurried. "As much as you would believe the contrary, not everything is about you. I have friends everywhere." He lowered his voice. "Secret friends."

He was smirking, waiting for a reaction, but she refused to give it to him. He was playing games, talking in circles. She was beginning to think he didn't know what the truth was.

"Then, when you left the girl, I knew." His eyes were fixed on hers, somehow empty and incredibly focused at the same time. She had to suppress the urge to squirm under his gaze. "You'd sensed my presence and left the girl for me. I—"

"No." She shook her head. "It wasn't like that. What I did to Andrea was wrong, but I never thought anything would happen to her." She hated the defensive whine in her voice, but couldn't seem to stop herself. "If I thought she was in real danger, I'd have never left her."

He shrugged. "Did you tell the police what happened?"

The question threw her. The last thing she'd expected was for him to ask about the police. "Where is she?" she snapped, ignoring his question.

"I'll take that as a *no.*" His voice, Mina realised, sounded quite different to the one he'd used when showing her the house and chatting at the pub. Gone was the cheerful enthusiasm, even the pitch seemed lower. There was a flat quality to the way he spoke. The result was almost robotic. "Getting back to my original question, does it strike you as strange that you came to me?"

"Tell me where she is."

"I followed you home from the college that first night," he continued, as if she hadn't spoken. "Very risky with the Do—with Andrea in the van. But, I had to know where you lived. I visited you, watched the house, so I know the police were there—"

"Where *is* she?" Part of her wanted to hear what he had to say—needed to know. But the longer she sat and listened to him, the more she wanted to do something… something violent. Her skin felt cold, almost feverish as if something wild had leapt from him and burrowed its way under her flesh. *No,* she couldn't blame Briggs for this. *I've always known it was there.*

"I know you're eager to hear about the girl, so I won't let your interruptions upset me, but please try to be patient."

In spite of everything, she almost laughed. He still thought he was in charge. Even in chains, he still thought he could call the shots.

"I planned to come for you when everything was ready. But." He raised his hands and pointed at her. "This is the really interesting part. *You* came to me." He chuckled, a dry and humourless sound. "You emailed me and set up a meeting. If I'd had any doubts, you laid them to rest. It's not a coincidence that we're together. There *are* no coincidences. We're the same, I can tell, and that's why we found each other. One conversation with me on the street and you couldn't keep away. People like us are magnets, we're pulled together by forces lesser people can't feel." For the first time, there was emotion in his voice; excitement. His arms moved in small jerks and his shoulders twitched.

"Maybe you're right," she said. His mouth dropped open in what looked like genuine surprise. He leaned forward as if waiting for her to touch him. "I don't believe in coincidences either. I am here for a reason, but not the one you think. I found you because I'm the one that's going to stop you."

Now it was her turn to smile as she watched the vacuous look in his eyes turn to confusion. "You're so used to snatching up women and doing God knows what to them, it never occurred to you that one day, you'd pick the wrong one." She leaned towards him. "If you don't tell me what I want to know, you'll die here."

Outside, birds twittered in the winter sunshine. The silence stretched out between them. Much to Mina's satisfaction, Briggs was the first to speak.

"You'll never find her without me." She could see the muscles in his face bunching.

"Then no one will ever find you." As the words left her mouth, she realised they were true. And so, judging by the look in his eyes, did Briggs.

* * *

The fever that had swamped Mina in the back shed—blistering under her skin, pushing her to act—hung around her like a cloud of toxic smoke. She opened the back door and entered the house, stripping off her coat and draping it over the chair. The powerful smell of cleaning products hung in the air.

It had been less than twenty-four hours and she'd let Briggs get under her skin. He wasn't going to give up his secrets, that much seemed clear. Running her fingers through her hair and scratching her scalp, Mina stared at the coat. Maybe the time had come to force the issue. But could she? Could she take the next step?

The house felt huge and empty, now filled with secrets whereas only yesterday the place had seemed homely and full of potential. She couldn't let this drag on. For Andrea's sake and for her own sanity, it had to end. Was it evil to want to rid the world of someone like Briggs?

Turning him over to the cops would take the burden off her. He'd be someone else's problem and she wouldn't have to get her hands bloody. The impulse to rid herself of involvement passed as quickly as it arrived. Without Andrea, the police would have no proof of Briggs' involvement. It would be Mina's word against his. Who would they believe? A well-liked local businessman or the woman who held him captive in her shed? She put her hand on the coat, the silky fabric felt cool and smooth. Slipping her hand into the pocket, she wrapped her fingers around the knife handle. Briggs' knife. How much pain and misery had he caused with this instrument?

The sound of wheels hissing over the driveway barely registered. It wasn't until the knocker rapped twice in sharp succession that she drew her attention away from the blade. She felt an instant of bewilderment, then alarm. No one knew where she lived. Who could be here? She shoved the knife back in the pocket, dumped the jacket over the back of the chair, and went to the front door.

In the lounge room, Mina stopped and listened. It had to be the police. Who else would know where to find her? She rubbed her hands together, palm against palm. It was the only explanation. Someone, whoever Briggs lived with, had reported him missing. He had mentioned his auntie, she'd probably called the police when he didn't come home.

Fear, like a panicked bird, thrashed around in her head with its wings beating an insane tune of dread. She took a breath and straightened her back. Maybe they were just checking everyone who'd seen him in the last week. If she played it cool, they might go away. *Or they might want to search the place.* She closed her eyes, *calm in the face of fear.*

The clatter of the knocker hitting the door jarred her forward. The door opened to flashing lights and blue uniforms. Mina sucked in a breath and the image in her head coalesced into what she really saw.

"Hi, I sent you at least six messages. You had me worried."

"Robbie." Mina managed to stutter the name out, still torn between the image her mind projected and reality. "I… how did you… I didn't tell you where I lived." It sounded abrupt, rude almost. "I mean–"

Robbie waved a hand as if shooing a fly. "Terry told me where you lived. There aren't many secrets in a small town." Her smile faltered. "Are you okay?"

Still trying to process what was happening, Mina forced a smile. It felt stiff and false. "Yeah. Just unpacking." She stepped back and opened the door wider revealing the lounge room. "Come in, but ignore the mess." *There aren't many secrets in a small town.* What, she wondered, did Robbie know?

Mina led her through to the kitchen hoping Robbie didn't notice the stacks of unopened boxes. Her legs felt awkward as if walking had become a conscious act that if done incorrectly could give her nervousness away.

"Sorry to just drop in on you, but it was a spur of the moment thing." Robbie spoke from behind her as Mina led the way into the kitchen. She couldn't see the woman's face but her voice sounded light with no hint of accusation.

"Do you want a coffee or something?" Mina picked up the kettle and gave it a shake. Her hands felt steady, but there were beads of sweat gathering on the back of her neck.

"Thanks, but just a quick one. I have to be at work soon. That's why I dropped by—on my way in and all."

Mina filled the kettle and switched it on. It occurred to her that she'd been in this exact situation with Briggs only the night before. She turned and faced Robbie, deciding it might be wise to keep the woman where she could see her. To Mina's horror, Robbie was reclined in the chair with her back pressed against the coat.

"Let me get that out of your way." Mina took hold of the coat, pulling it out from under Robbie with more force than she'd intended.

Robbie leaned forward. "Sorry. Nice coat, is it silk?" She reached out and touched the sleeve, then looked up at Mina with one brow raised. Her spiky blonde hair stood out in what looked like horns.

"Yes." Mina had the urge to rip the coat out of the woman's hands and tell her to get out of her house. Instead, she gave another stiff smile. "Thanks." She looked around for somewhere to put the coat and decided she didn't want it in the room. "I'll just put this out of the way."

After tossing the puffer coat on her bed, Mina returned to the kitchen just as the kettle clicked off. Trying to think of something to say, she busied herself making coffee.

"Thanks," Robbie said when she set the cup down in front of her. "Are you sure you're okay?"

"Yes, why do you ask?" Mina sat across from her and picked up her cup.

Robbie took a sip of coffee all the while keeping her eyes on Mina's face. "You seem jumpy. But," she paused. "I think I know what's making you nervous."

Mina swallowed a mouthful of coffee, her tongue felt dry and stuck to the roof of her mouth. She waited for the woman to continue, dreading what she was about to say. She'd wanted Dark Water to be a new start. It had been until now and, as everything spun out of control, she realised how much she'd also wanted her new friendship with Robbie to work out.

"You've only been here a few days and I've turned up on your doorstep. You're worried I'm some kind of local crazy who wants to live in your pocket." Her eyes, hazel and ringed with dark liner, twinkled. For the second time since meeting her, Robbie reminded Mina of her mother. The relief must have showed on her face.

"Don't worry." Robbie set her cup down then reached out and patted Mina's hand. "This is a one off. I won't be dropping in every day." She smiled and the dimples in her cheeks appeared. "It's just you're new in town and I couldn't get hold of you... and," she said, leaning back in her chair, "I wanted to let you know we're going to have to put off our shopping trip until next week. My boss has asked me to do a few extra shifts."

"That's okay." Mina had completely forgotten about the shopping trip. "I've got a lot here to keep me busy."

Robbie nodded and sipped her coffee when something struck Mina. It was so obvious, she couldn't imagine why she hadn't thought of it sooner. If she could find out where Briggs lived, it might lead her to Andrea. "You said Terry told you where I live." Mina let the comment hang in the air, hoping Robbie would fill in the blanks.

"Yeah. He was pleased about letting this place, apparently it's been on the books for quite a while."

"Are you and Terry seeing each other, right now?" She hoped the question sounded casual. She felt guilty, pumping her new friend for information, but she had to know more about the man chained up in her shed.

Robbie tipped her head back as if regarding the ceiling, it was a dramatic gesture, one that sat perfectly with the woman's over-the-top personality. "No, I wouldn't say that." She dropped her head and regarded Mina. All trace of humour had evaporated from her eyes. "When I was a kid, you know, in high school, Terry used to work at the fish and chip shop. He was older and I kind of had a thing for him, but it never really went anywhere."

"Why not?" Mina asked, leaning forward in her seat.

Robbie grimaced. "It's hard to explain, but he's a bit odd I suppose. Harmless, I'm sure, but odd." *If you only knew*, Mina thought, but kept her mouth shut. "It's like there's some kind of barrier between him and the world. We're just friends really." She shrugged. "I don't think he has many friends."

It occurred to Mina that Robbie was one of those people that collected strays. A kind-hearted woman, always surrounded by the fringe dwellers that didn't fit in. *That's probably what drew her to me.* She felt a pang of affection towards the woman and with it came the need to protect her. She wanted to tell her to open her eyes and realise that the world wasn't full of harmless people who just needed a friend. But what good would it do? Even if she did believe her, would Mina want her to change? To become more like... her?

When Mina spoke, it was to ask another question, the one that'd been burning in her mind since the conversation about Briggs began. "Does he live in town?"

Robbie drained her cup before answering. "What's with all the questions about Terry? Don't tell me you've got a thing for him." Robbie chuckled. Mina joined in, trying to sound relaxed.

"No, no." Mina held up her hands as if facing a robber holding a gun. "I'm still riding the bitter waves of my last dismal relationship. I'm just curious."

"Wow, that bad huh?"

Mina dropped her hands into her lap so she could grip her thighs under the table. "No, just ignore me," she forced another laugh and dug her fingers into her legs.

"Terry lives on Able Street, has done for years. Ever since his auntie died. I suppose that's one of the things I like about him, the way he took care of her after she had the stroke. Not many men would have done that, but she was all he had. I guess she was like a mother to him really."

"What happened to his parents?" She was getting side-tracked, but there was a sinking feeling in the pit of her stomach, like a heavy weight pulling her down—telling her there was more to the story. She had to know what had happened.

Robbie took her time answering. As the silence lengthened, Mina could feel her pulse race. Sure that her eagerness for answers was plastered all over her face, she averted her gaze, letting her eyes flit over the woman's features and uniform. Robbie wore black pants and a black T-shirt with the *Blue Smoke Café* emblazoned across the front. Her white skin and blonde hair looked stark against the black clothing. "They both died in a fire when Terry was eight or nine. I don't know the details, he's never talked about it. I only know because my dad knew his Auntie Dorothy."

Mina wanted to know more about the fire. Her gut instinct was that Briggs started his career as a killer early, maybe with his own parents. She had so many questions, but didn't want to keep pushing Robbie for answers. As it was, her interest in Briggs must have seemed strange. She tried to think of a way of asking what number on Able Street when Robbie looked at her watch and jumped up.

"Oh God, I didn't realise it's nearly three o'clock. I'm supposed to be back at the café by now." Before Mina could protest, the woman was already heading for the front door. "I'll text you about next week, okay?"

Mina nodded and watched her friend trot towards the car. She started the engine and the window slid down. "And remember, check your phone." Robbie gave her another dazzling smile and then drove away.

# Chapter Twenty-nine

Pieces of splintered wood littered the scarred and grimy floor. One more board and the gap would be wide enough for Andrea to pull her now thinner frame through. She'd been clamped to the wall like Spiderman for what felt like hours. At one point, she almost talked herself into climbing down and taking a break, maybe even a sip of water. But the floor looked distant and her legs quivered with the strain.

"If I go down, I'll never make it back up," she said to the empty room.

The sunshine through the gap was tantalisingly golden and the breeze tainted with something sweetly rancid, but fresh compared to the cloying stench of the room below. Andrea forced her numb fingers to keep working, imagining turning her face up to the sun and closing her eyes so that the rosy light shone through her lids and warmed her mind. It would be worth all the splinters and cramps her body could endure.

The last board proved the most difficult. The half metre slat was secured in place with four rusty nails. One had been hanging out when Andrea began, needing only a slight jerk of the wood to send it flying over her shoulder.

The other three, however, were less co-operative. If the board hadn't been running directly across the middle of the gap, she'd have given up and risked pushing through around the plank.

An asthmatic wheeze whistled through her chest making each breath laboured and painful. She tried to take small, even breaths hoping to stave off another coughing fit and so far, the technique seemed to be working. She grasped the slat in the centre and gave it a sharp backwards yank. The wood vibrated and another one of the three remaining nails broke away from its bed.

"I'm doing it." Her voice, a high-pitched squeal, cracked with excitement. The world beyond the gap seemed to shuffle a little closer and her heart gave a not unpleasant jump.

Wherever the Magician was, didn't matter. She'd be long gone when he got back. Maybe it wasn't far to the nearest house. If she could get help, get to a phone, the police might be right here waiting for him when he turned up with his toilet bucket and black garbage mask. These were the thoughts that went through her mind as she tugged on the faded grey board.

She licked her lips wishing she'd thought to tuck the almost-empty water bottle into the back of her pants. It had probably been only ten or fifteen minutes since she began her climb, but lack of food robbed her of what little stamina she once possessed. She had no doubt dehydration was also partly responsible for the light-headed feeling that swept over her every time she looked down. *I'll have a glass of cola soon*, she told herself and without realising it, smacked her lips together. *No, on second thought, I don't need to worry about the calories, I'll have a whole bottle.* She didn't think her stomach could manage food just yet, but a cold fizzy drink would do just fine.

One last heave and the board didn't so much come away as split down the middle with a groan. The wood broke in half and hung from the gap like a pair of jagged teeth. Suddenly the trees came into unobstructed view. Andrea laughed then coughed into the cold breeze that wafted through the opening.

She couldn't afford to waste time celebrating, her legs wouldn't last much longer. She had to get going before they gave out and she tumbled back to earth.

The gap was a little over half a metre deep and the same wide. At shoulder height, she'd have to go out head first. Making the drop on the other side would be the problem, but by wriggling through on her stomach, she thought she'd be able to turn half way so that her butt would end up dangling out of the building. From there, she'd lower one leg at a time and hang from the gap, then drop—and pray.

Standing with most of her weight on her right foot, she pushed up so her toes rested on the top of the door. Then, bracing her forearms on the concrete lip where the wood met the wall, she used the remaining strength in her shoulders to drag herself through the gap. She felt something sharp tug at her upper arm then jab into the flesh, tearing as she pushed forward. There wasn't much pain, just a pinching sensation, and then her breasts were over the lip and dangling out of the building.

There was no time to appreciate the sun on her neck or the caress of the breeze against her face. Her body rocked forward and, for a sickening breathless moment, she felt herself slide. Slapping her hand on the inside of the wall stopped the forward momentum and she was able to catch her breath.

What she saw below her, set her already pounding heart jack-knifing against the insides of her ribs. On the other side of the roller door was a small lean-to room not much bigger than a porch. The roof of the structure rested against the building just above door height, sloping downwards on a slight angle. Andrea gasped out another breathless laugh. Dropping from the smaller rooftop would greatly reduce the height *and* danger of her descent.

"Thank you," she said to no one in particular and began wriggling onto her back.

When her butt was all the way outside she leaned over, grasping at the wooden slats still in place near the gap and slid out her left leg. Her toes found the rooftop below and in seconds, Andrea was out and standing atop the small building.

After so long in the dimness of the room, the light and air felt unreal. There was a dreamlike quality to the moment, as if she were outside herself watching a hollow-cheeked girl in filthy, torn clothes stand in the sun like a refugee stumbling out of a prison camp after years of captivity. Turning her face upwards, she closed her eyes. *Just a few seconds*, she told herself, letting the rosy glow caress her face.

Opening her eyes and turning her face to the left, she noticed the tiled peak of a building nearby. A frightening image suddenly filled her mind. *Him*—the Magician—inside that house, waiting. He'd left her to die of dehydration and now he was waiting until the job was done so he could drag her lifeless body out into the surrounding bush. *You won't be alone*, a flat emotionless voice that sounded very unlike her whispered inside her head. *You've been smelling them since that first day.*

In that moment, she let herself acknowledge the truth. That smell, the sweetly rancid odour that hung in the air, was death. She'd been surrounded by it the whole time.

Another thought occurred with lightning speed. *What if he was in the room below her feet? Not just in there, but stood looking up at the roof, listening? Maybe he wants me to try and escape so he has a reason to kill me.*

Andrea crouched down, hands flat against the roof. She could go back, climb through the gap and return to the mattress. She'd clung to the stained bed for so long, it had become the only comfort she knew. At that moment, it seemed infinitely more appealing than climbing off the roof and into the hands of her tormentor.

She glanced over her shoulder at the opening through which she'd climbed. The jagged broken boards made it look like a huge insectile mouth ready to swallow her up. For a second, she thought she heard the clicking of wings echoing up through the gap.

"I'll die in there," she said to the trees. There seemed to be no answer; going back would mean a slow death and going forward… Going forward could lead to freedom.

She forced herself to stand, wavering slightly as a rush of blood filled her head. She hadn't heard his van in days. *You don't always hear it,* the very unlike her voice whispered. She couldn't deny the truth, sometimes she slept so deeply he'd be in the room grabbing at her legs with such suddenness she thought he really *was* a magician.

But, she realised, when she did hear it, it sounded close. Taking a step forward, the ground to the left of the lean-to came into view. A patch of reddish pea stones with a dirt track leading away from the structure. She recalled the crackle of stones under tyres and shuddered. Then another thought popped into her mind. That first night, when the nightmare began, he'd parked the van close to the building. She recalled the moment he flung open the back doors and pulled her out, the way her head had hit the lip of the van when she slid out into the darkness.

He wasn't in the lean-to. There was no vehicle, no sound. But that didn't mean he wouldn't arrive at any moment. The longer she stood there wavering, the greater the chance he'd return.

For a second she thought she heard an engine, but quickly recognised the sound as nothing more than a kookaburra winding up for a whoop of laughter. The bird was quickly joined by a second, then a third. She couldn't see them but their peals of laughter seemed to come from every direction. And why not? She probably looked pathetically funny to the wild birds.

A few feet and she'd be at the edge of the little structure then a short drop and she'd be free. Andrea took a step, a sound barely distinguishable above the clamour of the birds froze her movements. A creak turned into a snap. She dipped her chin to look down but, before her eyes found the source, the roof collapsed and the trees and the sunshine disappeared.

# Chapter Thirty

Mina's fingers flew over the keyboard. She couldn't believe the idea hadn't occurred to her sooner. The White Pages; all she had to do was look up Briggs' address. It had to be the place. If, as he'd said they were so alike, it made sense that he had Andrea somewhere on his property. *That's if he's telling the truth about her still being alive. He could be lying.* In fact, the chances of a psychopath like Terrance Briggs telling the truth were slim to none.

But, Mina realised it wasn't what Briggs told her that made her so sure Andrea was still alive, but something even less tangible than Briggs' grip on the truth. She felt an inner certainty that the girl was still held captive somewhere. Somewhere close by. She couldn't explain why, even to herself, but her gut was telling her to keep going.

She entered Briggs' name into the search engine and hit enter. Her laptop would need to be charged soon, but with the cord wrapped around Briggs' wrists, there was no chance of topping it up in the near future. Within seconds the information popped up on the screen.

"Damn." There were six pages of Briggs, but only two *T* Briggs listed. Neither of them were in Dark Water.

Mina shut the laptop and grabbed her keys. She had a street name; a good place to start. Before leaving the house she put on her coat. She doubted she'd need the knife yet liked the comfort of having it in her pocket. She considered leaving it in the coat, but decided that if the police found her snooping around Briggs' place it might look bad if she were armed with a hunting knife. Very bad.

She pulled the blade from the sheath and held it up. The steel captured a glint of sunlight streaming through the chink in the curtains. She'd been close to using it when Robbie knocked the door. *What will I do if I find Andrea?* Briggs would have most certainly outlived his usefulness. What then? Go to the police? Would they thank her for what she'd done or arrest her? She tossed the knife in its casing on the bed. There'd be time to worry about Briggs later.

During her earlier clean-up, she'd removed the battery from Briggs' phone and stashed it along with his keys high up on top of the air-conditioning unit in the lounge room. Dragging a chair from the kitchen, she climbed up and took the keys.

\* \* \*

Able Street turned out to be a side road with only a handful of houses, all set back from the road by large lawns. Six streets south of the main drag, it wasn't quite on the edge of town, but far enough away from the more populated areas to make it quiet even by small town standards.

Mina drove slowly, peering up driveways. When she reached a blue weatherboard house, she immediately spotted the silver-grey Hyundai parked to the right of the wide expanse of paved drive-way.

Although the street was deserted, she continued past the house and turned the corner. A small open area with a swing set and sandpit stood in front of what looked like an old church. Mina pulled into one of the handful of parking bays alongside the church and turned off the engine. Checking her watch, she saw it was almost four o'clock, time kept slipping away. People would be returning home from work soon, making the possibility of being noticed more likely.

She locked the car and headed back towards Able Street, hoping that to anyone watching she looked unnoteworthy—anonymous. She had to pass two other houses before she reached the blue weatherboard. As she made her way along the street she felt conspicuous, as if eyes watched her from behind curtains and hands reached for telephones ready to report a suspicious stranger to Crime Watch or skipping the middle man and just calling the police.

She was being ridiculous, there was nothing suspicious about a woman walking along a quiet street in the afternoon. If anyone did look out of their window, she hoped she'd be discounted as a threat. Just a woman on her way to visit a friend or taking a walk in the winter sun, easily dismissed and forgotten. Yet her trainers sounded like they thundered against the concrete foot path and her navy coat felt shiny and ostentatious in the bucolic setting.

When she reached the blue house, Mina turned and, without pausing, walked up the driveway. The lawn looked well maintained, it had been recently mown. An ancient garage loomed at the top of the drive with double doors, the kind that had to be pulled open before a car could enter.

She reached the small porch and, resisting the urge to glance over her shoulder, climbed the two stairs that lead to the front door. The partially enclosed wooden portico provided cover and the opportunity to let out a long, wavering breath. She fumbled Briggs' keys out of her pocket, found what looked like a house key, and slid it into the rather modern looking lock. Before turning it, she tried to swallow and found the saliva in her mouth had evaporated. After a few seconds' hesitation, listening for movement or voices from within, she turned the key.

In the seconds it took her to put the key in the lock and turn it, she'd become so convinced it was the wrong house that when the key actually turned and the door opened, Mina almost didn't believe her own eyes. So surprised was she that, for a moment, she stood frozen in place. The door swung inwards partially revealing a small sitting room.

Already rehearsing what she'd say if there happened to be anyone home, she stepped over the threshold. Before closing the door, she pulled the sleeve of her coat over her hand and wiped the outside of the lock.

The room was spotless apart from a thin layer of dust forming on the coffee table. The small sitting room reminded her of a display from a large furniture store— one of those set-up rooms made to look like it could be transported into any modern house. Only this house was far from modern and the almost industrial-style furnishings looked staged and out of place.

"Hello?" She forced her voice to sound friendly and cheery. The one-word greeting echoed off the highly-polished jarrah floor making the house seem larger, almost cavernous. Listening for any sound or movement, Mina noticed a faint smell of citrus in the air. Something flittered across her memory, but she couldn't quite put her finger on it.

She walked through the sitting room noticing a hallway to the right and kitchen on the left. Deciding the bedrooms seemed the most likely place to start, she entered the hall. There were two doors on the right and one on the left. Before she even started searching, Mina had a gnawing feeling that she wouldn't find any trace of Andrea.

The house was too quiet, too small. Throwing all the doors open quickly confirmed her suspicions: the place was empty. She wandered through to the kitchen and out to the laundry and toilet at the rear noticing that, like the sitting area and bedrooms, everything was spotless. She decided to check the yard and take a quick look in the garage.

The yard revealed nothing apart from a bare Jacaranda tree and a lawn as meticulously trimmed as the one at the front of the house. Not bothering to go around the front and open the double doors, Mina stood on her toes and peered through the window into the old-fashioned garage.

The interior sat in shadows. She cupped her hands around her face and leaned close to the glass. The centre of the building housed nothing more than a wide expanse of concrete with a few oil spots marking the otherwise pristine slab. This had to be where Briggs kept the van. That's why the Hyundai was parked to the side, he had to be able to get the bigger vehicle in and out with ease.

Mina rubbed her temples, she'd been sure he was keeping Andrea at his house. Unless she'd missed something like a trap door or secret room, the place was empty. Just to be on the safe side, she went in through the back door.

The scent of citrus hit her again, this time stronger than in the sitting room. She spotted a bowl on the kitchen table filled with mandarins. The fruit looked soft, like it was on the turn. She wrinkled her nose and walked back towards the hallway. This time she lingered longer in the master bedroom, using her sleeve to cover her hand while she pulled open drawers. Inside the wardrobe she found a row of neatly pressed white business shirts, three jackets along with several pairs of dark pants and two pairs of jeans. Shoes and trainers were arranged in neat row on the bottom and jumpers folded and stacked on the top shelf. *Jesus, only a psycho could be this neat.* Mina closed the cupboard.

The whole house struck her as odd in some way, she tried to identify why it troubled her but couldn't quite put her finger on it. The beginnings of a headache throbbed in her temples. She sat on the bed, a double covered with a plain grey comforter. *This is where he lives,* she told herself. These were the rooms where he planned his crimes, probably fantasised about the violent and depraved things he'd do to his victims. How could evil like that grow in a building and leave no trace?

Not that she expected his vile personality to leave a physical scar, but there was nothing. No books, no posters… Then it struck with the speed of a bullet—that maddening itch that had been bothering her since she entered the small blue house, now it made sense. There was nothing personal. Not one thing to mark Briggs' presence; no photos or magazines, not even a fridge magnet. Mina tapped her index finger to her lips, turning to take in the bland bare surroundings. *He doesn't spend much time here.* It hit her like a physical weight.

She stood and paced up and down in the small bedroom. That's why the house was spotless, it was little more than a shop front. Something to give the appearance of normalcy. The real action took place somewhere else, where he lived out his fantasies. Somewhere no one could hear his victims scream. Not on a suburban street, no, that would be too risky. He'd all but admitted to killing the other three women; to do that Briggs needed privacy. But where?

She'd been going non-stop since first thing in the morning, her mind felt fuzzy with exhaustion. She could tear the house apart, but she doubted she'd find anything. Checking her watch, she realised she'd been wandering around the house for more than half an hour. She couldn't afford to waste any more time, not if she wanted to get home and check on Briggs before it was dark.

She got all the way to the front door when it occurred to her that she'd only given the kitchen a cursory glance. Not that she thought Briggs had Andrea stashed in the fridge, but maybe another quick look would reveal some clue as to where he spent his time.

Mina walked back into the small neat kitchen. This part of the house, like the bedroom and sitting area, was freshly painted, but hadn't been modernised in any other way. Brown speckled Formica covered the cupboards and counter top. There was one plate sitting on the draining board, propped up on a yellow plastic drying rack.

Mina let out a tired sigh. The only thing in the entire house that showed any indication of being lived in was the bowl of mandarins. She felt that flitter again as if something had rippled across her mind moving too rapidly for her to grasp. An idea jumped into her head and she crossed the room and opened the back door. Just as she'd thought, no mandarin tree. She'd check on the way out, but was certain there were no fruit trees in the front yard.

While it wasn't unusual to have a bowl of fruit on your kitchen table, hell, her mother always kept green apples on their table, what struck her was the sheer volume. She studied the bowl noticing that some of the mandarins were irregular—lop-sided. Definitely not from a supermarket or grocery store.

"So, if there's no tree, where are you getting the fruit?" she asked the empty house.

# Chapter Thirty-one

"You're almost home," Regina's breath warmed Andrea's face. Her voice, a husky whisper, seemed to come from far away. But that didn't make sense because Andrea could feel the woman's lips almost touching her ear.

Her eyes wouldn't focus, they were clouded with something. She tried blinking, but couldn't bring Regina into view. There was an orb, brilliant and white, above her—the glare so bright it seemed to fill every inch of the world.

"I can't see you." Andrea heard her own voice, it carried the same hollow quality as Regina's. When the woman didn't answer, Andrea experienced a burst of panic. The feeling of being deserted, left alone, filled her with more than fear—a mixture of dread and despair woven together like a tight-fitting shroud.

*Maybe I'm dead.* The thought should have frightened her, but instead it seemed almost calming. If she were dead, the pain and the terror would end and she'd at least feel peace. But with the light blinding her, she could find no escape from the glare that pinned her to the spot, and the driving agony in her leg.

Andrea rolled her head to the side and the light, still above her, was at least partially blocked. Continuing to blink, she recognised something so alien to her grey cell and bleak surroundings that she let out a cry of surprise. A can of cola, its wavy red lines a cheery contrast to the dusty brown pavers.

Still confused, she reached for the can. Hadn't she been thinking about cola when... The memory came rushing back and with it the sights and sounds of the world around her: a rustle of branches, the sound of wind slapping at the walls. She could see a paved floor and bits and pieces of rubbish mixed with the odd dead leaf or dry stick.

But what really drew Andrea back to the world was the clothing piled haphazardly in one corner: jeans half rolled up like denim skins waiting for their owners to reclaim them. There were a few garments that might have been T-shirts scattered atop a pale blue sports bag. Nearby, one green trainer—an unnatural colour that only existed on hi-vis clothing—lay on its side as if someone had jogged right out of it and kept going. Draped over the T-shirts and random clothing was a jumper. One sleeve flopped out flat as if the owner had evaporated. But what made Andrea want to scream until her lungs collapsed was the pattern on the jumper: a puzzled looking bulldog with a circular black patch surrounding his right eye.

She got as far as opening her mouth and sucking in air before a deep rattling cough snatched the breath from her body. Her chest jerked and with each convulsive bark, a spike of pain ran up her right leg. Andrea rolled onto her side curling herself into a half-ball. The coughing lessened and then sputtered to a stop.

Using her elbow to push herself up, she managed to sit. She took in a small wooden structure littered with cans and discarded food wrappers. The smell of rot and something musky hung in the air. This was where he spent his time. The pile of clothes told her there'd been many before her, their lives reduced to a pile of rags. She looked up at the hole in the roof, the sunlight so brilliant and white, now appeared drained of colour and grey as if a dirty blanket had been thrown over the sky.

She'd come so close, for a moment up there on the top of the building, she'd actually believed her nightmare was nearly over. But that moment turned out to be nothing more than another cruel torture, like the beatings and starvation, just one more agony to be endured. It occurred to her that this was hell. Maybe that night at the college she died and since then she'd been in hell. But what was her sin? What had she done to earn this damnation?

She lifted her head and addressed the sky. "I didn't do anything wrong."

She wanted to be back on the mattress where she wouldn't have to look at the pile of clothes and be reminded of her life outside of this place. She sniffed and rubbed her nose along her sleeve. Even through the pain and misery, thirst bit at her. She was almost glad of the burning need, that endless longing reminded her she was still alive.

The cola can lay on its side, just out of reach. She tried to get up, but a shaft of pain rocketed through her right leg. Falling back onto her side, she bunched her ruined hands into fists and screwed her eyes closed. There were no more tears, although the dehydration had more to do with that than inner strength. After a few minutes, the pain in her leg ebbed enough for her to drag herself towards the can.

She could smell the contents even before she lifted the can and heard the liquid tinkle against the sides. The sweet smell of caramel mixed with cloves made her tongue tingle with anticipation. There were a few ants crawling lazily around the opening, but that didn't stop her putting the can to her mouth and drinking. The liquid washed over her parched lips and filled her mouth. Slightly gritty and without the slightest trace of fizz, the cola was the sweetest most delicious thing she'd ever tasted.

Miraculously, there was enough left in the can for two mouthfuls which she swallowed without pause. Then, wincing at the jarring agony in her leg, Andrea dragged herself farther using her left leg and arms to propel herself across the small room. When she reached the pile of discarded clothing, she rolled onto her back and sat up.

Stripping off the almost-unrecognisable-as-white fleecy top took some effort. The sleeves tugged at the scabs forming on the backs of her hands and her shoulder, still tender from the bite wound. But with some wincing and manoeuvring, she managed to pull the foul-smelling garment over her head.

Andrea held the top in her hands, trying not to remember the day he made her wash herself and then put on her captive's uniform. She dashed the garment into a ball and flung it across the room. She pulled on her bulldog jumper marvelling at how soft and clean if felt against her skin.

"I'm sorry," she said to the pile of clothes whose owners would never return. Without pause, she began to rummage through the abandoned garments.

She'd hoped for a mobile phone, but hadn't really believed the Magician would be careless enough to leave one, even on the other side of a locked door. What she did find was a packet of Life Savers which struck her as hilarious. When she held the brightly coloured tube in her hand, a fit of giggles bubbled up in her throat almost setting off another coughing fit.

The clothes turned out to be quite a bounty. Andrea found a strip of paracetamol with two cracked tablets still in the blister packs. She popped the tablets out and put the crumbling pieces on her tongue, grimacing as the bitter pills dissolved in her mouth. *I've broken my leg and I'm treating it with paracetamol,* the thought struck her almost as funny as the Life Savers.

The blue sports bag contained a silver drink bottle that was a quarter full and a zip-lock bag with a few half-melted M&Ms. Tears rolled in thin streams down her cheeks. She'd been working at staying alive for so long now, hadn't she paid her dues?

The door to the small lean-to room was made of wood, it reminded her of a garden gate. Even if it were unlocked, her leg was broken, either that or badly injured. She could barely sit up without stabbing pains in her chest and fits of coughing so violent, it seemed her body would turn inside-out. Maybe hard work just didn't cut it.

She peeled open the Life Savers and put a circle of sweet, sugary lolly in her mouth. Then, leaning on the pile of clothing, she closed her eyes.

"I'm Andrea Fields. My mother is Maureen and my dad's Norman. I live on Waverly Road and I work at the Busy Buy. I'm going to be a writer and buy a big house near the river." She repeated the words over and over. The chant-like quality of her voice lulled her until she lowered her head onto the discarded clothing.

# Chapter Thirty-two

"How you feeling?" Mina noticed Briggs didn't stand this time. Instead, he remained seated with his back leaning against the post. The water bottle lay nearby, drained of its contents. The light spilling through the open doorway had turned from gold to grey making it difficult to see. But even in the dull light she could tell his lips were dry and cracked and there were dark patches under his watery-blue eyes.

He shrugged. "Where have you been?" His knees were drawn up, legs spread apart. "You're not a very good host, Mina. I'm starting to feel a bit neglected."

Mina had taken up her position on the milk crate. Even with the door open the room had a stale odour of sweat and urine that seemed to coat the inside of her mouth.

"I know she's not at your house." Mina reached into her pocket and pulled out a mandarin, watching Briggs' expression. His eyes flicked to the piece of fruit in her hand and, for a second, she thought she saw something there that looked like uncertainty. "So, the question is," she paused dramatically. "Where would a freak like you take a girl so that you could play out your sick fantasies?"

Briggs stared at the mandarin then turned his gaze back on Mina. "That's what you're doing right now, isn't it? Playing out a revenge fantasy. But my question to you is," he paused just as Mina had done. "Who is it that hurt you so much that you'd like to chain them up and punish them?"

Mina wanted to look away from those oddly glittering eyes, but wouldn't give him the satisfaction. He was suffering, she could see it in the sag of his shoulders and the sunken look of his cheeks. Nevertheless, he seemed to be enjoying himself.

"My guess would be Daddy?" His voice was little more than a whisper.

Mina forced herself to smile even though blood pumped through her ears and every nerve in her body vibrated, alive with anger.

"You look hungry." She held up the mandarin. "I've read that a human being can go twenty-eight days without food but only three without water." She dropped the piece of fruit in her lap. "But what I've always wondered is, if you take that to the limit and say give that same person a drink every two and half days, can you keep them alive for the full twenty-eight without feeding them?"

Briggs shifted his legs, letting them slide out until they were flat on the concrete. "If you've read all about it, you'll know Andrea won't last much longer." He paused again, this time because his voice broke slightly. "I never wanted to hurt you. I still don't. If you let me loose, I'll take you to her."

Mina stood. "You're right about Andrea, she won't last much longer." She put the mandarin back in her pocket. "If you don't tell where she is, by this time tomorrow, I'll assume she's dead." She turned and walked to the door. "Once that happens, you'll only see me every two and half days."

He didn't respond, she hadn't expected him to. She locked the door and waited, hoping he'd call her back but only the sound of the wind rattling the leaves and her own breathing filled the space. Briggs wouldn't talk, at least not in time to save Andrea. She pulled the piece of fruit out of her pocket and hurled it into the trees.

She was getting close, she could feel it, but she could also feel time slipping through her fingers. Suddenly, the weight of what she was doing settled on her, a familiar burden that pushed her down until she could barely lift her head. Her legs buckled and she sunk to the ground.

Whatever decision she made now would be life or death. If she went to the police, they might have the resources to find his secondary residence. But that would mean handing over not only Briggs but herself to the authorities. And what proof did she have that Briggs was the Magician? The hairclips probably only had her fingerprints on them. The police knew she was the last person to see Andrea before she disappeared. However she looked at it, Briggs would win and the real loser would be Andrea.

Mina dropped her head into her hands. *How did things get so out of control?* The answer came to her simply and without thought—*when Mum died. No*, Mina corrected herself. *Not when she died, when I killed her.*

\* \* \*

Eight months from diagnosis to death. That's how long pancreatic cancer took to wipe away everything that held Mina's life together. She could pinpoint the exact moment when she gave up and decided to end her mother's suffering. By that time, the cancer was already eating away at Irene's lungs and bones. Not for the first time, Mina decided to play God with someone else's life.

"Your mother can return home for a while." The oncologist, Dr Flower, a small man with an oddly pretty name, delivered the news. The cluttered meeting room off the nurse's station smelled of coffee and hand sanitiser, a sickening combination. "Maybe a few weeks and then…"

His voice trailed off and he cleared his throat. "Then we'll probably admit Irene into the Palliative Care Unit."

Mina nodded, not sure what she was supposed to say or ask. Dr Flower had a deeply lined face, shadowed by thick dark brows that gave him a bear-like appearance. How many times, she wondered, had he given this news to numb, exhausted people. People who'd endured the months, sometimes years of dread, and dashed hopes.

"Your mother has fought a long battle." His voice was gentle—soft. "Now it's time for her to rest and let us take care of her."

*You mean die*, Mina thought but didn't say. She wondered if he used the exact words, *let us take care of her*, with all the other families. And what part would Dr Flower play in *taking care* of her mother? In that moment, Mina understood what *taking care* should mean.

"Okay, I understand." There was nothing left to say, so Mina stood. She would *take care* of Irene in a way that no one else could or would.

That afternoon, she telephoned Herbert Longfellow and asked if she could pop in to talk with him and his wife May about her mother's condition and certain financial arrangements. Over the course of her mother's illness Herbert and May had been a constant source of support. The couple visited Irene in hospital at least twice a week. May, childless herself but innately motherly, insisted on cooking meals and delivering them in Tupperware containers, three a week for the past six months. When Mina requested a meeting, Herbert seemed so genuinely concerned and eager to help, she felt a pang of guilt for what she was about to do.

May, a type-one diabetic since childhood was what Mina's mother described as old-school. Refusing to wear a pump, May injected herself with insulin twice each day and kept the drugs and pens in the kitchen fridge.

During what turned out to be a tearful meeting, Mina asked to use the bathroom. Listening to the elderly couple discuss the unfairness of Irene's illness, Mina stopped outside the bathroom. She pulled the door closed so it would appear she was inside then slipped farther into the house.

Without hesitating, she opened the fridge, wincing at the clink of bottles. There were two rows of vials. The small glass bottles filled with clear liquid were stored on a shelf in the door of the fridge. She took two vials, stashing one in each pocket of her jacket.

The whole side trip to the kitchen took less than a minute giving her ample time to return to the bathroom where she flushed the toilet and then turned on the tap. She let the water run, counting to twenty before turning it off. May would probably notice the vials were missing, but Mina doubted she'd suspect her of taking them. And if she did, what then? She couldn't imagine Herbert and May turning her over to the police.

As it turned out, neither Herbert nor May ever mentioned the missing insulin. When, two days later, Irene slipped away peacefully in her sleep no questions were asked. Dr Flower issued a death certificate without even seeing Irene's body. If May or Herbert harboured any suspicions, they kept them to themselves.

Irene's death, everyone said, was a mercy. She'd escaped the suffering that lay ahead. When Irene's hairless, emaciated, fifty-year old body was cremated, the consensus amongst the mourners was how lucky she'd been to die so peacefully.

Although part of Mina's mind understood the sentiment *and* agreed—wasn't that the final and only way she had left to care for her mother?—another part of her wanted to scream until her throat bled, smash the china, and turn over the tables of tea and sandwiches in the small room adjoining the crematorium. She wanted to make them understand that there was nothing lucky about anything that happened to Irene Constantine—the woman who married a monster and died at her daughter's hand.

Instead, Mina found a fixed point in the distance and kept her eyes trained on it, looking back only long enough to thank Irene's friends for coming.

That evening she drove to the bottle shop. Mina chose vodka because it reminded her of the insulin she'd injected into her mother's drip. The next eighteen months were little more than a muddy void of drinking and solitude, until the fog that surrounded her began to lift and she decided to sign up for a writing course, re-join the human race.

*  *  *

When Mina lifted her head, the sky had changed from grey to fiery orange. Her back ached, she'd been sitting against the door to the back shed for at least half an hour. Scrambling to her feet, she groaned like an old woman struggling out of an armchair. Her life was out of control, she recognised that but she intended to finish what she had started.

She walked back to the house listening to the sound of her trainers slapping against the uneven path. She wouldn't go to the police. Whatever had to be done, she'd do it alone.

"I can live with the consequences." She kept coming back to the gesture Briggs made when she asked him about the other girls: kissing his fingers and scattering invisible leaves on the wind. Briggs' death would cause her no grief.

Climbing the two steps to the deck, exhaustion swept over her, making the last few metres to the door seem like a marathon. She needed to eat, but her body wanted sleep more than nourishment. She pulled open the back door and registered the sound of her phone ringing.

The urgent peel of the simulated ring broke through her fatigued mind, and the headache that had been building behind her eyes ratcheted up a notch. She snatched up the phone, ready to tell whoever was calling to go to hell.

"Mina, it's me." Lee's voice, deep and soft, snatched the words out of her throat. In that moment, she wanted nothing more than to lay her head on his shoulder, let him chase away the demons and listen to him tell her everything would be all right.

"Mina, are you still there?"

"Yes." She felt wide awake.

"I need to see you."

Silence echoed across the line, for a second she thought she'd imagined the phone ringing and hearing his voice.

"I know you're angry with me and you have every right to be but… there are things you should know."

She didn't understand. Was he ringing because he wanted her back or just to try to explain his actions?

"What are you talking about?" She felt sick and tired of playing games, of listening to Briggs talk in circles. Now it seemed Lee was doing the same thing. "What things do I need to know?" Her voice had taken on a shrill edge, but she didn't care. "That you're a selfish prick who used me and now feels guilty? Because I already know that."

She could hear him breathing, trying to come up with something that would defend his actions. "Just let me see you so I can explain."

"Not—"

"It's not what you think. Just give me a chance." He spoke so quickly, she could barely keep up with what he was saying. "I'm not trying to justify myself or get you back, I know I've blown it. All I want is for you to understand the truth." He paused. "Please." There was desperation in his voice and something else that Mina couldn't quite identify. She thought of the way he looked last time she saw him; there were subtle changes in his appearance and that look of frailty was back.

"All right." Part of her just wanted to see him, even if it was for the last time. As hard as she'd tried, she couldn't hate him.

"What's your address?"

"No." She heard her voice and realised the word came out too fast and too loud. "I mean, I'd rather we met somewhere."

"Of course, that's fine." The line was silent, she couldn't even hear his breathing. "How about Fire Lake? Tomorrow at nine?"

She thought of that moment on the river bank, the way his lips tasted like mint and coffee. The feel of her heart fluttering when he held her. She didn't want an ugly scene marring that perfect moment. She wished he'd suggested anywhere but there.

"Okay?" he asked.

"Okay."

# Chapter Thirty-three

The door to the shed stood open, the interior a spider's web of shadows. Mina didn't want to step inside, but the sounds drew her in... slapping and sucking noises, as if someone were painting on a soft canvas. She tried to make her voice work, call out for help, but her throat clenched and all that came out was a weak gasp.

Inside, Briggs sat at the base of the post with his back turned. For some reason, he seemed to be encircled by light. She could see his head and shoulders moving, the jerky movements reminded Mina of a musician bent over an instrument.

She drew closer, not because she wanted to. Her feet kept moving and as she neared Briggs, the sounds were louder—wet. She could hear other things now, snapping and crunching. She didn't want to see what he was doing, every part of her wanted to turn away yet her hand was reaching out towards his shoulder. Her fingers looked bleached and stark as she entered the strange yellow light.

Her hand brushed Briggs' shoulder and his head snapped around. Blood covered his lips and cheeks in what looked like a sloppily painted clown mouth. He smiled, revealing teeth and gums stained red with ribbons of flesh caught like food scraps in his bloody grin.

"I *am* a magician, see." When he spoke, his lips smacked together spraying blood into the air like red mist.

Mina pulled her eyes away from his face to see what he was holding. His wrists were bloody stumps, raw and meaty with shards of white poking out from the centres. In his lap were the chains and cord resting on his severed hands. Mina stumbled back, her mouth opening and closing in a silent scream.

Her back hit the concrete but there was no pain, only a sense of falling. *This can't be happening, he ate through his hands!* In her mind, the words shrilled but still no sound passed her lips.

Briggs' weight dropped on top of her, driving the breath out of her lungs. "Abracadabra." His lips smacked together splattering her cheeks with blood. "You want to try some?" he asked, holding one fleshy stump up to her eyes.

Mina bucked, and twisted her head away from the disgusting pulpy mess. She opened her mouth and forced her throat to croak out a wail.

Her eyes snapped open and the room came into bleary focus. Thin chinks of light seeped in around the curtains making the outline of the wardrobe and night stand visible against the dark.

Her heart hammered inside her chest. The image of the gory stumps still filled her mind making the jump back from nightmare to reality almost impossible to grasp. Details slowly came into focus: the damp feel of her T-shirt clinging to her back, and the sound of her breathing. She wanted light, needed it.

There was no nightstand, so she untangled herself from the sheets and stumbled around the room searching for the switch. The layout of the bedroom was still new to her, so instead of heading for the doorway, she found herself walking into her suitcase and stubbing her big toe.

"Holy fuck." The sound of her voice in the dark reassured her. She almost laughed but the image of Briggs' face, grinning and bloody, popped back into her mind.

She groped around in the dark for a few more seconds before her hand landed on the doorframe, and then the switch. The stark and glaring light filled the room, chasing away some of the fear. She squinted at the sudden brightness and turned back to the bed. With the rest of the house still in darkness, she had no desire to wander any farther searching for switches. Instead, she sat on her bed, knees pulled up to her chest.

She'd had some weird nightmares in her time, but couldn't recall anything as real or horrific as the one she just experienced. The images faded slightly, but she doubted she'd ever forget the way Briggs held up his chewed wrists. She wondered what he was doing out in the shed. Was he sleeping or, like her, staring into the darkness waiting for the dawn?

\* \* \*

When Mina slid the key into the lock, her mind threw up images of Briggs' head and shoulders moving busily over his hands. She kept hearing the wet slapping sound his lips made and feeling the spray of blood hit her cheeks. The rational part of her mind, the area that functioned reasonably during the daylight hours, told her what she'd experienced last night had been nothing more than a vivid nightmare. Yet each movement she made seemed to pull her further back into the ghastly dream.

The door swung open. Entering the shed had become something of a routine: kick the door and let it swing open, survey Briggs' position, enter with caution. Mina took a step into the shed and halted, half expecting to hear the crunching and slurping sounds coming from the figure on the ground.

"I hope you brought me a drink." His voice came from the shadows, cracked and raw.

Mina felt her body relax. "Tell me where she is and you can have as much water as you want." She waited but Briggs didn't turn around.

His back rested against the post, his shoulders slumped. She couldn't see his face but could tell by his posture that the lack of food and water was working on him. Only then did she notice the smell and hear the buzzing of flies. Her stomach lurched and she clamped her hand over her mouth. The stench of human waste filled her nose.

She gagged and took a step back, turning her head towards the open door. For the first time since Briggs attacked her in the kitchen, Mina felt a wave of sympathy for the man. What she was doing was inhuman. She wouldn't leave an animal to suffer in this way.

Leaning against the door frame trying to take shallow breaths through her mouth, Mina tried again. "Tell me where Andrea is. Why are you forcing me to do this?" She could feel the tears building behind her eyes. She didn't want to cry in front of him, but the inhumanity of the situation overwhelmed her. "Just tell me."

She floundered, on the verge of running back to the house and fetching him water. She remembered seeing an outside tap near the galvanized shed closer to the house, if she attached the hose-pipe to the tap, she could use it to wash the mess off the concrete floor. She turned, and was half-way out the door when she heard the noise.

At first it sounded like choking, a crackling raspy sound. But then she realised what she was hearing—laughter.

Mina stopped and turned back almost unable to comprehend what was happening. "What the fuck is wrong with you?" Her voice wavered and broke. The tears were flowing now, she could feel them running down her cheeks.

"The first girl." His voice came out of the shadows like a wisp of poisonous smoke. "I don't remember her name. I barely touched her that first night and she shat herself." He chuckled. "It made me feel sick too, so I know what you're going through." The chains tinkled against the concrete as he swivelled around. "You can feel it, can't you?" His eyes appeared in the gloom like twin blue orbs.

"Feel what?" Mina wanted to slam the door but suddenly couldn't force herself to move.

"Our connection, it's getting stronger." His teeth appeared in the darkness and she realised he was smiling.

For a second, she wondered if she was still dreaming and the foul smell paired with croaking laughter were merely figments of her stressed mind. But the wood, coarse with flaking paint under her hand felt too solid to be anything but real. She dragged herself through the door on shaky legs. How she managed to pull it shut and get the padlock in place was little more than a blur.

With the sound of Briggs' guttural laughter still echoing in her ears, Mina ran back to the house. Once inside, she flopped into the nearest chair and tried to get her breath. Being in the back shed with Briggs was like stepping into another world, what she saw *and* felt terrified her. She lurched to her feet and switched the kettle on.

Mina made a strong cup of instant coffee, sweetened with two heaped spoons of sugar. The caffeine should have had the opposite effect, but the hot sweet drink calmed her jangling nerves and stilled her hands. By the time she had drained the last dregs, she felt able to think clearly. She was in over her head and there was no easy way out.

Briggs would never talk, that should have been clear from the start. He'd rather stew in his own filth and die a slow death than give up his secrets. She'd been crazy to think she could force him to cooperate. After what she'd just seen, she had no doubt the man was a psychopath with no understanding of human emotions.

*That's great*, she told herself. *Very insightful, but what are you going to do about it?* She hadn't quite worked that part out yet, but one thing she knew, it had to end today. Briggs was like a tumour, black and poisonous, growing and spreading. If she didn't do something soon, he'd infect her. *Maybe he already has?* No, she wouldn't accept that. Her conscience was far from pearly white, but she wasn't like him. Not yet.

She went into the bedroom and got ready for her meeting with Lee. As she dressed, the way ahead become clearer. She'd keep her date with Lee and then talk to Robbie. Only this time, she'd get the answers she needed.

Sitting on the edge of the bed zipping up her left boot, it occurred to her that in revealing her interest in Briggs, she'd also be revealing her involvement in something that would ultimately get her arrested.

Maybe the time had come to decide what was more important, protecting herself or finding Andrea. She stopped half way through pulling on the other boot. It came down to a simple choice: *Me or Andrea*.

The minutes ticked by while she sat with one black boot in her hands and tried to see a way out of the mess she'd fallen into. In the end, someone would suffer. She just hoped she had the courage to do the right thing.

\* \* \*

Dark clouds gathered, heavy and low in the morning sky. Mina drove the narrow entry road glancing nervously at the impending storm. She missed Lee, wanted him back in her life but with so much turmoil and uncertainty she regretted agreeing to see him. Could meeting up with Lee do anything but complicate an already dire situation? After today, her life might change forever. What good would it do to hear Lee's excuses?

The lake came into view and, in spite of the dread sitting in the pit of her stomach, her heart fluttered—not with fear, but nervousness. She spotted Lee's car; spraying up a shower of pea stones she pulled up next to it. A glance at her watch told her it was just after nine.

She found Lee sitting on a gigantic felled tree trunk. His head was turned towards the lake telling her he either hadn't heard her, or had better things to look at than her approach. *Stop it*, she told herself. What was the point of coming if she'd already judged him to be disinterested?

As if reading her thoughts, he turned away from the lake and stood. "Hi. I brought coffee." He held a cup in each hand, offering one to her as she drew near.

Mina took the cup, grateful to have something to do with her hands. For a moment, they both stood awkwardly holding the paper cups.

"Do you want to sit?" He gestured to the log and, in that moment, she noticed how dishevelled he appeared. His hair stood up in messy clumps and there was at least two days' worth of stubble on his face.

Mina ignored his offer and got straight to the point. "What's going on, Lee? You tell me you're going to Queensland, give me the brush off, and then turn up here looking like hell." She waited for him to speak, growing more impatient by the second. "Okay. This has been fun, but I have a lot going on right now so—" She started to turn away.

"I have cancer."

Mina stopped. She shook her head as if it would clear her thoughts. "What… What did you say?"

Lee sat down on the log and set his cup between his feet. "I have lymphoma. That's why I ended it with you." He ran his hand over the stubble covering his chin. "I thought it was better—easier that way. But then when I saw you the other day… the way you looked at me…" His stormy green eyes were red-rimmed suggesting that he'd been awake for days.

Mina tried to speak, but her thoughts were in disarray and she could feel something unpleasant churning in her stomach. He was sick, that's what Lee was telling her.

"Cancer?" She managed to get the word out and found that it tasted sour on her tongue.

Lee nodded. "I shouldn't have dragged you into my life in the first place, but I was okay. I'd been okay for a long time and you were..." he trailed off.

Her legs felt wobbly as if they might bow outwards. She sat on the log, not quite touching him but close.

"I don't understand any of this." She could hear the anger in her voice, but had no idea who she was mad at. "How can you have cancer?" Even as she asked, the memory of those moments when she'd caught a glimpse of something that she couldn't quite identify came to mind. Then, amidst the shock and disbelief another thought occurred to her. "How long have you known?"

He let out a long breath and leaned forward, resting his forearms on his thighs. "That last morning we were together, I rushed off because I had an appointment with my oncologist. Just routine." An edge of bitterness crept into his voice. "That's what they call it for people like me, routine. I'd had my regular screening the week before. I always get edgy waiting for the results, but I really thought I was okay." He gave a short humourless laugh. "Leukaemia at eleven and lymphoma at thirty-three."

"You should have told me." She wanted to say more, but the words wouldn't come.

He looked down, making it impossible for her to see his eyes. She wished he'd lift his head and look at her so she could get some idea how he was feeling. "Yeah? It's not an easy thing to tell someone you've just started seeing. By the way, I have cancer and probably won't be around long, wanna have dinner with me?" The anger in his voice took her by surprise.

"Don't say that."

His head snapped up and she could see just how angry and confused he was. Seeing him like this made her want to weep. "Sorry, Mina but I can't put on a happy face. That's one of the reasons I didn't tell you. I couldn't be strong for someone else and if I'd stayed with you..." He held up his hands, "I couldn't cope with what it would do to you. I suppose that makes me selfish, but I've been through this before."

The pained look in his eyes told her Lee was in desperate need of help. He'd become a man lost and in shock with nothing to hang on to. She'd seen the same look in her own eyes the night she bought the first bottle of vodka. Briggs was so convinced that they'd met for a reason, but it occurred to Mina that maybe *Lee* was the reason she went to Alice College that night and everything else that had happened was secondary.

She put her coffee cup on the damp grass and took hold of Lee's arm. He jolted at her touch.

"You don't have to put on a happy face *or* be strong for me." His skin felt cool under her fingers. She pulled him towards her. "I'm quite tough and ruthless."

This brought a smile and for a second it was like the sun had appeared from behind the clouds. In that moment, she realised she'd do anything for him.

He let himself be pulled into her arms. Once his body touched hers, he grasped her with enough force to take her breath away. They didn't kiss, instead she held him and listened to him quietly sob.

When they finally separated, Lee lifted her hands to his lips and pressed them against the skin on the inside of her wrist. "You're a good person, Mina. Too good. I feel better knowing you don't hate me, but I won't let you get sucked into my nightmare." He stood, still holding her hand. "I'm starting treatment on Thursday so I won't be in Dark Water much longer." The finality of his words frightened her.

The thought of him disappearing out of her life again was almost unbearable. Up until now, she'd managed to keep her emotions from overwhelming her, but she could feel her strength crumble.

"You're not walking out on me again." She managed to keep the quiver out of her voice.

He dropped her hand. "Look, I can't–"

"That wasn't a question." She stood. "You look like you haven't had a decent meal in days, at least let me buy you an early lunch."

He shrugged and nodded. "Okay, anywhere but Blue Smoke; my cousin works there and I haven't told her yet. Besides, if she sees us together she'll never let up with the questions."

Mina stopped walking. She felt off balance like she was standing on the edge of another world, one where coincidence and fate were a tangled mess and everything was somehow entwined.

"What's wrong?" Lee turned back and reached out his hand. "Are you okay?"

"Is your cousin's name Robbie?"

Lee's eyes widened in surprise. "Yes. How'd you know about Robbie?" Behind him, Mina could see the dark clouds building. What started out as an overcast day now had all the makings of an impending storm.

"She's a friend of mine." As the words came out, she realised their truth. Robbie was her friend; the first she'd made in years, and now it seemed she too was linked to Lee.

Lee held out his hand which Mina took. "How long have you been in Dark Water?" Lee asked as they walked to their cars.

Mina had to think for a moment. In many ways it seemed like years since Briggs turned up at her house but in fact, it had only been a few days. "Just a few days. I met Robbie at the café when I first came to town. She kind of befriended me."

"That sounds like Robbie." He let go of her hand and pulled his car keys out of his pocket. "Follow me, I know somewhere that serves a great burger and chips."

# Chapter Thirty-four

The burger shop turned out to be a sprawling winery fifteen minutes south of Dark Water. Heavy pine tables lined the tiled terrace that surrounded the impressive stone building. In view of the impending rain, they took a table inside.

It was still too early for lunch so they ordered a late breakfast from a plump redheaded waitress in her late forties. When they finished ordering, Lee leaned his elbows on the table. "What are you doing in Dark Water?"

It wasn't what she'd been expecting, but she couldn't blame him for wondering. "The easy answer is, I don't really know." She pulled her hair over her right shoulder and tucked it into the neck of her cream coloured jumper. "I just needed a new start and Dark Water was as good a place as any."

Lee didn't answer, his face remained unreadable.

"I didn't come here searching for you, if that's what you think."

He chuckled and for the first time that day, he seemed genuinely amused. "Okay, okay. I'm just asking."

Mina couldn't help smiling, it was good to see him relax. There were so many things she wanted to ask him about his upcoming treatment, but couldn't bear to ruin the moment. So instead, she searched for a safe subject. "Are you and Robbie close?"

"We used to be, but I've been away for a long time, so not so much anymore. She tries to keep in touch, but I'm not great at remembering to call or email." He frowned and she could almost see his thoughts turn inward.

"You should tell her."

He nodded, but didn't answer.

When their food arrived, Mina felt a sudden swell of sadness. Lee would be going back to Perth soon, to start treatment. She understood that an incipient relationship was the last thing he needed right now and for her... her thoughts were muddled, the overload of information catching up with her like a delayed shockwave.

Suddenly the sounds of other diners' chatter seemed too loud, and the smell of egg filled her mouth. She wished they'd sat outside—at least that way she'd be able to breathe. She reached out and tried to pour herself a glass of water and wasn't surprised to see her hand shaking.

"It's a lot to take in." Lee took the bottle out of her hand. "Let me." His hands were steady. He filled her glass and his own.

Mina took a few sips of icy water. She suspected that Lee's shocking news wasn't the only thing affecting her. She'd promised herself she'd end it today. Her plan had been to go from Lee to Robbie, could she still do that in light of the bombshell Lee was about to drop on his cousin?

She heard him speaking, saying something, but for a second Mina had drifted away. "Sorry, Lee. What was that?"

"I said, this place used to be an apiary. My uncle, Robbie's dad, used to bring us here to buy honey when we were kids."

As Lee talked, an idea popped into Mina's head. "You and Robbie would have hung out with the same people growing up?" Mina tried to make the question sound casual, but her hands were starting to sweat so heavily that she had to put her knife and fork down so she could use the napkin to wipe them.

"Yeah, well in a small town everyone either knows everyone or is related to them, so pretty much." He bit into a piece of toast. His green eyes still looked tired, but the raw, pained look had eased somewhat. "You know how it is, people come and go."

"Mmm." Mina picked up her fork and pushed the uneaten scrambled eggs around on her plate. "Do you know a guy called Bri—I mean Terry? Terry Briggs?"

The brown flecks in Lee's eyes looked darker as if burning through the green that surrounded them. "How do you know him?" There was a warning edge to his voice, Briggs' name hit a nerve.

"He showed me the house I rented." She could have said more but thought it wiser to wait and hear what Lee knew about the man.

He dropped the half-eaten slice of toast onto his plate and Mina noticed that like her, he'd done little more than push his food around. "You should steer clear of him, Mina."

She had a sudden image of Briggs, staring out at her from the depths of the shed, his lips drawn back in a humourless smile. "He seemed okay, bit of a geek." She hated lying to Lee, but he clearly knew something about the man and she had to know what that something was.

"He's dangerous." Lee wiped his mouth with a napkin and tossed it on his plate. "I know he seems okay, but there's something not right about him. Very not right. Trust me, he's not someone you want to know."

He stopped talking and stared off towards the counter where a couple of women were chatting to the red-headed waitress. Mina followed his gaze, wondering what had grabbed his attention, but when the women followed the waitress to a table near the window, she realised he hadn't been watching them, but became lost in thought.

"Are you okay? You look like you just saw a ghost." Mina tried to make the question sound light-hearted, but had a feeling she was getting close to something.

Lee dragged his gaze back to her. "Sorry. It's just, when you mentioned Terry Briggs, it brought back some memories. Bad ones."

"I didn't mean to upset you." She could feel the heat rising in her cheeks. Even with guilt burning her skin, she couldn't stop herself pushing for more answers. "Tell me what happened."

He picked up his coffee cup and took a sip. "I think I've laid enough on you for one day. You don't need to hear about my childhood traumas on top of everything else."

Mina slipped her hands under the table and gripped her thighs. "Tell me." Then she said something she knew would drive him to share what was obviously a painful memory. "I'll probably have to see Terry at rental inspections *and* around town, how worried should I be?" Her fingers dug into the thick fabric of her jeans, squeezing the skin hard enough to make her legs throb. She had to know what Lee knew about the man she'd been keeping chained up in her shed.

He held her gaze, his eyes boring into hers. It seemed like he was looking for something. She had the urge to look away but forced herself to maintain eye contact. Finally, he nodded.

"Terry was older than me, maybe by five years. He was always friendly, kind of funny. I was only twelve at the time, and having an older boy talk to me like I was a mate, made me feel," he sighed, "I suppose it made me feel important. I'd been sick the year before and because of the treatment, lost my hair. I was small for my age, skinny."

Mina felt the few mouthfuls of eggs she'd eaten churning in the pit of her stomach. Forcing Lee to talk about something so painful and personal felt like one of the most shameful things she'd ever done, but she let him continue.

"I was just starting to feel better, putting on a bit of weight and so I started begging my parents to let me ride my bike again. Well, finally my dad gave in. So on Fridays, I'd ride up to the chip shop and pick up my mum's order: three times snapper and chips." He swallowed and grimaced as if the words tasted sour on his tongue. "Part of the reason I liked picking up the order was talking to Terry. He always made jokes when I came in. You know lame stuff like knock-knock jokes."

As he spoke, she could almost see Briggs wearing that over enthusiastic geeky grin. She had fallen for it at twenty-nine, she could only imagine how easily he'd have charmed a kid with that nice-guy act.

"Then one day, he offers to let me ride his trail bike. He tells me not to tell my parents because he'd get in trouble if they knew he'd let me go on a real motor bike. I remember that day, he even walked me out of the chip shop. I felt like we were a couple of real cool blokes, talking about bikes and bush trails. It never occurred to me to question why a seventeen-year-old would invite a sickly little kid like me around to his house." Lee shook his head. "Why would it? My parents taught me to be afraid of strangers, but Terry wasn't a stranger, he was my friend."

Part of her didn't want to hear the rest, couldn't bear to watch Lee's face as he relived whatever nightmarish thing Briggs had put him through. But another part of her, a dark, angry fragment of her personality needed to hear the details. That shadowy piece of her wanted to feed the rage, fuel it with Lee's distress so that when the time came, she'd be able to summon that black, festering cloud and let it loose on Briggs.

"I told my parents I was going to visit Robbie," his voice tinged with bitterness. "When I got to Terry's place, his Auntie Dolly wasn't home."

"Hang on," she interrupted. "I thought his Auntie's name was Dorothy."

Lee looked surprised, as if he'd forgotten she was still sitting across from him. He frowned and a deep line appeared between his brows. "Yes, that's right, but everyone called her Dolly. It's a shortened form of Dorothy." He looked ready to continue, but then hesitated. "How do you know his aunt's name?" The question had a suspicious edge.

Mina picked up her coffee cup and shrugged. "He said something about his auntie when he was showing me the house."

Lee looked doubtful, as if he was weighing her story to see if it held water. Finally, he jerked his chin up and continued. "Terry said he had the bike in his shed and that we'd have to be quick before his auntie got home. There was no bike. He had a possum tied up with a length of fishing wire." Lee shook his head. "It was one of the most fucking gruesome things I'd ever seen—still is."

"The wire was tied around its back leg, sort of buried in the skin from where the animal had been trying to pull itself free. There was blood all over the floor, and I remember thinking I could see the possum's tiny bones where the flesh had been cut away." Lee poured himself and Mina a glass of water from the bottle on the table. Before he continued, he took a swallow.

"I didn't want to be in that shed. I remember asking Terry, *where's the bike?* He laughed and said this would be much more fun. I was only a kid, but I'd seen enough movies to know something terrible was about to happen. Terry closed the door behind him and stood blocking the exit. Then he picked something up off the window ledge. One of those homemade slingshots, you know the ones made from a $V$-shaped branch with rubber attached." He motioned with his fingers, using his index and middle finger to make the $V$.

"God that shed stunk, like animal shit, blood and sweat all rolled into one. Terry said, *watch this*. He started firing marbles at the terrified creature. And the more he fired, the more the possum jumped and yanked at its leg. I should have done something to stop him, but I just stood there and started to cry." He held Mina's gaze, his stormy ocean eyes watery with emotion. "I didn't even tell him to stop, I just stood there with my hands over my ears so I wouldn't have to hear the thing screaming, and cried."

"You were just a kid, he was bigger than you, older. There was nothing you could have done." It was true but she couldn't help thinking of the night she'd left Andrea standing in the dark empty parking lot. How many times since then had she tried to convince herself that there was nothing she could have done?

She wasn't sure if he'd heard her, he seemed to be thinking. Maybe hearing the long-ago echo of the possum's scream mixed with his childish sobs. "He tried to make me have a go, even pushed the slingshot into my hand. *You'll like it*, that's what he said but what he meant was *he'd* like to watch me do it. That's when I lost it. I'd been crying at first but when he shoved that thing in my hand, I really started blubbering. I tried to push past him and get out the door, but he grabbed me and kind of turned me around so he had me pushed up against the doorframe. He leaned into my neck and started saying stuff." Lee ran his hand across the back of his neck as if he could still feel Briggs' breath.

"I knew a bit about girls, but didn't really know much about sex." His voice was shaking now, if Mina had to guess, more with disgust than anger. "He pushed against me, grinding on me. Even at twelve, I knew he was doing something bad to me. I panicked, *I'll tell*. It was all I could think of to make him stop and it actually worked.

"He let you go?" Mina could feel the blood pounding in her ears.

"He stopped." Lee suddenly looked tired, more than tired—exhausted. "He spun me around and put his hands around my throat. I thought he was going to kill me. His eyes looked strange, like they were glittering or something." He gave a nervous chuckle. "I was twelve and so scared I came close to shitting myself, but it did look like there was something twinkling in his eyes. He told me if I said anything, he'd say *I* tied up the possum, that it was all my idea. Then he'd wait until everyone had forgotten about it to come and get me." He blinked twice, trying to clear his eyes. "Anyway, you get the idea."

"Did you tell?"

He shook his head. "I believed him. Not so much about people thinking I'd hurt the possum, but the part about him coming to get me. That, I believed and still do." The last part he said with a flat certainty that made Mina want to shiver. "I've never talked about it before. I'm only telling you because you might have to deal with the man. So, if he wants to do a rental inspection, don't let him in your house when you're alone."

*I wish I'd known that before Sunday night*, she thought but didn't say. "Jesus, Lee, that's incredible." Yet she had no trouble believing it. She wondered how many people outside of her and Lee had seen the other side of Terry Briggs and lived to talk about it.

Lee sat back in his chair. "I bet you're sick of hearing about my tragic life."

Mina unclamped her hands from around her thighs. "No. I'm glad you shared that with me. I know it wasn't easy." And she *was* glad, not just because she wanted information on Briggs, but because he'd opened up to her. She only wished she could be with him while he underwent treatment. She almost brought the subject up when he started talking again.

"It's stupid, but I've always had the feeling he was watching me." He scratched his forehead, squeezing his eyes shut. "Every now and again, I still think I see him.

Sometimes years go by and nothing. Then there he is again." He opened his eyes. "Even at the college, I was sure I spotted him. And then when I heard about the girl going missing, I almost went to the police, but…"

"But what?" The voices and movement around them seemed to melt away.

He shrugged. "I know it's all in my head. Post-traumatic stress or something." He laughed, but it was a dry sound, lacking any humour. "He really did a job on me."

She couldn't speak. *I have friends everywhere.* She'd wondered what he meant, but now it was clear. It wasn't enough for Briggs to assault and terrorise Lee, he had to keep the feeling of power going by inserting himself into his victim's life. Mina's fingers clenched, imagining the way Briggs enjoyed seeing Lee's haunted expression. Playing games with people, dragging out his fun for years. *I have friends everywhere.* Were there other victims like Lee?

"Mina, are you okay?" Lee was speaking, but she couldn't really focus on the words.

"Yes. Yes, I'm fine."

All this time, she'd believed the universe brought her to Briggs because she was the only one capable of stopping him. But it wasn't Briggs at the centre of everything, it was Lee. Briggs only saw Mina and Andrea because he was at the college stalking Lee. And Mina was drawn to Dark Water because Lee brought her here, not because Briggs gave her his business card. She realised it was her meeting with Lee that really set off this chain of events. All the coincidences and the things Briggs called forces, they were never really about Briggs or Andrea. Well not *just* about saving Andrea. Maybe Mina was supposed to be here for Lee. Or did she just want to believe her real purpose was more noble than killing?

"So now you see why I freaked out so much when we stopped at his auntie's house."

Mina's heart jumped a beat. She could feel her fists curling into balls so tight, her fingernails cut into her palms. Mina noticed the waitress approaching with a tray.

"What do you mean, his auntie's house?" Even as she asked, everything began to make sense.

"That place we looked at when we were leaving town, that was Terry's auntie's place. The first time I'd been back there since I was twelve."

"How was your meal?" The waitress cocked a harshly pencilled brown eyebrow at the two mostly uneaten breakfasts. "Was everything all right?"

"Everything was good, I guess we just weren't as hungry as we thought." Lee gave her a rueful smile and the waitress relaxed. "Can I get you anything else, more coffee?"

"No, just the bill. Thanks."

The exchange took less than a couple of seconds, but to Mina the time seemed to draw out into hours. Finally, when the waitress finished clearing the table, Mina spoke. "That house we stopped at belonged to Briggs' auntie? Does he still own it?" She could hear the urgency in her voice, but was powerless to control it.

She waited for Lee to answer. If he noticed the insistence in her voice, he didn't react to it. "I don't know. Why?"

She tried to think of how to answer him, but her mind raced, pulling her in all directions. And then it struck her, the niggling feeling hovering around the edges of her subconscious mind crashed into focus as clear and tangible as the room around her: that day, on the way out of town, she'd climbed out of the car and the first thing she'd smelled was citrus. That cloying, sharp and sweet odour of fruit lying on the ground, wasting in the sun.

"Lee, I've got to go." She stood up and pulled her jacket off the back of her chair, almost knocking it over in the process.

He didn't have to say anything, the look on his face—a mixture of hurt and surprise—told her what he felt. Lee had bared his soul and she'd responded by jumping up and trying to leave. Every second she hesitated could cost Andrea her life, if it hadn't already. Yet how could she leave him this way?

She stood beside him and took his face in her hands, she could feel the roughness of the stubble on his cheeks. He opened his mouth to speak, but she covered it with her lips and felt his body first jerk with surprise and then relax. His lips were as soft as she remembered, and she breathed in the mingled smell of soap and coffee.

When she pulled back, he tried to speak. "What are—"

"I can't explain, but trust me when I say this isn't about what you've told me today. If you'll let me, I'll go through anything just to be with you."

"I can't let—"

She cut him off again. "There's a friend of mine who needs help. Urgent help. Talking to you got me to understand what I have to do." His eyes reminded her even more of the stormy green waters of the Indian Ocean. "Trust me, okay?"

He seemed about to argue, but instead nodded. "Okay."

She moved to leave, and his hand shot out and grabbed her wrist. "Are you in trouble?" His fingers, tight around her arm, relaxed. "Whatever it is, I'll help you."

She felt her throat tighten. If she didn't leave soon, she'd begin to weep and then she knew he'd never let her go. "Seeing you again was all the help I needed." She disengaged herself from his grip. "Where are you staying?"

"I'm at the hotel behind the pub, you know the one."

"I'll be there before you leave, promise." With that, she turned and left the dining room.

# Chapter Thirty-five

Mina pushed the speedometer past the point of safety. If the police stopped her, she'd most likely have her car impounded but it was a risk she had to take.

She made it back to Dark Water at 12:15 p.m. The building storm blocked out most of the sun's rays turning the early afternoon sky something closer to dusk. As the thickly packed trees whirled past, she tried to formulate her next move. She felt sure now that Andrea was at the house on Huntress Drive, the place she'd visited with Lee.

She could go straight to the run-down house and start searching for Andrea, but how would she explain that she, the last person to see Andrea before she disappeared, had just happened to find her after she'd been missing close to three weeks? If she put herself in that situation, everything would come to light and she'd end up in prison instead of where she needed to be—with Lee.

A spatter of raindrops hit the windscreen as she turned onto Huntress. Her heart, not quite pounding, jacked up a notch. She considered making an anonymous call to the police, tipping them off about Andrea's possible location. But would they take the call seriously? With a high-profile case like the Magician, they were probably inundated with calls from crazies. Could she risk waiting for someone to pass on the information to the right person, and then the time it took for whoever made the decision, to send a uniformed officer out to check?

There was something else that clawed at her and held her back from taking immediate action. *Briggs.* If Andrea was discovered on Briggs' property, the police would be looking for him. Mina's mind flashed back to the dream: Briggs' mouth, teeth stained with blood and eyes burning. She couldn't risk getting the police involved, not while she still had Terry Briggs chained to a beam in her shed.

With the decision made, a plan formulated. Mina drove *past* the house on Huntress Drive. The entrance was just as she remembered it: overgrown with vines and natives, the *for sale or lease* sign little more than a blur of scratched red letters obscured by foliage. *How did I spot that thing in the first place?* Had the sign been more visible two weeks ago or maybe the sun had been higher in the sky? Whatever the reason, she saw the sign that day and now couldn't ignore those signs in her life that were telling her she had unfinished business on the property.

The car rolled past the entrance without stopping. Once the property was behind her, Mina headed for the turn to Fire Lake. With the rain falling, she executed a U-turn and parked on the uneven gravel lining the side of the road. Beyond the gravel lay dense forest, made wild and lush by the winter rain. Snatching a quick glance around to make sure she wasn't being watched, Mina exited the vehicle.

A light sprinkling of rain continued to fall. With slow persistence, the drizzle laid a fine damp mist over her hair and legs as she walked. She shrugged deeper into the warmth of her leather jacket, grateful for its water resistance, but at the same time cursing herself for wearing boots with a heel. The walk back to Huntress took longer than she'd anticipated. It was a full ten minutes before she came upon the entrance.

Without stopping, Mina strode past the crumbling driveway of Briggs' childhood house and continued towards her home. Andrea was somewhere on the run-down property, she could almost feel it in the marrow of her bones. But now was not the time to go searching. She had a few things to sort out before she could help the girl.

With every crunching step, her mind threw up images of the girl. First, as she was that night at Alice College: young, baby-faced, and needy. But as Mina drew farther away from what she was now certain was Briggs' hideout, her imagination conjured a stark, naked corpse laying on a bed of rocks and forest debris. As the road curved west, Mina had to battle the urge to throw her plans to the wind and run back to the property screaming Andrea's name.

Mina clamped her teeth together and buried her fists deep in the silk fabric of her pockets. She couldn't let herself give in to panic. Andrea had been missing for nineteen days, would a few more hours matter? *I hope not.* She picked up her pace.

\* \* \*

Hair clinging to her head in wet strings and teeth chattering, Mina unlocked her front door. The house sat in silence, broken only by the endless patter of rain on the roof. She stalked through the lounge room leaving wet prints on the hardwood floor, stripping off her clothes as she went.

The need to find warmth overtook the urge to keep moving. She padded into the bathroom in her underwear and grabbed a towel. Bent over, shivering, she dried her hair and then hurried back to the bedroom to throw on dry clothes. As she moved, a sense of calm and purpose returned. She had a plan. As long as she stuck to it, nothing would go wrong. The naked corpse flashed behind her eyes, only this time the rain lashed the white skin forming small puddles in the dips and crevasses of the lifeless body.

"I won't let that happen," she said to the empty house and continued to dress.

With time ticking by at what felt like an unnaturally fast pace, Mina threw on her puffer coat and grabbed the last few items she'd need. Before going through the back door, she shoved a tea towel in her back pocket and picked up the heavy-duty torch. She forced herself to pause and run a mental inventory of the items in her pockets.

With everything in place, she took one last look around the kitchen. The end was close, the next time she saw this room, the worst of the nightmare she'd been living would be over. *Or would it?* She couldn't help thinking that whatever she did, the memories of this day would never fade.

"She's alive." Saying the words aloud gave them more strength. "Something good will come out of this mess." With the words still repeating in her mind, she walked to the back shed.

Briggs seemed to be sleeping, his body lay slumped to the left of the beam. Mina took a step closer, trying to decipher the sound of his breathing through the maddening rhythm of the rain. Each time she breathed in, the thick stench of faeces assaulted her mouth and nose. The shed had become a black hole of madness and despair, only made worse by the puddles of rainwater gathering in shiny dots around the concrete slab.

"Briggs." At the sound of her voice, his body twitched and came alive. Mina felt a drop in the pit of her stomach... *disappointment.*

Briggs rolled over dragging the chains across his body. His movements were sluggish as if the weight of his restraints were more than he could lift. Lack of food and water were clearly taking effect. The shape of his hunched shoulders and narrow neck looked feeble and pathetic. *He can't last much longer.* The thought didn't bring her any satisfaction, only a gnawing guilt and anxiety. She wanted him to disappear from her life like a puff of smoke, but there was one more thing she needed first.

"Briggs, do you hear me?" Her voice bounced off the damp walls.

"You can't keep away, no matter how hard you try."

It struck her as a strange thing to say. He spoke like someone sleepwalking, his tongue not quite making the right sounds.

The approaching storm darkened the sky beyond the doorway, allowing only dull rays to penetrate the room. To be sure she got what she needed, Mina had to be able to see Briggs clearly. She turned on the torch and aimed the wide arc of light at his face. Briggs winced and raised a hand that looked darkened by filth.

*I'm inflicting this cruelty. Me.* Mina steeled herself and pushed away the guilt. "Where is she?" The question, now so familiar between them seemed to please him. He smiled through cracked lips.

"You want to know where the girl is, but you give me nothing in return."

Knowing she was playing with fire, she couldn't resist baiting him. "What do you want, water?"

Briggs pushed himself up to a sitting position. "I want you to take my hand." He held his two hands out letting the chain dangle between them. "Touch me and I'll tell you."

Mina kept the torch trained on his face when she replied. "All right."

She watched his expression change from dreamy to excited. His hands reached out, fingers extended and she was struck by how large and white they looked in the glow of the torch.

Mina took a step towards him and raised her left hand, extending it until it was just centimeters from his. She could hear his breathing now, harsh and urgent. Something danced in his watery blue eyes reminding her of the way a cat manages to look focused and blank at the same time, as if they possess no emotion beyond the hunt.

Just as he leaned forward and his fingers almost brushed hers, she pulled her hand back. "Then again, I think I'll just go take a look at your Aunt Dolly's house."

His eyes widened revealing bloodshot whites. For an instant, she thought she saw fear, it was very similar to the look in her father's eyes when he realised she was cutting off his air supply. The look told her all she needed to know.

"Thanks, Briggs," she said and clicked off the light.

When she turned the key in the lock, he called her name, just once before the final click.

# Chapter Thirty-six

With the hood of her coat blocking the rain, Mina hunched her shoulders and took long strides. The track veered south, she remembered catching a glimpse of the shed as she drove deeper into the bush. The mist of rain intensified, not yet a deluge but certainly heavier. She checked her watch: almost one. How could it be so late in the day? It seemed like only moments ago she'd stepped out of her car at Fire Lake... now it was nearly mid-afternoon. Time swept her along as it sometimes did in dreams, only this was no dream.

The bush seemed thicker on foot, oppressive and dangerous as if it was a living entity. Unable to stop herself, she turned and looked back the way she'd come. The trail, drenched in dark liquid, stretched out behind her. She could almost imagine someone—Briggs—moving from tree to tree, keeping step with her.

Mina forced herself to keep going. She'd overcome fear in the past, this was no different. The only thing out here she needed to worry about was her own imagination.

A branch shuddered and a shower of raindrops hissed through the leaves of a nearby wattle. The suddenness of the movement sent Mina staggering left in fright. She held up the torch, not for light but to strike whoever came out of the bush.

The sound of her breathing amplified in the interior of her hood. She waited, heart thumping, eyes wide. A black blur surged forward and before she could stop herself, Mina screamed. A large crow swooped low then flapped its lengthy wings as it barrelled past her.

"Oh God." The words escaped in a rush of air. She bent at the waist and then at the knees. Crouching, she dropped the torch and placed her hands on the track. "It's nothing. It's nothing." She used the words to calm her jangling nerves. "You've done harder things."

It was true. She'd done worse, but how much could one person take before their will crumbled? Judging by her jelly legs, she was getting close to her limit. *Calm down*, she told herself hoping to find her equilibrium. It was then that the words surfaced in her mind. *The woods are lovely, dark, and deep, But I have promises to keep, And miles to go before I sleep. And miles to go before I sleep.*

The simplicity of those words and quality of the rhyme soothed her fears. She repeated them in her mind and walked on.

She came close to missing the entrance to the side road, it was only a swatch of purple and orange that caught her eye, colours so vivid, they were almost out of place amongst the varying shades of grey and green. Head tilted down, rain dripping from her hood, Mina recognised the dead bird. It remained where she'd placed it, the leaves used to cover the small body now gone. She guessed they most likely had been picked away by scavengers. The once lovely lorikeet was torn open down the middle, its internal organs ripped out.

Mina turned away grimacing. The silver gum stood almost directly opposite. Positive that the tall, smooth-barked tree was the one she'd marked, Mina crossed the trail. Sure enough, she spotted the crookedly carved circle, easily visible if you knew where to look.

The back of the van stood in sharp contrast to the green of the waxy bushes that surrounded it. There was something ominous about the shiny doors protruding from the foliage, it reminded her of a living beast trying to hide from unsuspecting eyes. She wondered what horrors had taken place in the back of Briggs' van, but decided she didn't want to set her imagination loose on that course.

Squeezing through the water-logged branches to reach the driver's door, Mina's already damp coat became saturated. By the time she crawled behind the wheel, she could feel the coat's padding weighing her down. Slipping out of the wet garment, she turned over the engine and flicked on the heater. Warm air flooded the cab. Without hesitating, she activated the wipers and threw the gearstick into reverse, backing out of the bushes.

Once the back of the van bounced out onto the main track, Mina turned in a tight arc, narrowly avoiding the silver gum which stood as her marker. It was a close turn, wet branches squealed against the sides of the cab and slapped at the passenger window. When the front of the vehicle finally came to rest pointing forward, she realised she'd been holding her breath, biting her lower lip.

It was a crazy notion, but it seemed to her the bush had grown thicker and more inhospitable in the few days since she'd hidden the van. Branches appeared longer, like spiky arms grasping at the vehicle trying to prevent its escape. *I'm losing it.* She had no doubt that the consistent strain worked to erode her nerves and mess with her head. Still, the sooner she made it off the trail and onto solid road, the better she'd feel.

The main track was littered with twigs and gum nuts, she could hear them snapping and clunking under the chassis as the van bounced towards the front of the property. At one point, the wheels spun and the steering snapped to the right. For a nightmarish second, the van threatened to become bogged in a patch of soggy sand.

Mina applied slow pressure to the accelerator, relieved to find herself moving effortlessly across the rack.

The drive back to the side of the house took less than ten minutes, although to Mina it felt like hours. By the time she exited the property, her knuckles were white and her fingers cramping. Once on Stilltree Road, the drive became smooth. The only danger now was being spotted.

She needn't have worried about other vehicles between her place and Briggs' Auntie's—only a hand full of cars passed. She doubted anyone would remember seeing a white van on the road, and it would be even less likely that they'd be able to identify the driver through the rain-drenched windshield.

The weatherboard house was just as she remembered, dilapidated with an air of neglect that marked long abandoned dwellings. She brought the van to a standstill alongside the rusty wire fence. The rain was heavier now, fighting the wipers as they swept back and forth with a sloshing monotony. A glimpse of colour caught her eye. Mina leaned forward, squinting to see through the downpour.

Suddenly the memory that had been playing around the edges of her mind crashed into place. The stand of fruit trees, lemon and mandarin stood just beyond the rusty fence. She remembered the smell of spoiled fruit rotting on the ground, the way the odour hung in the air. She'd noticed it when she was with Lee, but until a few hours ago, it had barely registered.

"You crazy shit," she said aloud, staring at the ancient fruit trees. "After you finish terrorising the girls you abduct, you pick fruit." She could almost see Briggs, a vacuous smile lighting up his almost feminine features, plucking mandarins from the trees and placing them in a plastic bag.

Her gaze moved away from the trees and towards the house. She wondered how many sleepless nights she'd spend trying to wipe away the images of the horrors she might see. Would she find Andrea's lifeless body? Would there be others? In spite of the warm air in the cab, Mina shivered. She'd come this far, no backing out now. Only the thought of finding whatever grisly remains Briggs left behind in the house kept her frozen in the driver's seat.

She closed her eyes and Briggs' face swam in her mind, then Lee's. He needed her whether he realised it or not. She had to finish this, it was the only way to get her life back on track. If she backed out now, she'd never find any peace.

And then there was Andrea. As much as she'd tried to convince herself otherwise, Mina had played a part in bringing the girl to this desolate place. For once, she had to put things right.

A roll of thunder sounded in the distance like an ancient cannon. The *boom* startled her into action. She turned off the engine and climbed into the passenger seat. Mina pulled on her coat, noticing the heater had dried the silky fabric but the inside padding still felt clumpy and wet. It wasn't ideal but it would have to do. She pulled the tea towel out of her back pocket and leaning back across the cab, wiping down everything she'd touched. Holding the tea towel over the handle, she exited the van.

The long grass, almost hip height, painted her with moisture as she pushed her way towards the sagging porch. The last time, she'd shied away from climbing the steps for fear of trespassing. This time she approached the front door with a sense of grim determination.

The porch groaned under her feet. There were several keys on Briggs' plain silver hooped keyring including the van key and the one that opened the house on Able Street. Of the three others, only one looked like it might fit the old-fashioned lock. The door and surrounding weatherboard had once been red, but the faded and blistered paint now looked more like streaks of rust clinging to the wood in jagged smudges.

Mina slid the key into the slot and was relieved to hear the dull click of the lock opening. The door swung inwards with little more than a croak from the pivots. Although the building seemed abandoned, someone used the front door frequently enough to keep the hinges oiled. Stepping over the threshold, the powerful stench of damp and age filled her nostrils.

A hallway cluttered with stacks of newspapers and rusty cans led to a small sitting room. Unlike the hallway, this room had a few pieces of furniture. A television set with a cracked screen sat on top of a tallboy with only one remaining drawer hanging out and to the side like the last tooth in an old man's mouth. The room also contained a dark pink armchair, the only intact item in the room which sat next to a shredded piece of carpet and an empty suitcase.

This house was so different to the one Briggs kept on Able Street—probably what he thought a normal person's home should look like. This random array of crazily placed junk represented the real Briggs. Just standing amongst the clutter and decaying furniture made Mina feel dirty and somehow contaminated.

Listening for movement or cries for help, she moved through the room and farther into the house. Following a short stretch of hall, only illuminated by grey light creeping through a lone window, Mina came to the kitchen. This area looked more lived-in with a sturdy table and two chairs in the centre of the room. The smell coming from the stove told her this was where someone had been preparing food. Surveying the litter of dirty pots and pans and the row of dead flies lining the grubby window sill, she felt her stomach lurch.

*I'm wasting time.* Even though she knew she wouldn't find Andrea in the kitchen, Mina couldn't resist opening one of the cupboards. What she found was more disturbing than the foul smelling congealed food splattered over the top of the stove. Rows of tinned food and packages of snack bars. Mina flung open another cupboard only to find more of the same. There was enough food stock-piled to last Briggs months.

She thought back to the night he'd attacked her in her kitchen. Was it possible that this is what he had in mind for her? Mina rubbed her hand over her mouth. Briggs was in the process of tying her up when she'd bashed him over the head. Why would he bother to do that if he just meant to rape and murder her? Until this moment, she hadn't really thought through his plans for her. Maybe she was to be his unwilling guest too?

Mina slammed the cupboard door, wiped the handles with the tea towel and returned to the hall. There were three doors, all closed. Would she find Andrea in one of the rooms? She took a deep breath and instantly regretted it. The stench coming from one of the doors almost overwhelmed her. Even before she pushed the door open, she knew she'd stumbled upon the toilet and bathroom. Turning away with her hand clamped over her nose, Mina opened the next door.

Peeling wallpaper hung down in lazy tongues as if lapping at the bare, dusty floorboards. It took her less than a second to understand this was Briggs' bedroom. The single bed, bare mattress, and yellowing pillow told her someone used this room. Even over the other competing odours, she could smell the sour sweat that had come to greet her in the shed.

There was a length of fabric nailed to the window frame, the pattern of aeroplanes looked childish, like it had once belonged in a little boy's room. *This* was a place where a man like Briggs fantasised and planned. Whatever evil things he enacted, grew in this desolate space. Mina backed away from the doorway and turned to the next room.

A silver bolt screwed into the wood, large and shiny, told her this had to be the room. Before opening the door, she pulled her hair over one shoulder and tucked it into the neck of her jumper. As she'd done on the others, Mina used her sleeve to cover her hand before touching the door. The light from the end of the hall fell across the door in dull bars. She could hear nothing from the room, only the constant volley of the rain against the window. Sliding back the bolt and turning the battered brass knob, she pushed the door open.

A breath caught in her throat. If there had ever been any doubt that this was where Briggs spent his time, the sight of the boarded windows, bolted down bed and lengths of chain made it clear he'd created this room to be a cell. *Is this where I was to be kept?* Mina wrapped her arms around her body. If things had been different on Sunday night, this would be her prison.

Her eyes fell on the red plastic bucket near the foot of the bed and a tremor built in her legs. The shaking spread like fire, taking hold and rocking her body. This was what she'd so narrowly escaped. Chained like an animal and then what? Torture, humiliation, and finally death. She dropped her arms and clenched her hands into fists. Had Andrea spent her final days in this room?

The impulse to turn away, run from the house, gripped her. It seemed wherever she turned, darkness always followed. First her father, then her mother. Even her relationship with Lee was shadowed by tragedy. Now this. Body still quivering, she forced herself to slow down and take in the details.

The sheets were spotless and still showed the fold lines. They were new, just out of the packet. The bucket, glossy and red, had never been used. Scanning the floor, she could see no signs of blood. Grimacing with disgust, she moved closer to the bed. The chains were shiny, similar to the ones she'd used on Briggs. She couldn't be sure, but it looked like this room had never been used, not to keep someone captive anyway.

*The way he looked after his auntie after she had the stroke. Not many men would have done that, but she was all he had.*

Robbie's words came to her. What must the woman's last days have been like in this room? Was this where the idea of abducting women and having them at his mercy began? Even though she'd never met the woman, Mina felt a wave of sympathy for Briggs' auntie. She didn't want to imagine the horrors that had taken place in this house.

Another roll of thunder, this one closer, pounded her ears. Time to move. Andrea wasn't here *nor* did Mina believe she ever had been. Her only hope now was the shed. She remembered catching a glimpse of it that day with Lee. It had to be where he was keeping the girl. If not… Mina's thoughts faltered.

She turned away from the stark grimness of the make-shift cell. She couldn't think that far ahead. For now, she had to focus on searching the property. If, in the end, she didn't find Andrea, she'd deal with what had to be done.

Using the front door, Mina left the house. In spite of the continuing rain, the air tasted clean after the cloying smells that inhabited the decaying house. She skirted the building, taking care to watch her footing in the long grass. Somewhere to the west, a bird cawed as if protesting the premature gloom. Mina hurried past the rusty Hills Hoist and noticed a single shoe wedged near the base of the lilting pole. There was something menacing about the shoe as if it had been left behind by someone trying to warn of the horror that lay ahead.

The small, galvanised tin shed stood less than ten metres from the back of the house. The tiny building lilted to the left like it had been pushed over by giant hands. The size and condition of the shed made it easy to discount. A roar of thunder, first rumbling and then clapping, filled the sky. Mina ducked instinctively and moved to the right.

With her hands over her hooded head, she caught sight of a flash of red. It was the same glimpse of brick she'd seen when Lee was with her, only in the fading light it looked darker. Taking a moment to look around, Mina noticed the long grass farther to the right had been flattened, perhaps driven over by large tyres.

Scurrying to the flattened area, Mina followed the banked-down grass as it meandered through the trees and past a thick snatch of tangled native shrubs. Judging by the yellowing weeds and grass, something came this way often enough to create a rudimentary track, probably only visible to someone who knew what they were looking for.

The track widened and the building came in view. A burst of thunder exploded overhead. The sound reverberated off the building and nearby trees then rolled on with ear-spitting force. Mina clamped her hands over her ears and a sense of déjà vu took hold of her. The building appearing in the long grass while the thunder pounded overhead was so familiar that it threw her off balance for a second.

The sensation had to be a nervous reaction to the stress of the situation. Mina was afraid. It seemed only natural to start imagining things. She couldn't stand in the rain with her hands over her ears all afternoon. If Andrea was inside the building, dead or alive, Mina intended to find her.

She wiped damp fingers across her forehead and kept moving. On the east side of the structure, there seemed to be some sort of tacked-on room, shack-like and flimsy. Still at least five metres away, the smell hit her like a gut punch. Pungent and overpowering, unlike anything she'd experienced in Briggs' house, although there was an underlying odour of human waste. This stench was something much worse, a combination of rotten meat and some sort of sweet gas.

Instinctively, her hand went to her mouth, but before she could clamp it in place, a stream of vomit burst out. She staggered to the right and clutched her stomach. Another cramp gripped her middle, tipping her forward to choke out a thin stream of watery bile.

When the gagging stopped, Mina straightened up and swiped at her mouth with the sleeve of her coat. Her vision blurred by tears, she stumbled towards the little shack on the side of the building.

A bolt, similar to the one she'd found on the bedroom door was fastened to the wood. It looked older, well-used. Mina slid it back and pushed the door inwards. There was more light in the shack than she'd been expecting, her eyes were immediately drawn upwards. Rain spilled through a jagged gap in the roof, puddling on the roughly paved flooring.

Her eyes scanned the shack, barely taking in the details. One shaky hand still clamped the open door. Mina sucked in air and tried to blink her vision clear. Still woozy from the vomiting fit, she unzipped her coat and lifted the corner of her jumper, using it to wipe her eyes and mouth.

The smell still set her teeth on edge, but some sense of what she was seeing fell into place. The far end of the shack was dominated by what looked like a large scarred metal door. The floor, uneven and dirty was littered with soft drink cans and rubbish bags. To the left of the doorway lay a pile of rags.

Mina let out a long breath. Another room filled with junk. She didn't know how much more of this she could take, searching room after room, opening each door terrified of what horrors she might find, only to come across more junk.

The pile of rags rippled and something pale scraped at her ankle. Mina screamed, a sharp and panicked sound. Her feet skidded over the pavers as she tried to step away from whatever scurried out of the heap of rubbish. Trainers sodden and caked in dirt, her feet slid out from under her. Her back hit the door which swung wide, leaving Mina with nowhere to go but down.

Her butt bounced onto the pavers with jarring force. Without warning she found herself staring into a pair of terrified eyes.

# Chapter Thirty-seven

The pain in Andrea's leg changed from burning hot to chilling stabs that struck without warning and tore her from sleep. She curled on her side and fumbled with the cap on the metal cylinder. The drink bottle, liberated from the sports bag, now held little more than a few drops which she emptied onto her tongue.

She had no idea how long she'd been asleep *or* if it had been sleep. The total lack of dreams seemed more like death. *Anything is better than this.* If the blackness she'd emerged from *was* death, she wanted to fall back into it and never come out.

Tossing the bottle aside, she caught sight of the sky. With very little light and no stars, all she could see was grey. Had the night come again? If she had the strength to wish, she'd ask for daylight. It felt like the darkness never ended. She could barely remember the sunlight, her mind reasoned that she must have seen it. There was even a vague memory of lifting her face and feeling its warmth, but curled up in the gloom she doubted herself. *Maybe I've always been here and my memories are dreams.*

Something sounded overhead, a deep rolling boom that reminded her of the way a tent flap sounds when the wind whips it back. She tried to make sense of what she heard, straining to catch the sound. Another noise, distant but distinct. The rumble of an engine, this she recognised immediately.

"He's back." The words were little more than gasps. Her body shook as her hands slapped at the concrete trying to find purchase so she could hide.

She couldn't let him find her. He'd punch and bite and tear her to pieces. Images of his eyes, glowing with delight as the blows turned her inside out, sent her into a fit of coughing. An explosion in the sky, ear-splitting and sudden heralded his arrival with startling intensity. Andrea tried to scream but it felt like someone had laid bricks on her chest, squeezing the breath from her lungs.

Moving only her hands, she pulled the pile of clothing over herself. Burrowing under the stack of abandoned fabric in a desperate attempt to hide, her heartbeat echoing in her ears. *I wonder if I can make my heart stop before he finds me? Just turn it off like a switch on an old radio. And then... and then I'll be free.*

\* \* \*

The thing curling out from under the rags slid back and disappeared. Mina stared open mouthed at the heap near the door. Too startled to move, she waited. It occurred to her that the building might be infested with rats, yet somehow, she doubted that's what she saw. The movements had been too slow.

A sound, faint at first, then louder came from the pile. The hairs on Mina's arms stood on end as an invisible, icy finger crawled its way up her spine. It wasn't the noise of an animal, but a *human being*. Above the drumming of the rain, she heard whimpering.

Still on her butt, Mina pulled herself forward until she was on her hands and knees. Shuffling across the floor, she came within touching distance of the pile of rags.

"Is that… Andrea, is that you?" Her voice was little more than a whisper.

Mina touched the clothing, pulling back a thin piece of fabric that might have been a T-shirt.

"No. No. Don't hurt me." A voice came from the tangled mass of garments which Mina realised with horror wasn't a lifeless heap but a girl covered in a discarded layer of jeans and shirts.

"I won't hurt you," she answered the faceless voice. "I won't hurt you." She had no idea what to say to ease the girl's fear.

Pulling away the last of the fabric, Mina inhaled sharply and pulled her hand back. Huddled against the concrete, filthy and gaunt, was a figure barely recognisable as female. She let out a wail of pain that cut through Mina's shock and propelled her to action.

"It's okay. Are you Andrea? Andrea Fields?" Mina tried to make her voice sound strong and reassuring, but could hear the halting fear behind each word

The girl's eyes looked abnormally large in her sunken face. They moved from Mina to the door like glassy pendulums. There was no understanding, only terror and confusion in her gaze. Mina spent the last few days hating herself for what she was doing to Briggs, but seeing what he'd done to this young woman made her wish she'd used his knife to cut him to pieces.

"He's coming." The girl's lips moved, revealing a bloody socket in her gum. "He… Hhh… his van. I *heard* it." Tears spilled over her lower lids and ran through the layers of grime coating her face.

Mina leaned closer. "No. You're safe. I promise." She touched the girl's forehead attempting to brush back a strand of hair. The girl whimpered and shrank back.

"Are you hurt?" It seemed like a ridiculous question, but she needed her to focus. "Andrea?" She snapped out the girl's name hating the way she winced at the harshness of Mina's voice. "Andrea Fields."

Something in Mina's tone got the girl's attention, her eyes focused on Mina's face and there seemed to be a flicker of recognition. "Yes. I'm Andrea. I'm Andrea. Andrea." She repeated her name over and over as if only just remembering it.

Mina, still on her hands and knees, leaned back next to the girl. "Okay. Good. Now listen to me. I—"

"I heard his van. You have to go, he's coming." Andrea's hand shot up and grabbed Mina's wrist with surprising strength. "He'll hurt you, Regina. Don't let him find you."

Andrea was confused, traumatised. She looked at Mina and saw someone else. Someone named Regina. Mina didn't bother to correct her, it was better if she didn't recognise her. Mina looked down at Andrea's hand and stifled a gasp. It looked like the back had been through a mangle: clumps of skin hung off her knuckles in fleshy hunks.

Moving carefully to avoid touching the injured area, Mina disengaged Andrea's hand. She put her own hands on either side of the girl's face.

"It's over." She stared into Andrea's eyes. "He's not coming back. That was me in the van." She paused. "Do you understand?"

Andrea's lips moved but she made no response.

"You're safe. He's gone forever, I promise." As the words came out, she knew she meant them. She'd never let Briggs hurt anyone again.

"Safe?" There was a spark of understanding in Andrea's eyes.

"Okay," Mina continued while she had the girl's attention. "I'm going to call the police." She reached into the pocket of her coat. "See." She held up Briggs' phone. "I'm calling triple zero and the police and ambulance will come."

"Yes. Yes, the police." Andrea nodded and then a wet barking cough overtook her.

Mina dialled and waited. In the seconds that it took to be connected to an operator, she watched Andrea's face. The girl had been through hell, but she'd hung on. Whatever Briggs had put her through, she'd survived. Mina could only imagine what was ahead for Andrea, this nightmare would colour every day of her life. Mina hoped that whatever inner strength got Andrea through the days and nights of torture, would carry her through the difficult recovery that most surely lay ahead.

Her thoughts were cut short by the operator's voice. "Do you require Police Ambulance or Fire Department?"

"I'm Andrea Fields, I need help." Mina did her best to alter her voice. "I'm being held in a shed at the back of a property in Dark Water. Number two, Huntress Drive."

"Please stay on the line." Mina heard the distinctive *clack-clack* of typing. She wiped the phone over with the edge of her coat.

"You hold this now," she spoke to Andrea while covering the phone with her thumb. "Stay on the line with the operator, they'll come and get you." She pressed the phone into Andrea's hand and helped the girl lift it to her ear. "I can't stay with you, I have to go now."

The panicked look was back in the girl's eyes. "Don't leave me." The words came out in a breathless wheeze.

Mina felt a stab of guilt, this would be the second time she'd refused Andrea's plea to stay with her. *This time I'm leaving her in safe hands.* Even so, she'd still be alone and terrified until the police arrived. "I can't stay. I …" How could she possibly explain? "I have promises to keep." It was the first thing that came to mind and in many ways the best explanation.

Andrea held the phone to her ear and nodded. Not sure if she was nodding that she understood Mina's reasons or in response to something the operator was telling her, Mina leaned in and pressed her lips to the girl's forehead. Her skin was hot, feverish. There was nothing left to say and time was ticking away. Soon the property would be crawling with police and paramedics. Mina had to go.

From the doorway, she glanced back. She could see the top of Andrea's head and her fingers clinging to the phone. She wondered what the girl would remember about this moment, hopefully Mina's presence would be a blur.

Pulling the tea towel from her back pocket, she wiped the doorframe and bolt then zipped up her coat and ran. At one point, she stumbled and fell onto her knees in the long grass. For a second, she gripped the slippery blades, gasping and out of breath. The van was less than ten metres away, she had one job left and then her work here would be done.

When she reached the white van, Mina opened the driver's door. She fumbled the keys out of her pocket. The urge to toss them on the seat and run hit her with an almost overwhelming force. She wanted to be done with this place, with this endless day. But one slip up could ruin everything. She'd taken so much care, now was not the time to get sloppy.

Allowing herself a minute to catch her breath, Mina leaned against the side of the van. No wail of sirens—yet. She wiped each key individually and the ring. When she was satisfied that her prints were erased, she put the keys on the seat and left the driver's door open. Pounding rain poured into the cab, if there were any traces of her presence, she hoped the weather would obscure them.

Thunder roared, but this time with less power. It seemed the storm was moving away. Mina started to run, letting her hood fly back and the rain saturate her hair. The chilly water felt cleansing and fresh on her skin.

By the time she reached the turn off to Fire Lake and made it back to her car, Mina's legs were heavy, as if filled with mud. She climbed behind the wheel and started the engine, rain running off her hair and clothing. In the distance, she heard sirens. She wanted to pull her dripping coat off but didn't dare hesitate. Instead she drove towards home, straining to see the road through the rush of the wipers.

The drive was uneventful, roads not quite awash but wet enough to keep traffic to a minimum. Few cars passed, nor did she see any police. It seemed the sirens were approaching from the opposite direction. Mina turned on the heater and let the warmth wash over her. She should have felt joy, or even satisfaction at finding Andrea alive, but instead there was only a sense of numb exhaustion.

Perhaps in the days to come, the emotions would hit; for now, she wanted rest and warmth. But all that would have to wait, there was still work to be done. Mina gripped the steering wheel and pulled into her driveway.

She turned off the engine and let her hands fall into her lap. The magnitude of what lay ahead filled her with dread. The time had come to keep her promise. A promise to Andrea *and* herself. Time to make sure Briggs never hurt anyone again. This, like so many things in her life, was something she knew only she could do. It would be the last step and one she would take no pleasure in.

* * *

Briggs had been without water for two and a half days. He was weak, Mina had seen just how weak with her own eyes. Still, the man was dangerous and capable of anything. Mina stripped off her coat, letting it fall to the ground. The rain had dwindled from a downpour to a patter.

Her clothes clung to her like a second skin. Shivering, she slid the key into the lock and let the door swing open. She'd come prepared. Briggs' knife held behind her back, she picked up the torch and entered the shed.

The air was cold, more so inside the shed. Briggs lay near the beam unmoving. Her heart beat a steady rhythm, not hammering but heavier than normal. She held the light on him searching for movement. When there was none, she crossed the floor and set the torch down. *I can't hesitate.* There could be no pause between actions. She rehearsed the sequence in her mind: pull back his head, use the knife—point first.

It could only work if she didn't stop to think. She recalled the way her father struggled, the strength in his grip as he fought for life. *Don't think about him*, she warned herself. *Don't think about anything.* But no matter how hard she tried, the images kept coming. Her father's terrified eyes; the way her mother's hand felt in hers as it cooled; Andrea shrinking from her touch; and finally, Lee … The way his green eyes filled with tears and his voice shook with shame and disgust when he told her what Briggs had done to him.

It was as if a switch had been flicked in her head, a cool breeze played over her face and her clothing felt tight—her body too big to be contained. She stepped up to the prone figure and buried her fingers in his hair, hardly noticing the greasy texture. With a sudden jerk, she tipped his chin up exposing his neck. That's when Briggs' eyes opened and his elbow drove into her chest.

The blow almost lifted her off her feet. She doubled over gasping for breath and felt his hand close around her calf. His grip was impossibly strong for a man badly dehydrated and starving. Unable to straighten up, Mina felt her leg jerk and without warning, she was on her back.

Her arm struck the torch which rolled to the right, illuminating the shadowy area towards the back of the shed. In the seconds between hitting the concrete and Briggs climbing on top of her, Mina saw something that made no sense at first. A streak of gold, almost glowing in the torch light.

It wasn't until Briggs' face appeared above her that she realised what she'd seen. The water bottle she given him that first morning, she'd left it in the shed. *The crazy bastard's been drinking his own urine.* The croaky voice, the slumped posture, all an act to lull her into believing he was harmless.

"What have you done?" His teeth snapped near her face and the acrid stench of piss filled her nose. His voice rose to a shriek, "What have *you* done?" He stretched the *you* out until it was almost a scream.

Still breathless from the elbow to her ribs, Mina forced out, "You're finished. She's safe and the police are looking for you." Suddenly the situation struck her as funny and she laughed up into his bulging eyes. "You crazy fuck, I saw that shithole you live in." As she spoke, she remembered the knife still in her right hand.

"I'll kill you, you bitch!" He screamed in her face spraying her with spittle. His weight dropped onto her hips and his hands closed around her throat. She tried to scream, but only a gurgle slipped through her windpipe.

"You've ruined it. We could have been like giants, but you ruined it." He squeezed his thumbs into the hollow at the base of her throat.

Mina felt his hands crushing the air out of her. Tears blurred her eyes. She raised the knife but instead of stabbing him, she let it slip from her fingers and tried to pull his hands free of her neck.

"I told you, I'd hurt you if I had to." He loosened his fingers long enough to give her neck a jarring shake.

Mina's head hit the concrete with enough force to clang her teeth together. The momentary respite from the pressure on her throat gave her time to suck in a breath and then cough it back out again. Dark blotches danced in front of her eyes.

Briggs held her but the pressure decreased. He seemed to be thinking. Mina could see his chin turning as if looking for something. "We're going to do a bit of role reversal." He smiled down at her and he looked very much like he had in her dream. There was an unguarded savagery on his face that made her think of a bird of prey.

He let go of her neck and slid his hands downward. "You're all wet." His fingers trembled over her breasts and then slid down her belly. "I'm going to give you the keys." He dug into the front pocket of her jeans and fished out the keys to the padlock. "And you're going to unlock me."

Mina's hands were flat on the floor, as the air moved in out of her lungs, her mind spun. She felt something under her right hand. *Don't think.* She curled her fingers around the knife's grip. She clenched the weapon and brought it up in a fluid arc, sliding the point straight into the side of Briggs' neck. The blade hit something solid and stopped.

Briggs' smile drooped and a string of red ran over his bottom lip. His hand, still dangling the keys, dropped to Mina's chest.

She gritted her teeth and twisted the knife like a corkscrew, then pushed. The blade slid through his flesh with a wet scrape, stopping only when the grip hit skin.

He seemed to regain some control of his limbs, lifting his hand and batting blindly at his neck. Blood covered his dark clothes, moving like an unstoppable river. His eyes, wide with shock, rolled back then righted themselves. Briggs swayed as if moving to music only he could hear. Mina twisted under him trying to buck him off, but his weight refused to budge.

Coughing and gagging, she swivelled her shoulders and threw her upper body to the left just as Briggs, choking now and spraying a froth of pink blood, crashed down on top of her.

He hit her right shoulder, but missed her head leaving enough of her upper body free that she was able to use her arms and shoulders to wrestle his weight. Shoving and squirming, Mina managed to pull away. When her upper body was free, she turned onto her stomach and crawled elbow over elbow across the floor.

She felt the last of his weight fall away, but couldn't stop. She kept moving, her arms scraping across the concrete quickly joined by her legs. Mina continued to combat crawl until she came to the wall, then crouched against it covering her head with her hands.

The gurgling and coughing continued for what seemed like an eternity. She didn't dare move her arms or lift her head. Briggs was dying, bleeding to death nearby, and the horror of what she'd done kept playing over and over in her head.

In time, the noises ceased as did the rain. The only sounds were her breathing and the irregular drip from the runoff that marked the end of a storm.

# Chapter Thirty-eight

A fine mist hung in the air, backlit by an eerie whitish-grey of the early morning sun. The usually deserted hotel parking lot was crowded with cars and vans, most displaying TV news station logos. Mina remained in her car and watched as a group of four huddled next to the open doors of a news van. A woman with impossibly perfect blonde hair, and dressed in a heavy grey woollen coat, seemed to be lecturing the group. Her face, heavily made-up, looked stark in the gloomy morning light.

*"Believed to be Andrea Fields, the young woman who went missing from Alice College almost three weeks ago was transported to Royal Perth Hospital yesterday where she's in a serious but stable condition."* Mina looked away from the group and turned the volume on the radio up. *"Police and forensics are gathering at a property on the outskirts of Dark Water, a small town three hours from Perth. No arrests have been made so far, but the property is believed to belong to a local man. The Police Commissioner is expected to give a statement to the press sometime this morning."*

*"Traffic is moving well along the Mitchell Freeway with motorists—"* Mina clicked the radio off. Andrea was safe but now the vultures gathered. Dark Water would be a circus for the next few days, maybe even weeks. She ran

her hand across her cheek, rubbing at the spot where Briggs' blood had sprayed her face. She'd showered, scrubbed away every trace of the man, but her cheek continued to itch. She wondered if it would ever stop or if she would be like Lady Macbeth, forever trying to rid herself of the damn spot.

Lee appeared near the hotel's small office, she watched him enter and then minutes later exit through the same door. He carried a small overnight bag in one hand and his car keys in the other. She opened the car door and climbed out. It was only when he reached his own car that he noticed her approach.

"Mina." He opened the back door and tossed his bag on the seat. "After the way you took off yesterday, I …" His voice trailed off in a puff of mist.

"I told you I'd be here. I meant what I said." She tried for a smile but it felt weak, strained. "I meant everything I said."

He frowned. "Are you okay, your voice?"

She adjusted the thick woollen scarf wrapped around her neck. "I must be getting a cold. It's nothing." She could feel colour fill her cheeks.

"And your friend?" He looked over towards the news vans and then back. The way his eyes locked on hers was unnerving.

"Oh that." Mina forced herself to hold his gaze. "It's taken care of."

Neither of them spoke. Lee seemed to be waiting for her to say something.

"Did you tell Robbie?"

He nodded and looked down at his shoes. "She took it pretty hard. I don't know if coming here was the right thing to do. Telling you…" he paused. "And Robbie, just seems to be spreading the misery."

Mina stepped closer and put her hand on his arm. "I'm glad you told me. I don't want you doing this alone." He looked at her hand; for a second she thought he might pull away but instead covered it with his. Lee's hand felt warm. "You said you're starting treatment tomorrow?"

He drew in a breath before answering. "Yeah. Surgery tomorrow and if all goes well, chemo next week."

"Do you need someone to pick you up from the hospital after surgery?"

"Mina I don't—"

"Just as friends." She held up her free hand. "Promise." Her bruised throat burned with the effort of speaking. She did her best to make her tone light, but inside she readied for rejection.

He seemed about to argue, then thought better of it. "That would be really nice." He reached up and touched a strand of her hair, rubbing it between his thumb and forefinger. "If you're getting sick, you should go home and get out of the cold." He jerked his chin towards the gathering crowd of reporters. "You don't want to be in the middle of all this." He slipped his hand around her waist and pulled her closer. Mina bit her lower lip at the jab of pain in her rib cage. She felt his lips touch the top of her head. "I'll call you." He pulled away and got in the car.

She stood back and watched him drive away. He gave her a wave before his car disappeared into the mist. She stared after him for a moment and then turned and walked back to her car.

There was still work to be done, things to be tidied away. She looked at her watch: almost nine o'clock. Reliance Realty would be open soon. She intended to put an offer in on the house she was renting. The place wasn't for sale but Mina would make an offer the owners would be mad to refuse. It would be better if the house on Stilltree Road stayed in her possession—safer.

Her hands trembled on the steering wheel. Her heart began to pound. She had to pull it together; yesterday was over. Briggs couldn't hurt her anymore but the images, bloody and grim, kept jumping into her mind. She started the engine and pulled out of the parking lot. *It'll take time.* It seemed trite but she knew it to be true.

So much had happened to her in the last few days, she'd faced horrors most people never even contemplated. "And I'm still here," she said to the road ahead.

This time she wouldn't fall into drink and isolation. There had to be a way of living with the memories and not letting them drive her insane. She noticed the newsagents on the main street, a blow-up of the morning paper plastered the window.

*Missing Girl Found Alive!*

Whatever Mina had been through, paled compared to how Andrea had suffered. Briggs' blood was on Mina's hands, she couldn't escape that. But for the man himself, she felt no pity. It wasn't that she had ended his life, she could live with that, what she feared would haunt her was the sense of satisfaction she'd experienced when she twisted the knife. A momentary flicker in the pit of her stomach, a brief second of pleasure. It terrified her.

She turned left and parked on the street behind the real estate office. Her hands had stopped trembling. She checked her reflection in the rear-view mirror. *What do I expect to see?* In many ways she'd come full circle back to where she started, still wondering if she were a monster. *No*, she told herself. I've met monsters. *I'm no angel, but I'm not a monster.*

Mina opened the car door and stepped out into the crisp autumn air. She breathed deeply and felt a stab of pain. She'd read somewhere that ribs take a long time to heal. "But they do heal," she said aloud. An elderly man in blue nylon pants carrying the morning paper under his arm as he shuffled past gave Mina a quizzical look. She smiled at him and he nodded. It was an odd exchange, but she felt no urge to turn away or hide from the world.

Maybe keeping company with a monster had helped her understand how human she really was. Not perfect, but not one of the damned either. She picked up her feet and crossed the road, her steps felt lighter. It would be spring soon, she might start work on a vegetable garden.

# Chapter Thirty-nine

"Wake-up, love."

Maureen stirred in the chair and winced. She'd fallen asleep sitting with her chin resting on her shoulder. She felt a moment of panic and then the world fell back into place.

"Has something happened? Is Andrea all right?" She looked up into her husband's face searching for answers, ready to act.

He put his hand on her shoulder. "No. No, she's fine." He spoke quietly, his blue eyes gentle and reassuring. "The detective who was here last night wants a word. But I told him I'd see if you felt up to it."

Maureen looked over her husband's shoulder to where the man, Detective Worsten, stood in the doorway of the small waiting room. There had been two of them last night, she wondered fleetingly where the older one was.

"I... yes, that's fine." Maureen straightened her back and touched a hand to her hair. The two detectives had become something of a constant in their lives over the last three weeks.

Norman nodded for Worsten to come in.

"How's Andrea?" Detective Worsten seated himself across the narrow room. Maureen guessed he'd already spoken to the doctor and knew exactly how her daughter was doing, but was grateful for the courtesy.

"She needs surgery on her hands." Maureen rubbed her eyes. "Skin grafts. Her leg's fractured, but doesn't require surgery at this time." She spoke from memory, recounting everything she'd been told. "She's dehydrated, malnourished and has multiple bruises and… and…" Her voice trembled. Norman sat beside her and put his hand on her arm. She felt her emotions steady. "She has some bites." Maureen took a breath. "They… the doctors are most worried about the pneumonia. They won't operate until she's strong enough."

Worsten leaned his forearms on his thighs and laced his fingers together. He looked down, as if in thought. "She's a strong girl," he said and then looked from Maureen to Norman. "She's been through a lot, but you've got her back." His eyes were red rimmed as if he'd been awake all night.

*Yes*, she wanted to say. *No thanks to you*. It was unfair of her, cruel even, but the thought of her daughter in the hands of a madman—the things he'd done to her… Maureen wanted to jump out of the uncomfortable vinyl chair and scream in the detective's face. She could feel Norman's hand on her arm, he wanted her to be civil. She nodded.

"I know it's not a good time, but I have to ask you some questions." He looked from Maureen to Norman.

"We'll do whatever we can to help." Norman sounded strong, calm. Maureen knew he was holding himself together, for her. For Andrea. She'd heard him at night when he thought she was asleep, sobbing into his pillow. Wandering the house, lost—broken.

"Yes, of course." She slipped her hand over her husband's.

Worsten pulled a notebook from the inside pocket of his jacket. As the coat moved, she caught sight of his gun. There was a part of her that would like to use the weapon on the man who hurt her daughter. Worsten caught her glance and probably mistook the look on her face for fear, as he quickly pulled his jacket down covering the butt of his gun.

She watched the younger man flip through the pages. She remembered him doing that weeks ago, asking questions, making notes, his blond head nodding. She wanted this to be over so she could go back into Andrea's room and sit with her. She couldn't bear the thought of her girl waking up alone, maybe confused—frightened.

"I'm sorry, Detective but could we hurry this along? I want to go back in before Andrea wakes."

Worsten looked up, his blue eyes startled. He wasn't used to being told to hurry. Maureen guessed that he was a man used to setting the timeline and having others do as they were told. She felt the blood rush to her cheeks. She was being hostile again, a new habit. The man had been nothing but kind to her and Norman. She wished she could take the words back but they were out, and for a second no one spoke.

Worsten coughed. "I'm sorry, Mrs Fields." His eyes softened. "I have kids too, so I understand you want to be with your daughter. I'll be as quick as I can."

"It's all right, love." Norman slid his hand down her arm and took hold of her fingers. "The nurse said they gave Andy something to help her sleep, she'll be off with the fairies for a few hours."

At the mention of his pet name for their daughter, Maureen caught her breath. There had been times during the last few weeks—dark times—when she'd thought Andrea would never come back to them. In those moments, she wondered if there was any point in continuing. Could she get up every morning and go through the motions of living? She'd never said anything, especially to Norman, but if the worst had happened, she wouldn't want to try. In truth, she'd thought she'd seen the same in her husband's eyes.

"All right," Worsten began. "Does the name Terrance Briggs mean anything to either of you?"

"Is that him?" Norman's usually soft voice rose. "Is that the ratbag that took my girl?"

Now it was Maureen's turn to try to sooth her husband. "Norm, don't get upset. You'll make yourself sick."

"Mr Fields," Worsten broke in. "We're not sure of anything yet, but Andrea was found on a property owned by a man named Terrance Briggs. If you could both just think, have you ever heard that name before?"

When Maureen shook her head, he looked to Norman. "No. Never," Norman confirmed.

Worsten pulled his phone out of his pocket and Maureen caught another glimpse of the gun. He flicked the screen and then turned his phone. "Have you ever seen this man?"

Maureen stared at the picture, not sure what she'd been expecting, a monster maybe? Surely whoever did those things to her daughter had to be evil, yet the man in the picture looked normal: brown hair, a rather long nose, and a feminine mouth—an unremarkable face hiding such malevolence. Maureen shuddered and drew closer to her husband.

"I've never seen him." Norman's voice was soft, barely above a whisper. She could hear the pain behind his words.

"Mrs Fields?"

"No. I've never seen him before."

Worsten put his phone away. "One last thing before I go. You spoke to Andrea last night when she was brought to the hospital, did she say anything about the man who abducted her?"

"Why?" Maureen had the feeling he was leaving something out. If they had the man, why not wait until Andrea was stronger and then have her identify him? She'd watched enough American television to know there had to be plenty of forensic evidence to convict him.

Worsten shifted in his seat, and looked down at his notebook.

"You know who he is, you must have enough evidence to arrest him?" Maureen waited for the detective to answer her. A sinking sensation, starting in the pit of her stomach and then growing until it filled her chest drained her strength. "You *do* have him, don't you?"

Worsten flipped his notebook closed. "No. I'm sorry, we don't know where he is. When our officers found Andrea, they located his vehicle at the site." He stuffed the notebook in his pocket. "His phone was in Andrea's hand but Terrance Briggs wasn't on the property."

"You mean the man that did this got away?" Norman stood. For one horrifying second, Maureen thought he might grab the police officer. Instead, he covered his eyes with his large, work-worn hands and turned towards the wall.

"Mr Fields, I—"

"What do we tell Andrea?" Maureen swallowed. "When she asks, what do we tell her?"

"We'll find him." Worsten stood. "Sooner or later, he'll turn up."

"That's it?" Norman turned and she could see tears building in his eyes. "Sooner or later?"

Worsten was moving towards the doorway when his back stiffened. He turned back and for a second, Maureen thought she caught a glimpse of the man who faced monsters. His eyes were hard as if something cold lived behind them.

"There's evidence that indicates Andrea wasn't the first girl Briggs abducted." His voice was flat as if all the emotion had been sucked from him. "Those girls' parents are waiting." He looked from Norman to Maureen. "They're waiting for the bodies to be identified and when they *are*, I'll be the one who tells them their daughters aren't coming home." He buttoned his jacket closed. "So, when I say we'll find him, you can be sure I mean it."

# Chapter Forty

The water lapped against Mina's thighs, a delightfully cool contrast to the afternoon heat. She moved through the lake under the endless expanse of blue sky, tilting her face up to breathe in the sun's warmth. Afternoons at Fire Lake were the best part of county life. Well, almost the best.

She held her white sundress above the waterline and turned back to the bank. Lee, under the shade of a cluster of peppermint trees, shuffled through the daily newspaper. In the seven months since she moved to Dark Water, Mina had come to feel connected to the town in a way she never had in Civil Park. It was difficult to explain why, even to herself. Much of it, she supposed had to do with Lee and Robbie.

Their lives had become inexorably joined. It was as if the two other people had been waiting for her and now the circle was complete. She wondered if that was how it felt for everyone lucky enough to find their place in the world. Her thoughts, as they often did on days like this, turned to Andrea.

In the weeks after the girl's rescue, Mina followed the case closely. More than closely, obsessively. Andrea was released from hospital ten days after being found. Mina remembered watching the news and catching a glimpse of the detective, Willson or Worsten leaving the hospital. The sight of the blond detective had her on the edge of her seat. She'd paused the footage, her skin prickling with gooseflesh.

At the time, she felt like she'd been transported back to that first morning in the kitchen when the detectives came to ask her about Andrea's disappearance. The determination in the set of his mouth troubled her. His eyes were hidden behind dark sunglasses, but she knew if she could see them, they'd be cold and intent. He was a man who'd never give up. He'd search for Briggs until his superiors asked him to stop, and then he'd ignore them and continue to search on his own time.

At that point, with the TV still paused on the detective's face, Mina had rushed to the kitchen and searched through her handbag until she'd found the card he'd given her. The name "Worsten" was written on it, in bold black letters. Once remembered, she'd never forget it.

In those first few months, Worsten's face haunted her, not Briggs'. She even saw Worsten in Dark Water once. Back from Perth between Lee's first and second round of chemo, Mina drove into town to meet Robbie. It was early November, the air already warm with the approach of summer. Mina drove with the windows down enjoying the way the breeze played over her face.

On her trips into town, it wasn't unusual for her to pass Reliance Realty. In fact, after the first couple of weeks, she barely glanced at Briggs' old workplace. But on this day, Mina happened to turn and look at the red shop front. It was then that she saw the blond detective stepping through the glass door and onto the street.

Her mouth felt dry, as if the saliva had suddenly evaporated. Seeing Worsten in the flesh brought back every secret fear that came alive at night and followed her to sleep. Driving completely forgotten, she must have veered to the right. The sound of a horn, shrill and alarming, filled the street. Instinctively, Mina had stood on the brake and felt the car slide with a sickening screech.

In that gut-wrenching instant when the impact seemed a certainty, Mina caught a glimpse of Worsten's face. His eyes were on the road, a slight frown creasing his brow. She imagined his frown deepening, him leaning in her window and asking to see her license.

"Mina Constantine, we've met before."

The three seconds between the blare of the horn and the screeching of tyres seemed to draw out for minutes. And suddenly the car shuddered to a stop, jolting her forward with enough force to make her teeth clang together; but mercifully without the grinding metallic thump of impact.

Mina risked another look at Worsten and to her relief, he'd turned away and was walking towards the corner.

"Sorry!" Mina had stuck her head out the driver's window to where a black Mazda had come to a stop only inches from the bonnet of her car.

The driver, a fortyish looking woman with a severe bun stared at her with round, shocked eyes, slowly shaking her head.

"Sorry." Then Mina pulled her head back inside the vehicle. Hands shaking, she steered her car around the Mazda. She snatched a glimpse in her rear-view mirror and noted that Worsten had already disappeared around the corner.

Whatever information Worsten was searching for at Briggs' office, it never led him to her door. For that, Mina was thankful, but never really sure if one day there *would* be a knock.

"Mina." She turned to where Lee reclined on the bank. "Are you coming out? I'm starving."

All thoughts of Worsten left her as she waded towards the shore, enjoying the feel of the sandy lake floor between her toes. When she reached the picnic rug, Mina flopped down and opened the esky.

Lee was sitting up now, legs crossed with the newspaper in his lap.

"I can't believe you still read an actual newspaper," Mina teased, flicking the top of the page.

"I like the way the paper feels in my hands, it makes the news seem real, not just something on a screen." He looked up. She could see flecks of gold in his newly sprouting hair. He was still thin, but colour was returning to his cheeks.

"Besides," Lee continued. "There's something in here I wanted to read to you."

"If it's my horoscope, I know what it's going to say." Mina lifted out a large lunchbox and two bottles of water.

"What's that?" he asked, leaning forwards and catching hold of a strand of her hair.

"I'm going to make love in a public place with a near bald man."

Lee tipped his head back and laughed, it was a healthy sound, full and deep. "You must be psychic," he said, suppressing another laugh. "Forget the lunch, it's time to fulfil your prediction."

"No." Mina batted his hand off her thigh. "Food first." She opened the lunchbox. "What did you want to read to me?"

"Oh yeah." He pointed to the open newspaper. "Remember that girl, the one who went missing? She was in your writing class."

Mina put down the lunchbox and let her hands drop into her lap. "Andrea." She turned and looked across the lake. "Andrea Fields."

"Yes, that's right. Well there's an article in here about her."

Despite the sunshine, she felt a chill crawl over her skin. The image of Andrea's torn and bloody hand snaking out from under a pile of rags popped into her mind.

"Twenty-year old, Andrea Fields was abducted in July last year and kept captive for almost three weeks. It is believed the man who abducted Miss Fields, Terrance Briggs, is also responsible for the abductions and murders of four other young women including: Madeline Hawks aged 22, Inderma Abah aged 25, and Emma Hauser aged 18. The fourth body, which police believe is that of a child, is yet to be identified." Lee paused. "Jesus, Mina. I know I've said this before, but it bothers me that Briggs showed you that house. I just don't like to think of you alone with that crazy fucker."

"Yes." Mina pulled her hair over her right shoulder. "I really don't like thinking about it." She wanted to tell him to stop. That the murdered girls were the last thing she wanted to hear about.

"I know," he said and kept reading. "Miss Fields, still recovering from her ordeal has been offered a book deal by Stills and Holmes." Lee looked up. "They're one of the biggest publishers in the business." He continued reading. "Miss Fields will write an account of her three-week ordeal including details of her amazing rescue which a spokeswoman for Stills and Holmes says will be unlike anything readers have seen before."

Mina closed her eyes and saw Andrea's glassy gaze shifting between the doorway and Mina's face. She wondered how much Andrea would remember of that day. She'd been barely conscious when Mina found her, whatever she remembered would be unlikely to point towards Mina. Still, the idea of Andrea putting her experience on paper was unnerving.

"When asked if rumours of a movie deal were correct, it was confirmed that there was some interest from a major US film studio. Miss Field, however, was unavailable for comment." Lee closed the paper. "I guess she really was serious about that writing class."

Mina nodded. Maybe something good *would* come out of Andrea's ordeal. Mina hoped so for the girl's sake. Writing about what happened to her might be a way for

Andrea to exorcise her demons. After what Briggs put her through, she deserved a good life.

"Are you okay?" Lee touched her leg. "I didn't mean to upset you. I just thought knowing that she was doing well would… I don't know, help. You don't talk about it, but I know it was hard on you."

"Hard on *me*?" Mina wiped a hand across her cheek and realised she was crying.

Lee moved closer, placing both hands on her hips. "You knew her and," he hesitated. "You knew the man who abducted her, that's hard. I understand why you're upset."

"I'm not upset." Mina wiped at the tears with her fingertips. "I don't even know why I'm crying really. They must be happy tears." She pressed her palm to the side of his face. "And I *am* happy. Happy for Andrea. Happy for you." She sniffed. "So happy that you don't need any more chemo."

And it was true, what she really felt at that moment was happiness and optimism. For the first time in a very long while, things were going well. *Maybe*, Mina thought. *The darkness that's followed me for so many years has lifted.* She wondered if by helping Andrea she had exorcised some of her own demons.

"Okay," she said, wiping away the last of her tears. "It's time for lunch. I have cold chicken and salad." Mina took two plates out of the esky and laid them on the rug.

"Sounds good." Lee watched her heap his plate with salad and a generous serving of chicken.

Mina handed him a plate and cutlery. "Don't forget Robbie's coming over tonight with her new boyfriend." She picked up her knife and fork. "I said we might go with them to the pub, if you feel up to it."

"I'm looking forward to it," he said around a mouth full of tomato. "You know these tomatoes are amazing, I can't believe you grew them."

"Why is it so shocking?" Mina asked, pretending to be offended.

"I just never had you pegged as the gardening type." He took a bite of chicken.

"There's a lot about me you don't know," Mina said around a smile. "Like with gardening for instance, the key is to feed your soil. You can grow almost anything if you have the right kind of fertiliser." She popped a wedge of tomato in her mouth and smiled.

He put down his plate and leaned forward. "You're lovely," he said and kissed her on the lips.

She pulled back and cocked an eyebrow. "Dark and deep?" The words were out before she could stop herself.

Lee looked amused. "But I have promises to keep. And miles to go before I sleep."

Mina couldn't hide her surprise. "You know it?"

Lee nodded. "Robert Frost, I read his work at uni. Amazing poet."

Mina shook her head. "Is there anything you haven't read?"

He picked up his plate and frowned as if considering the question, his eyes—slightly tired—looked like the ocean on a calm day. "Twilight."

"What?" She wasn't sure she had heard him correctly.

"You asked if there was anything I hadn't read. Twilight, that's one I definitely have never read."

She let out a gale of laughter that came from deep down in her belly. It felt wonderful to be this happy and free. When the laughter finally subsided, she watched Lee finish his food. Her thoughts turned to what she'd said earlier about being happy for Andrea *and* for him. She realised she was also happy for herself—she'd finally found peace. She loved Lee with all her heart and would do whatever was needed to take care of him.

The End

If you enjoyed this book, please let others know by leaving a quick review on Amazon. Also, if you spot anything untoward in the paperback, get in touch. We strive for the best quality and appreciate reader feedback.

editor@thebookfolks.com


www.thebookfolks.com

Also by Anna Willett:

**BACKWOODS RIPPER**
**RETRIBUTION RIDGE**
**UNWELCOME GUESTS**
**FORGOTTEN CRIMES**

31042520R00183

Printed in Poland
by Amazon Fulfillment
Poland Sp. z o.o., Wrocław